PAGAN'S
SCRIBE

PAGAN'S
SCRIBE

CATHERINE JINKS

CANDLEWICK PRESS
CAMBRIDGE, MASSACHUSETTS

Copyright © 2000 by Catherine Jinks

Map illustration copyright © 2005 by Tim Stevens

First U.S. edition 2005

Library of Congress Cataloging-in-Publication Data

Jinks, Catherine.
Pagan's scribe / Catherine Jinks. — 1st U.S. ed.
p. cm.
Sequel to: Pagan's vows.
Summary: In France in 1209, Pagan, now an archdeacon, takes on a
new scribe named Isidore, a fifteen-year-old epileptic and an orphan,
and together they try to survive the siege of Carcassonne.
ISBN 0-7636-2022-X
1. Carcassonne (France)—History—13th century—Juvenile fiction.
[1. Carcassonne (France)—History—13th century—Fiction.
2. Epilepsy—Fiction. 3. Orphans—Fiction.
4. France—History—Philip II Augustus, 1180–1223—Fiction.
5. Middle Ages—Fiction.] I. Title.
PZ7.J5754Pai 2005
[Fic]—dc22   2004061836

2   4   6   8   10   9   7   5   3   1

Printed in the United States of America

This book was typeset in Weiss.

Candlewick Press
2067 Massachusetts Avenue
Cambridge, Massachusetts 02140

visit us at www.candlewick.com

*To Margaret Connolly,
for her endless support*

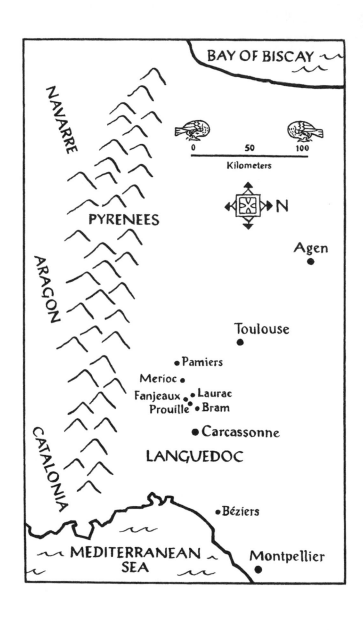

‡CHAPTER ONE‡

14 JULY 1209

Hear my cry, O God; attend unto my prayer.

Lord, I'm sitting here like a pelican in the wilderness. Like an owl in the desert, Lord. Is it truly your divine wish that I should spend the rest of my life in this miserable village? In this howling wasteland? Did you look at this dung heap and say: That's where I'm going to send Isidore, so he can eat the bread of sorrow? Because that's what I've been doing, Lord, ever since I arrived. I've been eating the bread of sorrow and licking the dust like a serpent.

Lord, it may have escaped your notice, but the nearest manuscript is a full day's ride from here. A *full day's ride.* Surely you must understand what it's like for me if I don't have any books? It's worse than not having any food or water. I can't live without books, Lord—you must know that. And the people here are so stupid: their heads are as empty as pots. And just look at this church I'm sitting in! Have you ever seen such a horrible church? Have you ever seen such horrible paintings? Look at that painting on the apse: that one of the four-and-twenty elders, with their white raiment and their crowns of gold. Do they remind you of anything? Of four-and-twenty poached eggs, perhaps? And do you see the way Our Lord Jesus Christ seems to be sticking his finger up the nose of that angel? It's blasphemous, Lord, it really is. Whoever painted it ought to be crucified.

Father, did you create Merioc just to punish me for my sins? Because if you did, it's the perfect penance. I hate this village, and everyone in it. I hate the way they're all married to their cousins. I hate the way they're all named Bernard. I hate the gossip, and the lice, and the sticky, smelly cheese they produce here. I especially hate the shepherds' bagpipes—have you heard those bagpipes, Lord? But of course you have. They're loud enough to drown the Last Trump, so you must have heard them in heaven.

O Lord, I know I'm a sinner. I know I have a devil in me, but I'm trying very hard to get rid of it. Can't you please punish me in some other way? If I don't get out of here soon, Lord, I think I'll go mad.

"Hello?" A man's voice, echoing around the church like the sound of bells. "Hello? Is the priest here?" Who can this be, marching onto consecrated soil as if he owns it? He stands there framed by the western door, dark against the light, and I can't really see him from this distance. But he moves forward, and it's obvious at once that he's not from the village: no villager walks like that, so briskly, with such a firm tread. All the villagers ever do is amble, like cows. He's peering into the dimness, and of course he sees me, because my white surplice gleams in the shadows like a wolf's eyes.

"Who's that?" he says. "Are you the priest?"

"No, I'm the parish clerk—"

"Where is the priest?" He's small and wiry, with thick black hair and a neatly trimmed beard. He also has a tonsure. I can see it now, on the crown of his head—that distinctive, circular, shaven patch of scalp.

So he's a cleric, then. How interesting.

3

"Where is the priest?" he snaps. "Have you lost your tongue? I just asked you a question!"

"The priest is at a deathbed, Father."

"Sweet saints preserve us." He stamps his left foot. (What a restless little man he is.) "That's typical," he rages. "That's all I need. What's your name, boy?"

"Isidore."

"Isidore? Good. Then you can come here, Isidore, because I need your help."

Come here, Isidore. Go there, Isidore. I'm like stubble before the wind, in this place. Ah, well. Better it is to be of humble spirit with the lowly, than to divide the spoil with the proud.

And speaking of the proud, this little man is no parish priest. Out in the sunlight, it's possible to see how supple and expensive his boots are. He's not wearing any jewelry, but his black robes are glossy and full, finely woven and finely stitched, like the feast-day vestments back in Pamiers. And look at his horses! At least, I assume they're his horses. None of the locals can flaunt a pair of beasts like those. In fact no one in this village owns any horses at all.

Perhaps that's why these two have drawn such a big crowd. At least half a dozen staring peasants

4

have gathered near the church steps, wary but fascinated: the usual crew of eavesdroppers, including Bernard Lagleize and Bernard Belot and Bernard Lagleize the Younger, chewing like cows, spitting and scratching and picking their noses. When they see the little man beside me, they cross themselves, because he has very dark skin—strange, dusky skin—and these people are so dense, so incredibly insular, that they're frightened by anything out of the ordinary. Witness the way they behaved when I first showed up. Anyone would think that red hair was a mark of the Devil.

"Look! Just look at him!" The little man points at one of his horses: there's a hunched figure on top of it. "See that steaming heap of garbage over there? That used to be my scribe. He's not fit to travel, because he's evacuating continuously from both ends. That's what happens when you're a greedy pig and eat bad fruit against the advice of your elders. Where's the priest's house, Isidore? I'll have to put this idiot to bed."

The priest's house? Oh, no. I can't invite you into the priest's house, little man. The priest's house belongs to the priest.

"It's all right." He's looking at me, squinting in the harsh noonday glare. "My name is Father

Pagan," he says. "I am the Archdeacon of Carcassonne. If your priest objects, he'll have me to
answer to. Now, where does he live?"

"Over there." Pointing. "Around the corner."

"Good. Let's go, then. You can lead that horse,
and I'll lead this one."

Lead the horse? But I don't know anything about
horses. What am I supposed to do with it? What if
it bites me? Just look at its great yellow eye, rolling
like the stone of Sisyphus. Just look at its great yellow teeth.

"Go on, she won't hurt you." The Archdeacon
has seized the reins of his scribe's mount, right up
under its bristly chin. But when I try to do the
same for mine, it snorts and tosses its head.

Help! This animal doesn't like me. Somewhere
in the crowd, someone laughs: the village square
seems to be full of mangy peasants, all waiting for
me to make a fool of myself. God curse them. May
their increase be given unto the caterpillar, and
their labor unto the locust.

"Come." The Archdeacon crooks a finger. "I'll
give you these reins, and I'll take yours. There. All
right, now? Just pull him along gently, and you
won't have any trouble."

Gently. Pull gently. One little tug, and the horse starts to move: I can feel its hot breath on my wrist. The scribe moans with every step it takes; he's curled up in the saddle, his greenish face pillowed against his mount's neck. He wears a canon's robe and a tonsure.

"Julien!" The Archdeacon speaks from behind me. "I warn you, Julien, if you dare throw up on my beautiful horse, you'll be *licking* the mess off, understand?"

But there's no response from Julien. The crowd follows us around the side of the church, toward the little mud-brick dwelling propped up against its southern wall. Ernoul is standing on the threshold, open-mouthed and popeyed: with his skinny frame and spiky hair, he looks exactly like a broom.

"Who's that?" the Archdeacon inquires. "Does that fellow belong to the priest?"

"Yes, Father, he's our servant."

"Good. Then he can hold the horses. You, there! Fellow! Come and hold these horses! And you—Isidore—you can help me with Julien."

Julien certainly needs some help. One small nudge and he tumbles down like an autumn leaf, emitting the most monstrous fart in the history of

7

the civilized world. It puts me in mind of a bison's fart, which (as everyone knows) sets fire to every tree within three acres.

"God preserve us!" the Archdeacon exclaims, staggering under Julien's unwieldy tangle of limbs. "You smell like a leper's latrine, you dung-bag!"

"I'm going to be sick," Julien moans. But the Archdeacon won't have that. He sticks one small brown finger into Julien's heaving breastbone. "No, Julien," he snarls, "*I'm* the one who's going to be sick. *You're* going to be sorry. Now, stand up and stop whining. Come on, Isidore—take his other arm."

It seems a very long way to Father Fulbert's kitchen. Julien doesn't have the strength to put one foot in front of the other, so it's a matter of dragging him, step by step, through the front door. And here to welcome us is the mountainous Mengarde, displaying her toothless gums in sheer astonishment. Her hands are covered in flour.

"Mengarde, this is the Archdeacon of Carcassonne, and this is his scribe, Julien. Julien is feeling sick—"

As if to demonstrate, Julien suddenly erupts. A spray of vomit hits the earthen floor in front of us, and the smell of old bacon fat is overlaid by an even nastier smell. Mengarde jumps backward.

By the blood of the Lamb of God, this is disgusting.

"Julien," says the Archdeacon through his teeth, "you are without doubt the most obnoxious individual ever to impose on my good nature. I'm finished with you."

"What do you want?" Mengarde's high, quavering voice. "What are you doing?"

"We're putting this man to bed." (So kindly get out of the way, old woman.) "You must take care of him."

"I?" She raises her hands in protest. But the Archdeacon is looking around: at the low, smoky rafters, hung with hams and garlic; at the greasy table and benches; at the hearth and the woodpile and the baby pig asleep in one corner. "Where shall we dump this useless sack of swill?" he demands. "Through there, do you think? What's through that door?"

That door? "That is the priest's room, Father."

"Oh." He frowns. "And where do your guests usually sleep, Isidore?"

"They sleep in my bed."

"Which is where?"

Which is over there, beside that barrel. He peers as I point, noting the grimy old sheepskin on

9

top of the lumpy straw palliasse. He seems surprised. "I see," he says. "And where do you sleep when your bed is occupied?"

"On the table, Father."

"Hmm."

Julien is making ominous noises again. I can feel his shudders, and the sweat soaking through his clothes. The Archdeacon turns to Mengarde.

"Get a bucket!" he snaps.

"But—"

"*Get a bucket!* Or would you prefer to clean up some more mess?" Whereupon Mengarde begins to waddle around frantically, wailing and whimpering, because all her buckets are full. She's fat and slow-witted, and she keeps bumping into things.

She makes me think of a big, stupid cow on the loose in a marketplace.

"Oh, no, you don't," the Archdeacon splutters as Julien gags. "Come on, Isidore—we'll put him on the table; I don't want him soiling your bedclothes. By rights he should be out with the pigs—he doesn't deserve anything better. Shut up, Julien. I'm not talking to you." He leads the way across the floor and almost throws his scribe onto the tabletop. (For such a small man, he's remarkably strong.)

"Incidentally, Julien, if you think I'm going to wait around here, cleaning up your vomit and wiping your loathsome spotty behind, you can think again," he says. "I have far more important things to do. And I'm also in a hurry. Isidore? I want a word."

With me? But why? I'm just the parish clerk— I'm as lowly as the chaff on the summer threshing floors. There's nothing *I* can do for anyone. Nevertheless, he grabs my arm and pushes me through the door, back into the sunshine, away from the sickroom smells of the kitchen. Out here the air is fresher, though not much, because of the dung heap along the side of the house. And of course there's the pungent fragrance of our delightful neighbors, who are still hovering about, discussing the new arrival and looking for all the world like hens at a trough. They fall silent when we make our appearance.

"Tell me, Isidore," the Archdeacon says, standing there with his gaze on the crowd, "can you read, by any chance?"

Can I read? Little man, that's an incomplete question.

"Can I read what, Father?"

11

"Why, *books*, of course!" He frowns at me, squinting. "Can you read books?"

"That depends on the language they're written in."

His eyes widen: they're very big, and very dark, as dark as the Third Horse of the Apocalypse. I wonder what he's thinking. I wonder if he thinks at all. So many priests don't. Take Father Fulbert, for example: Father Fulbert's head is full of air, like an empty stomach. He must have stopped thinking years ago.

"Very well," the Archdeacon says quietly. "I'll rephrase my question. Can you read Latin, Isidore?"

"Yes, Father."

"Can you read any other languages?"

"Yes, Father. French, German, and the *langue d'oc*. But not Greek."

"How old are you?"

"Fifteen."

"You're very well educated."

"Yes, Father." I am indeed. I'm very, very well educated. But what does it profit me? As the Preacher says: He that increaseth knowledge, increaseth sorrow.

The Archdeacon makes an impatient noise. "Damn, but you're a difficult person to talk to," he mutters. "*Why* are you so well educated, Isidore?"

Why? "Because I chose to be."

"Hmm." He's squinting at me again, as if he can't quite focus his eyes; his forehead is tense with concentration. Suddenly he pats my elbow. "Just sit down here on the doorstep, will you?" he remarks, and shoots across to where Ernoul is holding the horses. The crowd immediately takes a step backward, all together as one man. The Archdeacon fishes around in his saddlebag and draws out a leather satchel.

"This," he announces, in tones that ring out across the sunbaked square, "is my portable writing desk. I designed it myself." He returns and places the satchel on my knees: it smells of leather and horse sweat. There's a hard, thin wooden board sewn into a leather pocket, and a flap covering several sheets of high-quality parchment, and a piece of blue ribbon holding everything together. And what's this? A little drawstring bag, containing a vessel of ink, a stick of sealing wax, and a knife to cut goose quills. What a wonderful invention! What beautiful objects!

"I want you to write a letter," he says, removing the seal from the ink bottle. "A letter to your Bishop. Is he the Bishop of Pamiers?"

"Yes, Father."

"Yes, I thought as much." He dips a quill in the ink for me and points at the smooth, pale surface of the parchment. "In Latin, of course. Begin 'To blessed Odilo, Apostolic Father of the See of Pamiers, greetings from Pagan Kidrouk, Archdeacon of the See of Carcassonne . . .'"

Kidrouk! Of course! I remember now. This must be *the* Father Pagan. The man who—yes, I recall, he was from the East. A foreigner. And there was something else, too. . . . Was he an Infidel? An Infidel converted to the True Faith? Something of the sort. They used to talk about him, back at the cathedral.

No wonder his complexion is so dark.

"Come on, Isidore. I haven't got all day." He prods me in the ribs. "'To blessed Odilo, Apostolic Father of the See of Pamiers, greetings from Pagan Kidrouk . . .'"

Beato Odilo, patri apostolico . . . How good this pen feels. How sweetly it glides across the page, like a duck across the surface of a pond. How much I've missed this glorious sensation!

"' . . . In accordance with the command of my beloved Father, Bernard Raymond de Roquefort, Bishop of Carcassonne, and to fulfill his most ready devotion and his deepest wish in Christ, I

14

have been pursuing the good of the Faith in your territories, as I informed your paternity when I last spoke to you.'"

Secundum mandatum patris mei . . . Slow down, slow down!

"New paragraph. 'By divine grace I am well in myself, but my scribe, Julien, has been struck down by a grievous illness, just a few miles out of Pamiers. Beloved Father, without a scribe, I am as a barren fig tree, for my eyes, which discern the world clearly at a distance, are crippled when presented with the forms of things close to my face.'" The Archdeacon pauses: there isn't a sound to be heard except the scratching of my nib against the creamy parchment. "'Therefore,'" he continues, "'because my scribe lies ill in the village of Merioc, I have been obliged to secure the services of your loving son, Isidore . . .' Do you have another name, Isidore?"

"Yes, Father."

"What is it?"

"Orbus."

"Orbus?" He sounds surprised. "Isidore the Orphan?"

"Yes."

"I see. That's interesting. Well—where was I? Ah, yes. '. . . the services of your loving son, Isidore

Orbus, whom you sent there as parish clerk, through God's inspiration. My own scribe, Julien, will remain in his place until you have chosen a substitute, and my venerable master, the Bishop Bernard, will make worthy satisfaction to you for your pains. May the angel of good counsel be with you, so that you understand what is right and act in accordance with it. Farewell.' Have you got all that?"

Angelus consilii boni . . . vale . . . "Yes, Father."

"Read it through to me, then."

"*Beato Odilo, patri apostolico . . .*" (I can't believe this. Is it really happening? O Lord, have you answered my prayer?) "*. . . petebam salutem Fidei . . .*" (But it won't be easy, serving this little Archdeacon. Not only is he a profane, bossy, discourteous man—he's a former Infidel, too! How can I bow my neck to his yoke? It will be very difficult.) "*. . . iuxta faciem meam . . .*" (However, I'm in no position to pick and choose. As the old saying warns us: *Selde cumet se betere*—rarely does a better one come next.) "*. . . servitia filii dilecti . . .*" (After all, if I don't take advantage of this God-given opportunity, I may never have another chance to get out of here.) "*. . . secundum quod sit iustum. Vale.*"

"Excellent." The Archdeacon nods, and peers at me with his crippled eyes. When he peers, he doesn't push his head forward, but draws it back. "Is there anything in that letter you would prefer to remove?"

"No, Father."

"Nothing?"

"No, Father."

"Good. Then I'll give it to the servant, and he can give it to your priest. I daresay someone will pass by soon, on their way to Pamiers." He takes the leather satchel and stands up. "Can you ride a horse, Isidore?"

"Um . . ." That depends on your definition of the word *ride*. "I rode to this village, Father." (Although I spent more time on the ground than in the saddle.)

"Then you shouldn't have any difficulty," the Archdeacon declares. "Any fool can sit on a horse. Besides, this horse is so intelligent, you won't need to do anything but sit." All at once he grins, and he has the grin of an urchin, wide and disrespectful, with one tooth missing. "A few falls won't hurt you," he says, slapping me on the back. "Hurry up—we'd better get a move on."

"Now?"

"Of course. I have to be in Fanjeaux before sunset."

By the blood of the Lamb, he doesn't waste time, does he? Even his stride is quick and impatient as he approaches Ernoul and shoves the letter into his grubby hand. "Here, take this. Give it to your priest when he returns. Tell him that Isidore is safe in my care." Seizing the reins from Ernoul, he looks around and beckons to me. "Isidore! Come on! It's time to go."

Yes, indeed. It is time to go. But where in the world am I going?

Hear my cry, O God; attend unto my prayer. From the end of the earth will I cry unto Thee, when my heart is overwhelmed.

Please don't lose sight of your humblest servant.

✝CHAPTER TWO✝

14 JULY 1209

O Lord, what a marvelous work is this country. How vast are its spaces; how lofty its skies. Look at the way the golden fields alternate so beautifully with those patches of rich green forest, in a pattern that yields both refreshment to the eye and varied gifts of produce to the zealous laborer. O Lord, how manifold are Thy works! In wisdom hast Thou made them all: the earth is full of Thy riches.

"Would you like a drink, Isidore?"

The Archdeacon is holding a wineskin. He rides so easily, so smoothly, rising and falling with the swing of his horse's gait, his left hand hanging free. What skills he must possess, to sit like that. How difficult it is not to slide all over the saddle. And what an astounding mystery presents itself when you get up onto a horse! For how can something look so narrow from a distance, when in fact it's so incredibly wide? The measure thereof is longer than the earth, and broader than the sea; the measure thereof is higher than the vaults of heaven.

"Isidore? I'm offering you a drink—do you want one?"

"No, Father."

"Are you sure?"

"Yes, Father." I don't want to reach for that wineskin, or I might fall off. It's so hard keeping my balance, way up here.

"You must think I'm very unsympathetic, treating my scribe like that," the Archdeacon observes, quite suddenly, as if he's been giving the matter some thought. "The fact is, my scribe Godric was a wonderful man, and we got on well until he died. Then I was given Julien. Julien was bearable just as long as he was comfortable. But he didn't like traveling, and as soon as we set off, he started to moan and sulk and carry on. It was driving me insane." His voice shudders with the impact of each step, as his horse picks its way around the potholes; peering across at me, he adds: "*You* don't look like a moaner. In fact you don't look like anyone I've ever seen before. What's a person like you doing in these parts?"

A person like me? What are you saying? There's nothing wrong with me, nothing at all.

"I don't understand."

"Well, look at your hair, for a start. It's so red it's like wine. And look at your skin: it's as white as snowflakes. That's northern skin. Northern hair. Where were you born?"

Curse you, little man. Curse you and all your increase. May you be smitten with blasting and mildew, and may you bring forth emerods in your secret parts.

"What's the matter?" he says. "Can't you tell me? Don't you know?"

"No."

"Why not? What happened?"

By the blood of the Lamb, can't you leave me be? Do I ask about *your* parents? Do I pry into *your* secrets?

"Listen, Isidore, I'm not going to laugh. I don't even know who my father was—he raped my mother, and she gave me away when I was born. So I'm not in a position to feel superior." He's staring at me again: I can feel that bright, black gaze boring into my left cheek. "Are you a bastard, too?" he inquires.

"I don't know."

"But your parents are dead?"

"Yes, they are."

"What happened to them?"

"They were killed by brigands." (Why do you want to know this? What will it profit you?) "They were pilgrims, returning home from Compostela. They were with some other pilgrims. But the brigands killed them all and stole their possessions. I was found among the bodies."

There's a long pause, filled only by the buzz of flies, the creak of leather, the thud of hoofbeats. When the Archdeacon speaks at last, his voice is very gentle.

"That's a sad story," he murmurs. "How old were you then?"

"I was twelve months old."

"And you don't know who your parents were? Where they came from?"

"No, Father. The brigands left nothing. Not even their clothes."

"I'm sorry."

No, you're not. How can you be? They weren't *your* parents.

The Archdeacon thinks for a moment, his eyes on the road in front of us: it's a terrible road, covered with rocks and gullies, and I feel like a locust being tossed on the wind.

"So the Church took you in, and looked after you?" he says.

"Yes, Father."

"And I suppose you went to the cathedral school, at Pamiers? It has quite a good reputation." He steers his horse around a particularly big hole. "I gather you're still an acolyte, since you're only fifteen. Did you like it, living with the cathedral canons?"

Did I *like* it? What's that got to do with anything? Why can't you leave me alone? Why can't you ignore me, the way everyone else does?

"Isidore? *Isidore!* I just asked you a question, boy. Did you like living at Pamiers?"

"I liked the books."

"But not the people?"

This is excruciating. I don't have to answer. I *refuse* to answer. I'm not in confession.

"Because I can't help wondering what you were

23

doing in Merioc," he continues quietly. "With your level of education, you're wasted on a village like that. You should be at university, or at least working where your skills can be properly employed. Why aren't you?"

Because I have a devil in me, that's why. Because I have a devil that would make your hair stand up and your sweat turn to ice on your brow.

"Isidore!" He shakes the wineskin at me. "By God, but you make people work! Why aren't you at university?"

"Because universities are expensive."

"And your superiors weren't interested in helping you?"

"No."

"Why not?"

Will you please leave me *alone*? If you think I'm going to tell you my secret, little man, then you're wrong, wrong, wrong. My face is harder than flint, and my tongue is bound with bars of iron.

"Why won't they help you, Isidore?"

"I don't know."

"Don't you? How strange. But maybe you just sat there, looking like that—it's enough to scare anyone."

Like what? What do you mean? He's smiling a

24

little as he raises the wineskin to his mouth. One sip and he's finished: he hangs the wineskin on his saddle and wipes his mouth with his free hand. How I wish I'd had the courage to take that wineskin. It's been such a long afternoon, and the sun is so hot . . . though not quite as hot as it was, of course. Everything is dusty and parched, and the birds are all silent, and when the wind blows, the leaves rattle like coins in a pot.

Far away, across the fields, golden hills gleam like the brass mountain of Zechariah.

"Well, now." The Archdeacon yawns, and stretches until his joints crack. "I suppose I'd better tell you what I'm doing, rushing around the countryside like this. Do you know anything about heresy, Isidore?"

Of course I do. I'm an educated person. "It comes from the Greek word *haeresis*, meaning 'choice,' because each heretic decides by his own will whatever he wants to teach or believe, against the authority of God and the apostles."

"Hmm." Once again, the Archdeacon smiles. "I see you've been reading the *Etymologies*. Is there anything else you can tell me about heretics?"

"They gather in cellars and fornicate, and when the babies are born, they cut them to pieces and

25

throw the pieces on the fire, and then they mix the ashes with the baby's blood, and drink it."

This time he seems lost for words. I must have stunned him with my knowledge. At last he says, "Where on earth did you hear that?"

"I didn't hear it; I read it."

"Where?"

"In Guibert of Nogent's *Monodiae*."

"I see." He smoothes his beard with one hand and cocks his head like a bird. "That's a very old tale you've read, Isidore. It comes from the ancients, via Michael Psellus. It was written about various ancient heresies, but it doesn't apply to the modern ones. If you want a more correct account of what today's heretics do and believe, you should read someone like Alan of Lille. He's a little more balanced."

"But it was *written*. About the modern heretics." (Do you think I'm stupid?) "It was written in a book."

"Just because it's written, Isidore, doesn't mean it's right. In the *Disciplina clericalis*, Pedro Alfonso warned us: 'Read everything you find, but do not believe everything you read.' You should remember that."

"But how do you know it's not right? How *can* you know?"

"Because I know heretics." He drags his sleeve across his sweaty forehead. "At least, I know the heretics around here. They're called Cathars, and they don't eat babies. They're perfectly normal people—which is why they're so hard to distinguish from everyone else."

"But how can they be normal? They are children of Satan!"

"Perhaps. Perhaps not. They're not entirely bad, Isidore."

"'A good tree cannot bring forth evil fruit; neither can an evil tree bring forth good fruit.' Christ said that."

"And Saint Augustine said that heretics are needed, just as we need the darkness to see the light."

He did? "Where?"

"In his treatise *De vera religione liber unus*. You should read it. It's very good."

How can I read it, when I don't even have it? I've never had enough books, not ever. How can I argue, when I have no books? It's all right for you: you can argue better, because you've read more.

"In any case, whatever else the Cathars might be, they're certainly a problem." The Archdeacon sighs. "They're all over the place, and they have a lot of power. For the last few years I've been involved in various preaching missions, sent to this country to convert the Cathars back to the True Faith, but none of these missions was very successful. In fact one of the mission leaders was killed last year. He was a papal legate called Peter of Castelnau."

"Did the heretics kill him?"

The Archdeacon hesitates. "We don't know," he says finally. "We don't know who killed him. But the Pope wasn't very pleased. He's called on the King of France to send an army down here, to chastise the lords of this land for protecting heretics. Lords like the Count of Toulouse and the Viscount of Carcassonne."

"An army?" Oh, no. "Coming here?"

"Don't worry, it's nowhere near us yet." He reaches out and plucks a switch from a tree he's passing: the flies scatter as he waves it across his horse's flanks. "A muster date was set for Saint John's Day, at Lyon, but these things never get started on time."

An army! An army of lords, coming here! But there are priests here—good, faithful priests. And monks, and nuns. Surely there must be some other way of converting the heretics? Why should the Pope send men with swords?

"Anyway, my Bishop is getting a little worried," the Archdeacon explains with an irreverent, sarcastic note in his voice. "He's sent me on a mission to speak to the Cathar nobility, like the lady you're going to meet tonight, in Fanjeaux. He thinks that if I persuade them to band together and go to the Pope to make their submission, then the army will be stopped."

But of course! Of course it will! What a brilliant idea!

"Needless to say, it isn't working. I've just been to see the Count of Foix, at Pamiers, and he laughed in my face." The Archdeacon is speaking so quietly that it's hard to hear him. He's gazing across a field of millet, toward the huddle of stone houses beyond. "Without the Count's support, none of the other lords will even consider such a proposal. Well, why should they?"

"Because of the army!" (Isn't it obvious?) "Because of the Holy Father!"

"No one down here in the south believes that any army can get past Carcassonne," the Archdeacon points out. "And they're probably right, too.

29

As for the Holy Father—well, they don't give a damn about the Pope around here. Never have, and never will."

"Then they *deserve* to be attacked!"

"Do they?" He turns and looks at me: his eyes are expressionless. "Do you know what they're calling this invasion, Isidore? They're calling it a Crusade."

A Crusade? But—

"The Pope is granting an indulgence to all those who fight against our local lords. That means that everyone who joins the invaders will receive absolution and remission of their sins."

"But—but *we* are not Infidels." I don't understand. "This is not Jerusalem. Crusaders go to the Holy Land, to fight the Turks."

"Not anymore, they don't." When the Archdeacon smiles, it's not a happy smile—it's more of a grimace, sour and scornful. His teeth are clenched, and his face looks very dark. "After all, why should they go all the way to the Holy Land, when they can come down here? It's closer, it's cheaper, the wine is better, the roads are safer—"

"But I don't understand." This still doesn't make sense. This is illogical. "You just said that Cathars were difficult to distinguish from normal Christians."

"That's right."

"Then how will these Crusaders distinguish between the people they should kill and the people they shouldn't?"

The Archdeacon raises an eyebrow. For some reason, he doesn't look so angry anymore: in fact he looks rather gratified. He even laughs a little, through his nose.

"Isidore, that's a very good question," he says, squinting as he studies me. "And I have to tell you that I haven't worked out the answer yet. But as soon as I do, I'll be sure to let you in on the secret.

"Until then, I suggest we both keep our heads down."

✝CHAPTER THREE✝

14 JULY 1209

So this is Fanjeaux. I remember hearing that it was built on a hill, but not that the hill was such a high one. How lofty and white its walls are! How fine its church looks, up there near the castle. And how incredibly, unbelievably steep this road is.

"Give her a nudge," the Archdeacon advises as my horse slows to a standstill. "Just a little nudge, in the ribs. That's right. That's the way." She lurches forward, reluctantly, the loose stones rolling from under her hoofs. "It won't be long now," he says. "Only a few steps farther. I told you we'd reach it in time."

Yes, but only just. The sun is low and red; the shadows long and dark. Up ahead, there are hardly any people at the gates. Only one man, a garrison soldier, is lounging under the archway: he peers at us suspiciously as we pass through. When the Archdeacon raises a hand in blessing, that oafish creature actually spits on the ground.

I can't believe it. What disrespect!

"Not very keen on their clergy around here," the Archdeacon remarks, with a twinkle in his eye.

O Lord, have the workers of iniquity no knowledge? Wickedness is in the midst thereof; deceit and guile depart not from these streets.

"Of course, there's a strong Cathar influence," the Archdeacon adds. He's sitting very straight in the saddle, his alert, restless gaze flitting from house to house, from face to face. "They even have a community of Cathar priests living here. They call their priests 'Good Men' and 'Good Women.'"

"They have *women priests?*"

"Oh, yes."

Women priests! I don't believe it. And yet this place looks so ordinary, just like Pamiers, with its narrow streets and stone houses, its dung heaps and chickens and flapping laundry, its shingle roofs and shuttered windows. Even the smells are the same: the smells of wood smoke, of pigs, of boiled cabbage and bacon fat. And the people don't look very different, either. That woman over there looks just like Mengarde.

"Of course, their women priests don't actually live with their men priests," the Archdeacon continues. "The women live in a separate house, run by a member of one of the town's leading families. Guilhelme de Tonneins, her name is. A very pleasant woman."

"But—but—"

"But what?" Suddenly a small child darts across the road in front of us. My horse jerks its head and whinnies, retreating a few steps. The Archdeacon grabs my bridle. "I think perhaps I should lead you, from here on," he says. "This place is too dangerous for an inexperienced horseman. All the noise, and the movement—"

"But why are there so many?"

"What?"

"Why are there so many heretics?"

"Oh." He twitches his own reins, and we round a sharp corner. The road is still rising, but it's wider now, covered with worn and irregular paving stones. There's a ditch full of rubbish, and a cheesemonger's, and a well—a fine well, made of dressed stone, with seats set all around it. The houses are bigger, two-storied, rambling, each possessing a poultry yard, a dovecote, a garden, a barn. People are slouching in doorways, talking and drinking, some of them picking their teeth, some of them nursing infants, enjoying the last rays of the setting sun. As we pass, they stare and whisper.

"To be honest," the Archdeacon observes, eyeing the women who are sitting around the well, "I would speculate that the number of Cathars in this town is probably related to the degree of support they receive here."

"You mean from the Lord of Fanjeaux?"

"No." The Archdeacon smiles, but he's not smiling at me: he's smiling at a tall woman in a green gown, who's carrying a basket of eggs. As he inclines his head, she turns away, looking flustered. What in the world can he be doing? Does he *know* that woman? "There is no Lord of Fanjeaux," he says absent-mindedly. "Dame Cavears is the mistress here: she has seigneurial rights, and normally lives in the castle when she's not visiting her relatives. In this town, Isidore, it's the women who run things."

The women? How shameful. The Archdeacon

squints at me and laughs aloud: his laughter echoes down the street, where the people fall silent, and turn, and glare. He has an unrestrained, disconcerting laugh. "Don't worry, Isidore," he crows. "It's not so bad."

"Saint Paul said—"

"Yes, I know what Saint Paul said. 'Neither was the man created for the woman, but the woman for the man.' Well, that may be so, but here it seems to work the other way around. To our advantage, I may add." He's still grinning broadly, without discretion, like a common child of the streets. How dare he laugh? How dare he mock my words, and taunt me, and say such things? It's unjust. It's undignified. "The men in this country hate priests," he says, "but the women love them. Even the Cathar women. Even Dame Cavears." He's squinting at me again. "What's the matter, Isidore?"

May the dust of your land become lice. May your carcass be meat for the fowls of heaven.

"You're not angry, are you?" He sounds startled. "You always seem to be angry. What did I say this time?"

May your blood be poured out by the force of the sword.

"I'm not angry, Father."

"Yes, you are; I can tell. Is it something I said? About the Cathars?" He sighs, and carefully guides us around a stack of wood that's been left in the middle of the road. "Let me tell you something, Isidore. One of the finest women I ever knew was a Cathar. A Cathar priest. She may have been misguided, but she was very good. Her name was Esclaramonde."

"You—you—"

"What?"

"You actually seem to *like* the heretics!" (You little heathen. You shameless, noisy, stunted little heathen.) "Is that because you were an unbeliever yourself?"

"What?" He blinks. "What do you mean?"

"You were an Infidel, once. They told me so."

"Who told you?"

"They all did. At Pamiers."

He's shaking his head in disbelief. "I was never an Infidel," he says. "I was born a Christian."

"But you came from Jerusalem—"

"When I was in Jerusalem, Isidore, it *was* Christian." He's watching the road, because it's getting very rough, but he keeps glancing at my face as he steers the horses. "That was before the Turks invaded the Holy Land and defeated the Christian king. I

37

am a Christian Arab. I was born in Bethlehem and brought up in a monastery. I was never an Infidel."

Then why are you so impious? Why do you favor heretics? Why do you have such strange ideas?

"Mind you," he adds with another sly, taunting grin, "one of the finest *men* I've ever known was an Infidel. In fact he was the commander of the Infidel forces that seized Jerusalem. His name was Saladin."

Saladin! Lord Jesus, protect us.

"Saladin was a noble man. A chivalrous man. Most worthy of respect." (What a monster he is. Just look at the way he's laughing at me, secretly, behind that solemn expression. I can see it in his eyes. I can hear it in his voice.) "You know, Isidore," he says, "I realize that when you're brought up in a cloister, things look very simple. But the world isn't as clear as the writing in a book. It's not plain black on plain white. It's a lot more complicated."

So *you* say.

"However, we can't talk about that now." He lifts his head to look at the castle walls: they're looming in front of us, dark against the darkening sky. The battlements are saw-toothed, like the horns of an antelope; the towers seem to spring up like trees from a sheer face of solid rock. "We'd better save our philosophical discussions until after we've talked to Dame Cavears," he says. "Otherwise I won't have the breath left to deal with her."

You mean we're going into the castle now? We're really going *in*? Oh, give thanks unto the Lord, for He is good: at last I'm going to see the inside of a genuine castle. Will there be troubadours, I wonder? Will there be dancing and music and golden hangings on the walls? Will they serve marvelous delicacies, like peacocks and sugar and apples of paradise?

Are we actually going to sleep there?

"One more climb," the Archdeacon says, pointing at the ramp leading up to the gateway. "One more climb, and we can all relax." He drops my reins and takes the lead: his horse begins to ascend, wearily, carefully, stumbling on the uneven surface. I'm glad we didn't arrive any later. It's already getting a bit dim—imagine trying to find your way up here in the dark! Someone hails us from above, and the Archdeacon shouts a reply.

"Benedicite! I come in peace!" he bellows. There are three people hovering near the gates of the fortress: three men in steel hats. One of them is leaning on a

spear; the other two are eating nuts and laughing. They stop laughing when they see us.

"It's a priest," says one.

"It's the priest from Carcassonne," says another.

"Yes, that's right." The Archdeacon addresses them in a friendly fashion, as if they're his equals. "It's me again. I've come to see your mistress."

"What for?" The one with the spear pushes his helmet back from his forehead. He's as fat as a heifer at grass, and his haircut surpasseth all understanding. "We've already got a priest here."

"Yes, I realize that," the Archdeacon replies. "But what can you do about the fetters of love, my friends? I just can't tear myself away from your enchanting mistress."

The three men burst out laughing. They howl. They shriek. They slap their legs and hold their sides.

I don't understand. What's so funny?

"Oh, my friends," the Archdeacon chides, "do you hold such little hope for my suit?"

"Go on," the fat one splutters. "In you go."

"On the wings of love, most fair."

"With a boot up your backside, more like!"

What brainless talk is this? Why should an Archdeacon stoop to such vulgar badinage? He jerks

40

his head at me, and the sound of laughter soon fades as we pass through the thick walls, emerging onto an open stretch of gravel with a great stone keep at one end. God be praised! What a work is this!

"You have to watch how you conduct yourself around Fanjeaux." The Archdeacon swings a leg over his saddle and drops lightly to the ground. "They're quite capable of refusing entry, if you put on airs. Come on, Isidore, down you get."

Down. I have to get down. But I seem to have lost the stirrup. . . .

"Here, take my hand," he says. "I'll hold the horse. Just bring your other foot—that's it."

By the blood of the Lamb! What's happened to my knees?

"Are you all right?" He peers at me as I sway and stagger. "Don't worry, it won't last. You'll soon develop the muscles to cope."

I'm coping perfectly well, thank you.

"Can you walk? Would you like to lean on my shoulder?"

No, I wouldn't like to lean on your shoulder! I'm not an old man! I don't need your help, and I don't need your sympathy.

"I'm fine, thank you."

"Are you sure?"

41

"Yes, thank you."

The Archdeacon looks around. There's a pall of smoke hanging over the clumsy huddle of buildings propped against the inner wall of the bailey: they're made of wood and mud brick, and there are lights showing through some of their doors. I can smell cooking, and see people lurking in the shadows, but no one moves or utters a word of greeting. Only the dogs approach, growling and sniffing our ankles.

Good dogs. Nice dogs.

"Useless bunch of ill-mannered pus-bags," the Archdeacon mutters. Undaunted by the hostile atmosphere, he raises his voice to address a man in a leather cap, who's slouching on a doorstep with his arms folded. "You there! Fellow! If you're not busy, you can take our horses."

"Where to?" A frightening voice, like a thunderclap, but the Archdeacon doesn't flinch.

"Why," he says winningly, "to the stables, of course. I am a guest of Dame Cavears."

The man grunts. He comes forward and snatches the reins from the Archdeacon—who takes a very deep breath, holds it for an instant, and slowly lets it out again.

"Come, Isidore," he murmurs. "I think we'd better announce ourselves."

I can hear a baby crying. I can see a ruined tower, all gaping holes and piles of rubble. There's a discarded shoe lying in the dust near my foot, and a goat nibbling at a cabbage stalk. But there's no music, no dancing, no silken flags. And that smell— it smells more like salted herring than roast peacock.

Oh, Lord, am I to be disappointed once again? Why are things never as good as the poets and philosophers tell us they are? Is it because I'm unworthy to drink of the river of thy pleasures?

Or am I simply in the wrong place, at the wrong time?

"Come, Isidore."

It's the Archdeacon; he's heading for the keep. How can he move so swiftly after all that riding? When he reaches the stairs, he bounds up them two at a time, like a young goat, and waits for me at the top with his foot tapping.

The door of the keep is disappointingly small, with no carvings or pillars to ornament it.

"Now, don't worry if Dame Cavears teases you a bit," he says in a low voice. "She's an old lady, and she's practically blind, so you have to be tolerant.

Just stand up straight and take it like a man. That's what I do." He grins at me, and winks. "Don't fret yourself, boy. Remember what I said? The women in this country love priests." He gives me a push. "Go on," he urges. "In you go. I'm right behind you."

✝CHAPTER FOUR✝

14 July 1209

Behold the house of Hezekiah, full of precious things. Behold the merchandise of fallen Babylon: the gold and the silver, the silk and the linen, the vessels of ivory and brass. Painted chests, as blue as sapphires and as red as rubies; tablecloths heavy with embroidered flowers; tapestry hangings like the pages of some great illuminated manuscript, glittering in the candlelight. Every surface seems to be enameled or gilded or painted or carved, busy with color, gleaming with richness. Only the floor is unadorned.

I feel like the Queen of Sheba coming before the wealth of Solomon. There is no more spirit in me.

"Who's that?" The colors shift as someone moves; it's so hard to distinguish the people against the patterns. But there she is—I can see her now. An old, old woman, with a face like a sun-dried apple and a gown as scarlet as sin. "Who's that?" she squawks. "Is that you, Enguerrand?"

"No, Madame, it is not," the Archdeacon replies. At the sound of his voice, there's a flurry of movement: heads turn; benches creak. I can count three faces, all of them female. The room is so abundant in candles—great bunches of them, made of beeswax—that every line, every hair, is clearly illuminated. The old woman is sitting on a kind of throne, with a back to it, as if she were a bishop. She wears a rich veil, embroidered with gold, and many golden rings. The other woman is dressed simply, in a dark robe and veil; she has a humble, careworn face, like the virtuous woman of Solomon's proverbs, who riseth while it is yet night and eateth not the bread of idleness. Her eyes are gray, just like those of the girl beside her—the girl who looks up, and looks away, and makes such a beautiful shape with her mouth; the girl who is as fair as a lily among thorns. Her skin is white, like the heavenly robes of the martyrs, but her hair is raven black through a net of woven silk.

46

Bless the Lord, O my soul, and forget not all His benefits.

"Why, it's Pagan!" the old woman cries. "It's little Pagan! I'd recognize that voice anywhere."

"Madame." The Archdeacon bows. "It's good to see you."

"Come here—sit down—look, Guilhelme, it's Father Pagan!"

Guilhelme nods. The girl beside her glowers. What a pity that such a beautiful face should be marred by such a sulky expression.

"You're just like a bird," the old woman says with a cackle. "He's just like a bird, isn't he, Guilhelme? Flitting in and out, surprising everyone."

"If I'm a bird, Dame Cavears, then I'm a golden oriole to your fruit trees." The Archdeacon smiles.

"Oh, will you listen to him? Off he goes, the little devil! Sit down, Father—I've been pining for a good joke. Guilhelme here doesn't know any. Have you met Guilhelme de Tonneins? Oh, of course you have. And this is her daughter, Aude."

Guilhelme de Tonneins! Isn't she the arch-heretic? The Evil Priestess? Lord God, protect us! The Archdeacon smiles and nods calmly, as if this nest of serpents is a field of flowers. Suddenly the old woman grabs him and points at me.

"Who's that?" she demands.

"That's my scribe," he says. "Isidore, this is the Dame de Fanjeaux."

"What's wrong with his head? Is he bleeding?"

"No, Sister, that's just his hair." The Evil Priestess sounds amused. (How could I ever have thought her humble?) "He has red hair."

"Red hair? Show me. Come here, Isidore. Come on! Over here." Her hands are so old and fat and unsteady—she has hairs on her face like a man, and little black eyes like a rat's. "Come closer, or I can't see you. No, down here! By the Virgin's milk, Father, there's no end to him."

"Yes, he is rather tall."

In Thee, O Lord, do I put my trust; deliver me in Thy righteousness. Her fumbling hands reach for my head; they drag it down and down until I'm almost in her lap—until I can feel her breath on my tonsure.

I can't believe this is happening.

"What a beautiful color, Guilhelme," she croaks. "It's like autumn leaves, don't you think? What a pity you're not a girl, young man—you'd break hearts with that hair." She laughs a wheezy laugh. "But I don't suppose I need to tell you that, eh? You must have broken a score of hearts already."

"Look, Mama." It's Aude's voice: I can't see her face, but I know it's her voice, young and high and spiteful. "Look, he's blushing. He's as red as his hair."

"Don't you tease him, young lady," the old woman retorts. "You've no cause to feel superior. It's disgraceful, a young girl like you living like a nun. And such a pretty girl, too. Don't you think she's pretty, Isidore?"

What are you saying? Leave me alone! When I pull back, she laughs and laughs, rocking from side to side, showing her slimy, toothless gums. And the Archdeacon—the Archdeacon is grinning too; they're all grinning, every one of them except Aude. Aude is scowling.

"What *he* thinks is of no interest to me," she says, and the old woman waves a hand at her.

"Go and tell Pons that we want some food, my dear. I'm sure these poor lads must be hungry. Off you go, now." She watches Aude rise and stalk off. "That girl should be married," she declares in a loud voice. "If she doesn't marry soon, she'll curdle."

The Evil Priestess shakes her head. "You know that's out of the question, Sister," she says, and the old woman turns to the Archdeacon.

"Our Good Men don't believe in marriage," she explains, taking his arm. "They say it's a sin."

"Yes, I know."

"Well, it might be a sin for some, but not for a girl like Aude." The old woman wags a finger at her heretical friend. "What that girl needs is a man. A man and a baby."

"But she doesn't *want* a baby." The Evil Priestess sounds tired. "She believes very strongly in the teachings of the faith. She believes that having a child is condemning another soul to hell. Sometimes I think she blames me for having borne her—though I did it long before I embraced the Truth."

By the blood of the Lamb! This is heresy, pure and simple. But the Archdeacon doesn't even cross himself. He just removes his arm from the old woman's grip and sits on a stool near her feet.

"You know, Madame, I didn't come here simply to pay my respects," he says. "I came here to warn you."

"Warn me? About what?"

"About the coming of the northern knights." He speaks quite casually as he sits there arranging the skirts of his robe—yet this is a crucial point in the conversation. "Have you heard about the army that is gathering up north?"

"The army? Oh, yes, I heard about that from

Aimery de Montreal. He dropped in last week and gave me a beautiful casket. Guilhelme, where's that casket? I want to show it to Father Pagan—"

"Madame, did he tell you what this army is going to do? It's going to invade Languedoc."

"You mean it's going to *try* to invade Langue-doc." The old woman waves her hand. "You mustn't worry about the northerners, Father—they'll never get past Carcassonne. Why, you know what the walls there are like. The Devil himself couldn't scale them."

"Yes, but—"

"Ah! Is that Aude? And here's Pons with the food. What's that you've got there, Pons? Not onions, I hope—you know they make me fart."

What a monstrous woman. As greedy as a pig, as lascivious as a goat, and as shrill as a manticore. Truly she walks in the streets of Babylon, and wallows in the mire thereof.

"I can smell beans," she complains. "Why did you bring me beans, Pons? You know they're as bad as onions. Oh, I see, the apples are for me, are they? Did you put honey on them? Good boy." Pons is covered in flea bites: you can hardly see his face for spots. He's carrying a big, steaming dish full of beans and bacon. Aude has the bread and the stewed apples. "Just put them down there, on that bench. Would you like some beans, Father?"

"I certainly would."

"Give him some bread, Aude, that's a good girl. I hope these apples aren't too hot." The old woman begins to push great handfuls of sweet, sloppy fruit into her mouth. The juice runs down her chin and drips onto her bosom. She licks her fingers with a long blue tongue. "Go on, Isidore, tuck in. That bread tastes better with beans."

No, thank you.

"Here." The Evil Priestess hands me the dish. "Take some."

Not from you, I won't.

"Aren't you hungry? You should eat more. You're much too thin. Isn't he thin, Father?" When the old woman speaks, she sends bits of apple spraying across the room in all directions. "He's as thin as a needle."

"What's wrong, Isidore?" The Archdeacon lifts an eyebrow. "Don't you like beans?"

"Of course he does. Everyone likes beans. Go on, my dear. I ordered them for everyone."

"No, thank you." (Just leave me alone.)

"But why not?" The old woman is beginning to sound plaintive. "What do you think I'm trying to

52

do, poison you? What's the matter with the boy, Father?"

"Just try some, Isidore—you're being rude."

I'm being rude? That's a joke! What about her?

"Beans are bad for clerics, Father."

"What?" He frowns at me. "What on earth are you talking about?"

"Pythagoras said that wits are dulled by beans. Varro said that bishops shouldn't eat them."

"But you're not a bishop!" the old woman cries. And suddenly Aude speaks, in drawling, sarcastic tones.

"Perhaps he's on a fast," she says.

"Oh, don't be ridiculous, girl. What kind of sins would *he* have to fast for? He's barely out of the egg." The old woman snorts, and wipes her mouth with the corner of her sleeve. "There's only one sin he could have committed, and that's coming out of his mother's womb backward."

"Perhaps he forgot to make a sign of the cross when he stepped in a cow pat," Aude says slyly. "Perhaps he ate too much roast pork and burped when the priest was saying grace."

"No, no, I know what he did. He looked down one day when he was pissing, and he saw what was there!"

53

Yes, that's right. Laugh away, old woman. You'll be laughing on the other side of your face when the Crusaders come. Then your joy will soon be ceased, and your dance will be turned to mourning.

"He's a good boy, Madame," the Archdeacon says mildly. "He doesn't deserve to be laughed at."

"Why, of course he's a good boy! It's written all over him. That's why his sin must be so very, very small." The old woman leans forward. "Go on, my dear, tell us why you're fasting. What was your sin? Was it a wink? A fart? A roll on the dung heap?"

"Whatever my sins are, they're not as bad as yours!" (Shouting.) "You're all heretics, and you're going to burn in hell!"

Dead silence. The old woman sucks in her bottom lip. The Archdeacon covers his eyes with his hand. Aude scowls ferociously.

"Why do you say that, Isidore?" It's the Evil Priestess. Her voice is quiet. Calm. Amiable. "Why do you say we're heretics?"

"Because you are! Because you believe that marriage is a sin!"

"But how do you know that it isn't a sin?" She's talking as if I were a child. "How do you know that this earth isn't Satan's realm and that giving birth

54

to a child isn't condemning a heavenly soul to a hellish imprisonment?"

"Because it's ridiculous!"

"Why?"

"Lady Guilhelme—" the Archdeacon begins. But she lifts a hand and continues.

"Why is it ridiculous, Isidore? Tell me."

"Because—because—" (Oh, what's the answer?) "Because in the gospel of Saint John it says 'The world was made by Him.' And it's talking about God, not the Devil." (So there.)

"But what if it's referring to our souls, which are God's, and not to our bodies?" she objects. "Remember what Jesus says later, in the same gospel? 'The prince of this world cometh, and hath nothing in me.' Satan is the prince of this world."

"So?" (You stupid woman.) "That doesn't mean that Satan is our God and creator. When the Scriptures say 'The king of the gentiles lords it over them,' does it mean that the king is their God and creator? Of course it doesn't."

"But Christ said 'My kingdom is not of this world.'"

Yes, he did, didn't he? But I know that he didn't mean—I know that he really meant—um—oh—

"Isidore," the Archdeacon says.

No! Wait, I've got it! "He didn't mean that his kingdom wasn't over this world. He meant that it wasn't *from* this world. He meant that this world didn't give him his power."

"Then," she replies, "why did he say to the crowd: 'Ye are of your father the Devil, and the lusts of your father ye will do'?"

Why did he? I've got to think. But I can't think. . . . There's something wrong . . . a strange smell . . .

Of burning.

"Isidore?" The Archdeacon's voice. "Isidore? What is it?"

Oh, no. No! The Devil!

Help!

✝CHAPTER FIVE✝

14 JULY 1209

My face hurts.

It's dark.

Where am I?

That's a ceiling up there, but it's not Father Fulbert's ceiling. It's too high, and there are no hams. No hams, no pots, no garlic. No swallows' nests, either. And what's this underneath me? A pillow? Am I in bed?

Oh, God. Of course.

My devil.

It came, and I must have hurt myself—I must have—I didn't—O God, why hast Thou cast me off forever?

"Isidore?"

That's the Archdeacon's voice. Where is he? It's so dark, and this room seems so big. . . . No, wait, there he is. Holding a lamp, his shadow looming behind him. He leans over the bed.

"Isidore?"

He reaches out, touches my hand. His skin gleams in the lamplight, because he's not wearing anything on his arms or his chest, although there's a blanket draped over his shoulders.

"Why didn't you tell me?" he says.

Go away. Please. I don't want to talk.

"Was it because you wanted to leave Merioc? Is that why?" He sits down: there must be a stool right there, beside my pillow. "You should have told me, Isidore. You could have fallen off your horse during one of these fits. You could have killed yourself."

Killed myself? Who cares? The truth is, I should have died at birth. Let the day perish wherein I was born, and the night in which it was said: there is a man child conceived.

"How often does it happen?"

The walls of this room are painted, but the paint is very old and blackened by smoke. There are holes and scratches scored deep in the plaster.

"Isidore? Look at me. How often does this happen?"

How often? Too often. Even in the dimness, I can see he's frowning, but he doesn't seem annoyed.

"Once a month?" he says. "Once a week?"

I can only nod.

"Once a week? You mean it happens once a week?"

"Sometimes more." My voice cracks; it's raw and ragged. I need a drink. "I'm thirsty."

"I'll get you something."

He disappears, and I can hear his footsteps fading with the light. But he's back in an instant.

"Here," he says. He has a fine glass goblet in his hand. "Can you hold it yourself?"

I'm not a cripple, Father. Of course I can hold it. The glass feels warm, because the wine has been mulled—and there are herbs in it, too, which leave a bitter taste. But at least it's wet.

He's peering at me with those big dark eyes.

"Is this the reason you're fasting?" he says, very softly.

Well, of course it is. Can't you tell? Didn't you see? I've heard that I even foam at the mouth, like a mad dog. And that I twitch and growl and piss and kick and lose everything—everything—like a monster. A monster.

"What did they tell you, Isidore? About these fits?"

"They told me it was a devil."

"Taking possession of you?"

"Yes."

"And do you believe that?"

"Of course."

"Why?"

Why? *Why?* Because of the smell, that's why. Only the Bottomless Pit could smell so infernal.

"It's the smell." Gasping. "It always comes . . . just before . . . "

"What smell?"

"The smell of burning. Burning flesh. I—I—" I can't explain. I can't bear it. Covering my face with one hand, because I don't want him to see.

"This is the reason, isn't it? The reason why you were in that village. The reason why no one would send you to university." He sounds so calm. So sympathetic. "They were frightened of you, weren't they?"

Frightened? I don't know. Perhaps they were frightened. Perhaps they were simply disgusted.

The other secondaries used to imitate me when the Bishop wasn't looking. It was the ugliest thing I've ever seen.

"You certainly frightened Dame Cavears," the Archdeacon continues. "She thinks you're possessed. It took a lot of careful negotiating before she would allow us to sleep in this room tonight. You've made things rather difficult, I'm afraid." He takes the empty goblet from my hand. "Tell me about your devil, Isidore."

My devil? Why? He's holding the lamp on his knee, and it throws strange shadows across his face; there's a long, jagged scar on his arm, and another across his shoulder. In fact there are scars all over him—on his forehead, on his chest, on his hand. They look very white against his dark skin.

"Do you remember what happens?" he inquires. "Do you remember anything else, besides the smell?"

"No, I don't."

"Have you ever tried to get rid of this thing?"

"Of course."

"How?"

"With fasting." (Let me think.) "With medicines . . ."

"What medicines?"

"Holy water. Hellebore. Mugwort and mandrake and wolf's flesh—"

"Exorcism?"

"Oh, yes. Three times. 'Therefore accursed devil, hear thy doom and give honor to the Lord Jesus Christ that thou depart with thy works from this servant—'"

"Anything else?"

"Well . . . they beat me." (I'll never forget that. Never.) "They tied me down and beat me."

The Archdeacon closes his eyes for a moment. He leans down to put my goblet on the floor and wraps his blanket more tightly around his shoulders. The silence is profound: I can't hear anything, not a single chirp or rustle. Everyone must be asleep.

I wonder how late it is.

"There was a man I knew at university, in Montpellier," the Archdeacon says. "He suffered from the same kind of attacks as you do. He was a good man, and very learned: he'd read more books than anyone else of my acquaintance. What's more, he used to say that his devil wasn't a devil at all, but a kind of fever. He told me that he'd filled his head with so much information that his mind would grow hot and boil over like a kettle." Pause. "I must say I'm inclined to agree with him."

A fever? Truly? But what about the smell?

"I've never believed in fasting for young people," the Archdeacon adds. "I think it's like bloodletting: good when you're strong, bad when you're not so strong. In my opinion, Isidore, you should stop fasting. You should eat more, and sleep more, and get plenty of fresh air and exercise." He grins at me and screws up his nose. "I can just imagine what kind of life you've been leading, shut away with a smelly tallow lamp, hunched over a book, stuffing your head with Virgil and Cicero and Cassiodorus—"

"There weren't any books at Merioc."

"And how long were you at Merioc?"

"Um . . ." It seemed like a thousand years. "About three weeks."

"Well, that's not very long, is it? No, it seems to me that you've got a fever, from reading too much. After all, when people have a fever, don't they often lose their wits? Don't they often forget where they are, and thrash about, and lose their power to communicate? Hmm?"

"I suppose so."

"Good." He rises. "Then you should keep cool, and drink lots of water, and eat lots of balm and lettuce—cold, moist foods—and make sure that you get enough sleep. In fact, I'll leave you to sleep right now, because you've got a big day tomorrow. A big day and a long journey."

"Back to Merioc?"

There. I've said it. He catches his breath and looks away, and I know—I know what he's thinking—I know what it means, that expression, that uneasy silence. Oh, it's not fair, it's not fair—why does this always happen? Why is light given to a man whose way is hid, and whom God hath hedged in?

"I can't risk having you fall, Isidore." He sounds helpless. "You must see that. You might hurt yourself badly, falling from a horse. You might kill yourself."

So what? I don't care. My soul is weary of life. I eat ashes like bread, and mingle my drink with weeping. What is my strength, that I should hope? What is my end, that I should prolong my existence?

"Isidore . . ." He's squinting at me through thick black eyelashes. "Try to understand, will you? I travel around a lot. I'm always visiting towns.

64

Abbeys. Villages. That's what I do. I take care of the Bishop's business throughout his diocese. How can I take you along, when you're not even . . . when you can't . . . oh, God." He runs his fingers through his hair. He turns away and turns back again. He spreads his hands. "If only you could warn me before it happened—"

"But I can!" (I'm not going back to Merioc. Not now.) "There's the smell of burning. I just told you."

He sits down. "You mean—"

"When I smell the fire, I'll warn you, and then you can help me."

"But what if I'm not there?"

"You won't be at Merioc, either." Oh, please. Please, Father, don't send me back. Nothing could be worse than Merioc, nothing could, not even you and your vulgar, impious, irritating jokes.

"Are you sure?" He sounds very stern. "Are you sure about this?"

"Yes, Father." Shame on you, Isidore—your molten image is falsehood. Forgive me for lying, O Lord, but I'm desperate—you know I am. The spirit of a man will sustain his infirmity; but a wounded spirit, who can bear?

"Very well." The Archdeacon sighs. "I'll give you another chance. I'll let you stay with me."

Praise ye the Lord! Praise ye, the name of the Lord! Praise Him, O ye servants of—

"But I'm warning you, Isidore: this is the one and only time." He wags his finger. "If you fall off your horse, then it's back to Merioc. Understand?"

"Yes, Father."

"And kindly see if you can produce the occasional smile, will you? It'll make things so much more pleasant." He stands up, hitching his blanket back onto his shoulders. "I'm going to bed now, so I'll leave the lamp right here. If you want anything . . ." He pauses, cocks his head, eyes my face. "If you want anything, you can get it yourself," he concludes, and disappears into the shadows.

I waited patiently for the Lord, and He inclined unto me, and heard my cry. He brought me up out of a horrible pit, out of the miry clay, and set my feet upon a rock.

Blessed is the man that maketh the Lord his trust.

✠CHAPTER SIX✠

15 JULY 1209

The pain! Lord Jesus, the pain! Every joint is groaning. Every muscle throbs.

"Is it bad?" the Archdeacon inquires. "Don't worry, it'll get better. The second day is always the worst."

Yes, yes, I know. The second day is always the worst. Good fortune deceives, but bad fortune enlightens. The greatest joy is ushered in by the greatest pain.

I've heard them all, and they don't help me one little bit.

"Anyway, it's not very far," the Archdeacon continues. "Look, see that? That's Prouille, over there. That's our destination." He points across the hazy expanse of fields and forest, toward the silhouette of distant mountains. There are five roads, converging on the very hill beneath us, and the sparkle of a river in the distance. "See that hummock, near the river? See that little speck on top of it? Well, that speck is a windmill. And the windmill belongs to Prouille. We'll be there before noon."

Noon. *Noon?* But that's a lifetime away!

"Come on, Isidore." He nudges his horse in the ribs, and the beast starts to pick its way carefully down the steep, dusty road, between rocks and roots and ditches. As soon as we leave the shadow of Fanjeaux's walls, the sun hits my scalp like a hammer; it stabs at my eyes and sucks up my sweat. By the blood of the Lamb, how sore my legs are! All around us there are people working in the vineyards, and people carrying water, and people laboring toward the city gates beneath huge loads of firewood—but none of these people is worse off than I am.

"We must stop at Prouille to see if my Bishop has written to me," the Archdeacon remarks in a loud voice. He's up ahead, sitting gracefully in the saddle, his backside rolling with a smooth, easy rhythm as his horse sets the pace. "My Bishop generally sends his letters to Prouille, if I'm in this part of the world: there's a nunnery there, run by a very reliable Austin canon who gets around a bit. Dominic Guzman, he's called. Originally came across the Pyrenees, to preach to the Cathars. On one of those missions I told you about." He glances back over his shoulder and grins. "Poor old Isidore. You're not having much fun, are you?"

Fun? What's fun? I survive, little man. I don't have fun.

"Never mind—you'll enjoy it when we get there." As we reach level ground, the road widens, and he pulls at the reins that have been dangling so loosely from his fingers, slowing his horse until I manage to catch up. "They have books at Prouille," he adds.

"Books?"

"Yes, I thought that might interest you." Another quick, sharp glance. "It's not a big place—in fact some of the Sisters are still living in Fanjeaux, because the convent isn't finished yet. But Dominic brought a fair number of books from Osma. Mostly theological texts, of course, and books of Christian thought: Jerome, Augustine, Ambrose. At least six of them."

Books! How I long to feel the weight of a book in my hand. How I long to turn a page, and pass

69

through the print as you'd pass through a door, into that world of wise and lofty spirits, of strange animals, of noble deeds and faraway cities. If only I could crawl into a book and stay there for the rest of my life.

". . . But you can't help admiring him." The Archdeacon is still talking, his eyes fixed on the road ahead. "Anyone else would have given up—everyone else *did* give up—but not Dominic. He stayed, and he kept preaching. He traipses from one smelly little village to another, living off scraps, patiently arguing with a bunch of boneheads who wouldn't know a syllogism if you slapped them across the face with it and stuffed it down their collective earholes." He laughs to himself. "Personally, I would have given up long ago."

Yes, but then you're not a holy person, are you? You have no humility. No restraint. You don't preach to heretics; you share meals with them. How can you hope to understand the actions of a truly pious soul?

But I mustn't be ungrateful. Don't be ungrateful, Isidore. At least this man has some charity in his heart.

"From Prouille we'll move on to Laurac," he says, "where we'll talk to Dame Blanche. She's the Cathar who happens to run that town. Then, when we've completely failed to convince her of anything, we'll visit my friend Roland, on our way back to Carcassonne. You'll like Roland. He's a wonderful man. Then we'll return to the Bishop, and inform him that this whole trip was a complete waste of time (as I said it would be), because these people are as stubborn as mules, and even if the Archangel Gabriel, in all his ineffable glory, appeared with a chorus of cherubim—"

"Bloodsucker!"

"Devil's priest!"

What? Who said that?

"Go away!"

"Go away—we don't want you here!"

I don't believe it. They're peasants! Ordinary peasants, standing in a field of oats. How can they say such things? How can they utter such blasphemies?

"Ignore them," the Archdeacon murmurs. "Just ignore them."

"Wine-swiller!"

"Bed-louse!"

"Look, it's a priest! It's a man who farts out both ends!"

Jeering laughter. Angry voices. A man with a

71

scythe steps onto the road in front of us: he's big and hairy, and built like the Tower of Babel.

"Don't stop," says the Archdeacon quietly. He kicks his horse into a brisk trot and sails past the scowling peasant with his nose in the air.

O Lord God, in Thee do I put my trust: save me from all them that persecute me—

Thunk! What's that? *Thunk!* They're throwing stones! *Thunk!* "Father Pagan—"

Help! What's happened? *"Father!"* Stop, horse, stop—it was only a stone! Help, help, I don't know what to do!

His hand, grabbing my reins. Pulling the horse's head down. His soothing voice, firm but quiet. "Shhh. It's all right, sweetheart. It's all right, girl. . . ." The horse stops rearing, but its ears are still laid flat on its skull.

Howls of laughter from somewhere nearby.

"Isidore? Isidore! Let go of her mane. You're safe now." Why does he look so angry? It wasn't my fault! Oh, I see. He's not angry with me; he's angry with them.

"Who threw that stone?" he cries. "Who did it? You—yes, you! Did *you* throw that stone?"

The man in question has a doughy, formless face like a bear pup (which, as everyone knows, is licked

72

into shape by its mother at birth). He growls something between teeth as black as the tents of Kedar.

"What? What did you say?" The Archdeacon lashes out with a voice that could flay the skin off a bullock. "Speak up, maggot-bag, or don't you have the courage? Would you prefer to wait until my back is turned, so you can throw stones at a defenseless child?"

What do you mean? I'm not a child!

"Oh, what mighty warriors! What noble adversaries! Brave wolves, hunting a flightless dove—a newborn lamb—doubtless you would have done the same to Saint Stephen!" (How vicious his tone is; he uses his tongue like a whip.) "But no, you're not wolves. You're dogs! Mangy dogs, snapping at our heels, preying on the weak and the gentle—"

"*You* are the wolf!" someone yells. "You take our lambs and grow fat on them, like all priests!"

"Fat? *Fat?* Have you waddled home and weighed *yourself* lately, grease-bucket?" The Archdeacon points at me. "Look at this boy! Look at his clothes! Is he fat? Is he rich? Is he a *priest?* Why don't you people use your brains, for once, instead of behaving like a bunch of mindless brigands—"

Thunk! A stone hits the ground in front of him.

73

Thunk! Another one sails over his head and bounces off the tree to his right.

"Devil!"

"Thief!"

The Lord God protect us! What are they doing? They're coming closer, all eight of them—no, ten—no, look, there are more of them, with scythes and spades! Quick, Father, quick, we must flee before they—

"Haah!" His horse bounds forward. The sunlight flashes on the blade in his hand, a long, swinging blade that cuts through the air, lunging, twisting, as he charges straight into the knot of peasants. It breaks up instantly; the peasants run and shout; they scatter their tools and duck their heads and plunge into the cornfield, hiding like rats, with the Archdeacon in pursuit. I can't—I don't—by the blood of the Lamb of God—!

"Father!"

But he's slowing now—he's turning—he's coming back. Is he insane? Has he lost his mind? What lunacy is this?

"Don't worry," he says in a loud, breathless voice. "I've scared them off." He brings his horse alongside me and sheathes his sword. (A sword! On a priest! I didn't even know it was there. . . .)

74

"They won't come back; they're a bunch of cowards. If I had been Roland, they would never have attacked us in the first place."

"How—how—"

"Are you all right?" He peers into my face. "You're not scared, are you? They're just rabble. Look, they're halfway to Fanjeaux already."

"You have a sword!"

"Oh, yes. I have a sword." He kicks his horse into a trot; my own mount follows without the slightest encouragement. "You have to carry arms around here," he says. "The roads can be very dangerous."

"But you're a priest!"

"Being a priest is no guarantee of safety, Isidore. Not in this part of the world."

That's not what I mean. That's not the point. A priest is a man of God; he doesn't bear arms like a mercenary. Christ said: "Put up thy sword into the sheath." He didn't say, "Cut off his other ear, Peter!"

"You—you shouldn't have to carry a sword." My voice sounds weak and thin. "You should have guards beside you, like the Bishops."

"Guards? Nonsense!" He waves a hand. "If I had guards, the brigands would only assume that I had something worth stealing. Besides, I don't need guards. I was a soldier, once, before I became a priest. I was trained as a squire by Lord Roland Roucy de Bram—the greatest knight in Christendom. I fought against the Turks in the Holy Land. Why should I need guards to handle a few miserable peasants?" He looks back at me and laughs. "I can take care of myself, Isidore. I always have, and I always will."

Conceited midget. Behold, he burns incense to vanity, and esteemeth brass as rotten wood. But just remember, Archdeacon: the Lord of Hosts shall be upon everyone that is proud and lofty, and he shall be humbled.

So don't be surprised if one day, at some crucial moment, all your skills fail to deliver you from the worst threat you've ever faced.

‡CHAPTER SEVEN‡

15 JULY 1209

Whatever can have happened to Prouille? It seems to be falling to pieces. First the crumbling walls, then the ruins of Saint Martin's chapel, and now this—this battered windmill, constructed on the remains of a fortified tower. They must have dismantled the tower to build the windmill, because they've used identical stones for both of them.

I wonder who's responsible for allowing the place to collapse like this.

The foundations of the tower are big and square and very thick. There's a communal oven built nearby, but no one's using it. A few dilapidated houses seem to be propping each other up; the sheep pen in the village square is empty; the only activity is concentrated around the fountain, where a handful of old men and young women sit on the steps, talking.

They fall silent as we pass them.

"See what Dominic's done?" The Archdeacon points to a low, bulky structure near the weather-worn church. It looks as if it's been thrown together hurriedly, out of rubbish and remnants: bricks, stone, wood, even ancient-looking tiles. "Not bad, is it?" he says. "They're more or less finished now — they just have to add another room, because of the number of people who want to join the convent. And they have full use of the church, of course, because the priest comes from Fanjeaux. Prouille isn't a parish any longer. Aha!" He raises a hand. "That looks like Sister Alazais."

She's carrying a bucket, whoever she is: probably heading for the fountain. But as soon as she sees us, she stops and darts back inside.

"Glad tidings," the Archdeacon mutters. He drops to the ground as lightly as a petal and stands there stretching: I can hear the crackle of his joints even from this distance. "Come on, Isidore, you can't sit up there all day."

By the blood of the Lamb, I'm going to have to get down. I'm going to have to move! Have mercy

upon me, O God, according to Thy loving kind-
ness.

"How do you feel?" He's looking up at me.
"Want some help?"

Oh! Ah! My knees! My back! My bottom!

"Come on, you can do it."

Of course I can do it! I just—I can't—ouch! Ah!
There.

"There, see? Not a problem. We'll make a horseman out of you yet." He laughs through his nose.
"Out of what's left of you, anyway."

"Father!" Someone hails us from the door of the
convent: a slim man in a white canon's surplice,
just like mine. He comes toward us with his hands
outstretched. "Father Pagan, what a great joy."

"Dominic." The two men exchange a Kiss of
Peace, with Father Dominic stooping to embrace
the Archdeacon. His hair gleams red in the sunlight. Or perhaps it's not red, exactly—more reddish. A reddish brown. He has a ruddy complexion
and bad teeth and long fingers. He looks very
tired.

"I've been expecting you," he says in a low voice.
"The Bishop has sent you a letter. Are you well?
How was your journey?"

"Not bad," the Archdeacon replies. "Could have

been worse. We had some trouble this morning, though."

"Trouble?" Father Dominic looks concerned. "Not brigands?"

"No, no. Just a bunch of peasants and a couple of rocks. The sort of thing that's always happening to you, Dominic." Laying a hand on my shoulder, the Archdeacon adds: "This is Isidore, my new scribe. He's from Pamiers."

Father Dominic smiles. He takes both my hands and presses them. "Welcome, my son," he murmurs. "It is a joy and a pleasure to welcome you here."

"F-father . . ." I can't even bow, because my back is too sore. But he doesn't seem to mind.

"Come," he says. "Come inside and rest. *Sister! Sister Curtolane!* Sister Curtolane will take care of the horses."

A woman appears, and another, and another. They're dressed in gray and brown and black; they hover around us like bees around a hive, and follow us into the convent. One of them is standing just inside the door, with a basin of water and a towel. Praise ye the Lord, that water feels good! So cold, so fresh, so soothing on my face.

I think I must be sunburned.

"Please—won't you sit down?" Father Dominic

80

steps aside, motioning with his hand. It's very dim in here, after all that sunshine, but I can just make out some tables and benches, and rushes on the floor. Is this the refectory, then? It's all very plain, although the drinking cups are of good quality, finely glazed in rich colors. A plump little woman is arranging them on the largest table.

"Why, it's Ermessende!" the Archdeacon cries. "Sister Ermessende, you're a happy sight for a weary wanderer."

She beams all over her round, red, surprised-looking face.

"Father Pagan!" she chirps. "We're so pleased to see you—"

"And Sister Alazais." The Archdeacon grins at a solid woman with heavy brows. "You're looking fit, Sister."

"I am," she says, with a slow smile. She has a mighty voice, the sort of voice that breaketh the cedars, and maketh the hinds to calve. "I am fit and strong."

"Well, that's good news. I know that this whole place would fall apart without you. Isidore, come here! You must meet the Prioress. Sister Guilhelmine, this is my scribe, Isidore. He's from Pamiers."

All these faces—it's so confusing—but this must be the Prioress. She's rather tall, with beautiful white teeth and a very large . . . a very large . . . bosom.

But I mustn't look at that.

"Sit down, Father—you must be so tired." They fuss around, all rustling skirts and fluttering hands, and the Archdeacon seems to be enjoying himself: he's grinning and joking and laughing in a most improper way, because you shouldn't behave like that to women, not when you're a priest. Suddenly he leans over and grabs my wrist and says, "Just wait till you taste the food here, Isidore. It's marvelous. Simply marvelous. I always do very well here, because Dominic gives all his food to visitors. He lives on boiled nettles and bits of old shoe."

Laughter from the women. "Oh, no," Sister Ermessende protests. "Father Dominic doesn't eat nettles—"

"Only because you don't serve them to him," the Archdeacon rejoins. "But I'm sure you could make even nettles taste delicious, Sister. You're such a superb cook."

She blushes and dimples, and the other women smile. I can't believe this. It's disgusting. A man of

his age, behaving like a troubadour! He must be—
oh, at least thirty. Probably even older. Why can't
he sit quietly, like Father Dominic, instead of chattering and winking and—well, let's face it, frankly
flirting with a group of holy women!

"Ah!" the Archdeacon exclaims as the crowd
parts to admit a girl with a very large dish in her
hands. "And here's Sister Gentiane with—now,
what are those delicious-looking tidbits you've got
for us?"

"They're stuffed cabbage leaves, Father. In olive
oil." She has a soft little voice and a face to match.
Lord God of my salvation, what a face is this! So
fair, so tender, with snow-white skin and golden
hair. Her neck is like a tower of ivory; her eyes are
like the eyes of doves by the rivers of waters,
washed with milk and fitly set.

Preserve me, O God, for in Thee do I put my
trust.

"Sister Gentiane, permit me to introduce my
scribe, Isidore. Isidore, this is Sister Gentiane."

Help. She's smiling at me. Even her teeth are
perfect.

"Brother Isidore," she coos. "You have a beautiful
name, Brother. Were you named after that revered
scholar, Isidore of Seville?"

Help! Help me! Looking around, and that wretched little man is grinning away, amused, diverted—may he be poured out like milk and curdled like cheese.

"Go on, Isidore, answer the lady."

I can't stop blushing. My voice is just a strangled squawk. I can't—I can't—

"What's that?" He's laughing now, really laughing. "You'll have to speak up, Isidore."

"I said *leave me alone!*"

"Yes." It's Father Dominic. "Yes, I think that's all, Sisters. If you could leave us now, please: the Archdeacon and I have business to discuss."

His tone is quiet but firm, and suddenly the women are gone. Every one of them. They've just faded out the door, soundlessly, like smoke in a strong wind. How obedient they are. How well they know their place.

As for the Archdeacon, he looks positively bereft.

"This came from the Bishop," Father Dominic continues, producing a sealed letter from somewhere beneath his surplice. "It's for you, Father."

"Hmmph." The Archdeacon grunts, takes it, and tosses it at me. "There you are, Isidore," he says as he reaches for one of the oily cabbage rolls. "See if you can decipher that."

"You—you want me to read it, Father?"

"Unless you'd care to wipe your backside on it."

Don't be crude! There's no need for such language. The letter is of vellum, which tears when I break the seal; the script seems to lurch and wobble like a drunkard.

"It's in the vernacular."

"Is it? Then it was probably written in haste." The Archdeacon is talking through a mouthful of cabbage. "Off you go, then."

"'Bernard Raymond de Roquefort, Bishop of Carcassonne—' "

"Yes, yes, you can skip the preliminaries."

Skip the preliminaries. Very well. " 'My son, the news is bad. I am told that the Count of Toulouse, bowing to the might of those forces massed against him, has made humble submission to the Pope's representative on the steps of the Cathedral of Saint Gilles. I am told that he has joined the crusading army, which numbers twenty thousand knights and so many more villeins that their number cannot be counted. They say that William of Porcelet has also submitted, and that his two fortresses in

Arles have already been demolished. It seems that the army has left Lyon and has almost reached Montelimar. Oh, my son, what times are these! God has given us like sheep appointed for meat, and has scattered us among the heathen. But the Lord is our defense, and the rock of our refuge.'"

A snort from the Archdeacon. "Scared witless," he mutters as Father Dominic sighs. "Go on, Isidore."

"'All is not lost, however, for the Viscount our lord, greatly afflicted by the Count's submission, has at last been enlightened and delivered unto our way of thinking. He has agreed to approach Arnaud Amaury, the Abbot of Citeaux, and other leaders of the crusading forces, to beg for clemency. My son, you must make haste to join him, for he requires the persuasive powers of your sweet-tongued rhetoric. He will not leave without you. Make haste, my son, or the plagues of the Apocalypse will be upon us.'"

Dead silence. Father Dominic crosses himself.

Hear my voice, O God: preserve my life from fear of the enemy.

"Well," the Archdeacon says with a yawn, "it looks as if we won't be going to Laurac this afternoon. We'll have a rest, and leave for Carcassonne first thing tomorrow. If that's all right by you, Brother?"

"Of course. You're welcome." Father Dominic frowns. "But don't you want to go to Laurac? If the Viscount of Carcassonne is going to appeal to the Abbot of Citeaux for clemency, then perhaps the nobles of Laurac will want to follow his example. Isn't that what you're trying to persuade them to do? Isn't that why you were sent on this mission in the first place? To make all these Cathar lords beg for mercy?"

The Archdeacon shakes his head.

"It won't make any difference," he declares. "They won't stir themselves until the Crusaders are mining their walls. They live in a world of their own around here."

"'The blind that have eyes, and the deaf that have ears,'" Father Dominic agrees, with a desolate look on his face. "It's true. So true. They are blind to the teachings of God."

"No, no, just blind to the realities of international politics." The Archdeacon reaches for another cabbage roll. "Things are changing. It's impossible to hide away anymore. The lords of this country have no idea of the forces massing against them."

"Some would say that they were the forces of

good," Father Dominic observes quietly. But the Archdeacon laughs behind his hand.

"Only those people who haven't met Abbot Arnaud Amaury of Citeaux," he says, thrusting the roll into his mouth.

"Surely you cannot doubt the Abbot's spiritual zeal," Father Dominic objects, and the Archdeacon quickly swallows the food in his mouth.

"No," he replies, "but I doubt the way it manifests itself. I'm not comfortable with zealots. They always end up with blood on their hands."

"The Abbot has already tried peaceful means, Father. He came here with the preaching mission several years ago. You saw him yourself. He traveled these roads like a pilgrim, patiently exhorting the heretics to humble themselves before the glory of the True Church."

"He was here for four months, and he failed. So he goes whining to the Pope, and now he's back with half the population of Europe behind him. Do you think that's a reasonable response?" The Archdeacon raises an eyebrow. "I think it's the action of a man with a serious problem, don't you?"

Father Dominic stares down at his hands, which are carefully arranged on the tabletop. He has such a still, cool, impassive face. "Arnaud Amaury didn't call this Crusade, Father," he points out. "The Pope did, because his very own representative, Peter of Castelnau, was killed—"

"Look." The Archdeacon hammers on his knee with a clenched fist. "All I'm saying is that there's a perfectly simple solution to this entire business. If we had an equitable system of tithes, and a higher standard of parish priests, then the Cathars would lose at least half their support around here."

"But—"

"You know it's true, Dominic! God preserve us, I'm an archdeacon, I know what some of our priests are like. You might as well ordain a bunch of grape pips." (Turning to me.) "I bet Isidore knows what I'm talking about. What was your priest like, Isidore? Was he a complete sepulcher-head?"

Don't. Stop. This isn't fair.

"Well? Come on. You didn't like him, did you? Why not?"

"Because I don't particularly like anyone."

There. That's shut him up. He blinks, and opens his eyes very wide.

"Dear me," he says. "That's a bit of a blow. You don't like *anyone*, Isidore? Not even me? Not even the man who saved you from the insufferable torments of Merioc?"

89

"Perhaps he's tired." Thank God for Father Dominic. He lays a gentle hand on the Archdeacon's arm. "Perhaps he needs a rest. Is there anything you'd like, Isidore? Anything to eat? Anything to drink? Perhaps you'd care to lie down for a while?"

Opening my mouth. Taking a deep breath. But the Archdeacon answers for me.

"No," he says, "I'll tell you what he'd like. He'd like a book, wouldn't you, Isidore? A big, fat, juicy book." (Winking.) "He prefers books to people, don't you, eh?"

To some people, little man. Especially to some people.

"Only because books are better than people, Father."

"Is that so?"

"Yes, it is. Because they are masters who instruct without a rod. If you approach them, they are never asleep; if you are ignorant, they never laugh; if you make mistakes, they never chide. They give to all who ask of them, and never demand payment." (How sweet are their words unto my taste!) "All the glory of the world would be buried in oblivion if God hadn't provided us with the remedy of books."

90

A long, long pause. The Archdeacon's face has changed. Suddenly he's very still.

"Sweet saints preserve us," he says softly. "What a find you are."

And he isn't laughing.

‡CHAPTER EIGHT‡

15 JULY 1209

"Isidore!"

Oh, go away.

"Isidore! Are you there?"

Leave me alone. Can't you leave me alone? I'm *busy.*

"Ah!" He appears at the door and stands there, grinning. (Why doesn't he go and flirt with the nuns?) "So you found Dominic's room, did you? I thought you would. Found yourself a book, too, I see." He strolls across to the window and looks out at the gathering dusk. "What book is it?"

"Saint Augustine's *Confessions.*"

"Really?" He seems surprised. "But surely you must have read that before?"

"No, Father."

"I'm astonished."

"Our copy at Pamiers was very old. I wasn't allowed to touch it." As if I would have harmed Saint Augustine! Oh, Saint Augustine, you are the spring whose waters fail not. You are a soul enriched with the manifold grace of God's holy spirit.

"So what do you think?" The Archdeacon turns his head and leans one elbow on the windowsill. "Do you like what you've read so far?"

"Well of *course*!" (Who wouldn't?) "It's — it's —"

"Magnificent."

"Yes! Yes, it is! It's magnificent!" So real. So vivid. I can almost smell the schoolroom. "The way he remembers everything! And he's so wise. That bit where he talks about being scolded —"

"It's a long time since I read it, Isidore."

"But you must remember! It's so true — so very true — where is it? Oh, yes. 'For we wanted not, O Lord, memory or capacity, whereof Thy will gave enough of our age, but our sole delight was play, and for this we were punished by those who yet themselves were doing like. But older folks' idleness is called "business"; that of boys, being really the same, is punished by these elders.' Isn't that *exactly* what happens?"

He laughs. "Isidore, I don't believe you've ever played a game in your life."

"And isn't it amazing the way Bishop Ambrose used to read? Without making a sound? 'His eye glided over the pages, and his heart searched out the sense, but his voice and tongue were at rest.' How could you do that? It doesn't seem possible."

He's shaking his head at me; he's smiling and stroking his beard. What is it? What did I say? What's so funny?

"I can't believe this is you," he remarks. "I can't believe I'm listening to Isidore. When you're talking about books, Isidore, it's as if you're another person." Pause. "A happier person."

Well, of course I'm happier. What's that got to do with anything? He crosses the floor and sits down beside me on the bed: his breath smells of wine and garlic.

"I don't know if you realize this," he adds in a low voice, "but you've got a terribly forbidding manner, for someone so young. Half the time you look like a fifty-year-old bishop. A fifty-year-old bishop with dyspepsia. You have to learn to be less icy. Less aloof. Especially with women."

Oh, *please!*

"Yes, yes, I know what they say about women. But women are important, Isidore. Believe me. They have a lot of influence in this world." He waves a hand. "Why, just look at Dominic! He's only able to stay here because he has the support of some wealthy women. Now, I know you're probably frightened of them—"

"I am not!"

"Oh, yes, you are. Why shouldn't you be? You've been brought up by celibates, and most celibates are terrified of women—"

"Well, at least they don't flirt with them!"

That's stopped him. He draws back, startled, and lifts an eyebrow. He doesn't look too pleased.

"Flirt with them? Who flirts with them? I hope you're not referring to *me*, Isidore."

Then you hope in vain.

"I don't *flirt*, my friend. What you witnessed today was diplomacy. I was being diplomatic." He narrows his eyes. "It's a skill that *you'll* need to develop, if you want to get along in the world."

Oh, go away, will you? I'm reading. Why should I waste time talking to a bunch of women, when I can learn so much from Saint Augustine? Let's see, now. Alypius . . . Nebridius . . . Ambrose . . .

He's staring again.

"Why are you always staring? Don't you know it's impolite?"

"I'm sorry." He looks away. "I know what it's like to be stared at."

Yes, I'm sure you do. The way you carry on.

"But in my defense, Isidore, you must remember that I can't see very well—and that you rarely open your mouth. So if I want to know what you're thinking, I can only do it by watching your face." He scratches his cheek and smiles. "You're very like Roland, in that respect. My friend Roland. He would never tell me what he was thinking, either." A bright, black, sidelong glance. "In fact, you remind me of Roland in many ways. He has a long nose, too, though it's not quite as beaky as yours. But he tends to look down it in just the same fashion—as if a slug had crawled onto his shoe."

What are you talking about? I don't look like that, do I?

"Of course, he's not as educated as you are. In fact, he can't even read. Twenty years in a monastery, and he still can't read. It makes you wonder. . . ."

"But I thought you said he was a knight? How can he be a knight if he's in a monastery?"

The Archdeacon throws me another piercing

look, as sharp as the tongue of a serpent. "So you remember," he says softly. "Yes, Roland was a knight. The greatest knight of all. He left his home when he was just nineteen years old, and went off to the Holy Land. He wanted to fight for God and find salvation. That's why he joined the knights of the Temple. He wanted to become a Monk of War— to protect Christians and fight unbelievers."

The knights of the Temple! But that means— that must mean—

"Then you were a Templar!" (I don't believe it.) "You were his squire, so you must have been a Templar!"

"Yes. I was a Templar squire. I fought beside him all through the siege of Jerusalem, and when the city surrendered, I was there when he offered to sacrifice himself for the sake of others." The Archdeacon stares off into space, his eyes misty. "He wouldn't let the Order pay his ransom, because the same ransom would have freed fifty children. He said that it was better for fifty children to go free than one knight."

By the blood of the Lamb. What nobility! "Did he escape, then?"

"No, no. I begged Saladin to spare him, and my petition was granted." A taunting smile creeps across his face. "Didn't I tell you that Saladin was a great man?"

"But what happened then? Why did Lord Roland become a monk? Why did he leave the Templars?"

"Oh, it's all a bit complicated. . . ."

"Tell me!"

The Archdeacon's smile widens into a broad and gratified grin. "You really want to know, don't you?" he says. "What a strange boy you are."

"You haven't finished the story!"

"Ah." He nods. "Of course. I understand. It's the story you want, isn't it? Well, now . . ." He covers his eyes with his hand and thinks for a moment. "After Jerusalem fell, we took a ship to Marseille, and rode back to Roland's birthplace. His father was the Lord of Bram. Do you know Bram? It's north of here, about a day's ride from Carcassonne. We were going to persuade his father to join the Crusade against Saladin." A short, sharp snort. "That was in the old days, when crusades were really crusades. Not glorified territorial disputes."

The Crusade against Saladin! Of course! I've read about that Crusade. I've read about King Richard.

"Did you meet King Richard?"

"What?"

"King Richard the Lionheart. Didn't he lead the Third Crusade?"

"Oh. Him." The Archdeacon sniffs, and waves the subject aside. "I don't know much about him, because in the end we didn't join the Crusade. When we reached Bram, Roland's family was involved in a nasty little feud with their neighbors, the lords of Montferrand. One of the people involved—do you remember that Cathar priest I was telling you about? The one called Esclaramonde? Well, *she* lived near Bram, and Roland fell in love with her—"

"No!"

"Yes."

"But she was a heretic!"

"She was a very good woman, Isidore." He looks at me, and his eyes gleam in the lamplight. "All she wanted was peace. She was very small and young and pretty, with long black hair right down to her ankles."

"And Lord Roland? What does Lord Roland look like?"

"Oh, Roland looks like a saint. He's tall and strong, and his eyes are as blue as the sky, and his

99

hair—well, it's gray now, but it used to be the color of gold. Pure gold. He's as beautiful as a stained-glass window."

So his beauty surpasseth all men. How wonderful. It sounds just like a poem.

"And did he marry the pretty girl?"

"No." The Archdeacon sighs. "No, I'm afraid something terrible happened. You see, Roland brought Esclaramonde to Bram, to protect her from the lords of Montferrand. One morning, just before dawn, the Montferrands attacked Bram, and Esclaramonde was killed."

"Oh, no." Poor Lord Roland. "Couldn't he save her?"

"He wasn't anywhere near her. She ran in front of the Montferrands' horses, to try to stop them, but they went right over her. Trampled her to death." The Archdeacon drops his gaze to the floor and adds in a low voice: "I remember her hair, spread all over the ground. It was lovely hair."

"But what did Lord Roland do?"

"He threw his sword away. He threw it away, and he entered the Abbey of Saint Martin. I went with him, but I didn't stay very long. They sent me off to Carcassonne, to study at the cathedral school." He laughs, as if at some private joke. "But that's another story," he concludes.

So Lord Roland cast off his sword. He cast off his sword for love, and dedicated his heart to God's service. What a righteous soul. What a magnificent story. The golden knight and the dark-haired maiden.

"How I'd love to meet him."

"Meet who?"

"Why, Lord Roland." (Who else?) "He must be a great hero."

"But you *are* going to meet him." The Archdeacon lifts an eyebrow. "Didn't I tell you? We're visiting Saint Martin's tomorrow."

"Saint Martin's? I thought—"

"We'll stop at Saint Martin's first, and then Carcassonne. I never return to Carcassonne without visiting Roland." He slaps me on the back. "So you'll be able to ask him all about the Templars and Saladin and swordplay and falling in love and everything else that interests you."

"I'm not interested in falling in love." (Thank you very much.) "I've taken orders."

"Ah. But orders never stopped me. Didn't I tell you that Cathar women love priests?" He flashes his jauntiest grin and rises from the bed. "Come along, now, it's time for dinner. We don't want to miss any of Ermessende's cooking. Her seasoned pork is the closest thing we have, down here, to the glory of the incorruptible God."

By the blood of the Lamb! Has this man no shame? That's the most blasphemous thing I've ever heard.

"Oh." He stops suddenly, on his way out the door, and turns to address me. "By the way, Isidore, I thought I'd better remind you: that long, flexible thing under your nose, down there, is specially designed for smiling. So please make use of it when the Sisters serve you up the most delectable meal you'll ever have the honor of shoveling into your mouth. Otherwise . . ." He pauses. "Otherwise, I'm going to be *very displeased*.

"And you don't want to know what I'm like when I lose my temper."

‡CHAPTER NINE‡

16 JULY 1209

"Cheer up, Isidore. Look! We're nearly there."

Praise God in His sanctuary. Let us go into the house of the Lord: our feet shall stand within thy gates, O Saint Martin's.

"I could do with a cup of spiced mead," the Archdeacon continues. "They do a wonderful spiced mead in this abbey." He gazes down the road toward the big stone gatehouse, with its yawning archway and crenelated towers. Beyond it, a jumble of shingled roofs rears up against the sunset. The walls are very high, and well maintained. "You'll like it here," he adds. "It's small and peaceful, and they have an excellent library."

Oh, good. "Do they have Saint Augustine's *Confessions?*"

The Archdeacon smiles. "I'd be most surprised if they didn't," he says. "Poor old Isidore. I'm sorry I had to drag you away from your precious book. But I couldn't wait around Prouille until you'd finished it."

If you hadn't sent me to bed so early last night, I probably *would* have finished it. I'm swifter than a weaver's shuttle when I get my teeth into a good book. But of course no one ever listens to me.

"That looks like Beraldus," the Archdeacon suddenly remarks, and raises his hand. *"Oi! Beraldus!* I think I'll let him take our horses."

"Father Pagan!" A monk emerges from the shadows of the gatehouse. He has a harelip and an odd, misshapen face, as if someone has cut it in half and then stuck it back together again, without quite aligning the two pieces. "Father Pagan! *Deo gratias. Ave.*"

"Frater Beraldus. Felix sum et placet."

"Ave. Avete." The monk turns to me. *"Ave, Frater."*

All this Latin. My brain's turned to mush from so much jolting and bumping. I can't think of the word for "honor."

"Come on, Isidore, you can get off now." The

104

Archdeacon climbs down from his saddle, wincing slightly. He turns to Brother Beraldus. *"Mihi placeat ut meum caballum deduceres, Frater."*

Brother Beraldus nods and obediently takes the Archdeacon's horse. Ah! Ouch! My bones are as the dust of the wilderness; my liver is poured upon the earth.

"Can you manage, Isidore?" The Archdeacon sounds worried. "Do you need some help?"

"No, thank you." I can get down by myself. But he's hovering there, near the stirrup, and he slips his arm around my waist. "Here," he says. "Just lean on me. It isn't far to the guesthouse. You'll be fine in a moment."

"Fratres Deum adorant, Pater," Brother Beraldus announces. Oh, of course. All the monks will be at Vespers.

The Archdeacon waves his hand. "It's of no consequence. I don't need any assistance, Brother."

"Sed —"

"Thank you, Brother, I know my way."

Poor Brother Beraldus. Doesn't even get to finish his sentence. As for the Archdeacon, he shoots through the gates like an eagle that hasteth to eat. What's the rush? Are we late for an appointment? (It's so hard to keep up when your knees aren't functioning properly.) Beyond the gatehouse stands the church, large and simple, with three carved pillars on either side of its western door. The cloisters are built against its southern flank: they're a mismatched collection of stone walls, wooden shutters, and smoking chimneys. The only entrance seems to be that one, way over there.

The Archdeacon heads straight for it.

"This is where we'll stay," he says, pushing me across the threshold. "It's the abbey guesthouse. Woof! Something smells a bit ripe. Those rushes need changing."

I can hardly see a thing. Will we be sleeping in here? There seems to be a table, and a hallway off to the right. The floor is strewn with soggy rushes.

"This is where I lost my front tooth," the Archdeacon observes. "It was knocked out in a fight, twenty-odd years ago." He sniffs, and pokes at the rushes with the toe of his boot. "I wouldn't be surprised if it was still here, somewhere. They obviously haven't swept this place out since the turn of the century."

"Father?"

"Yes?"

"I can walk by myself now."

"Good." He lets me go. "I wonder where they

keep the candles. There was a storage chest, the last time I was here. . . ."

"Is this where we'll be sleeping?"

"Oh, no. This is the common room. There are bedrooms down the hall. Ouch!" (A crack.) "God curse it!"

"Are you all right, Father?"

"I hit my hand on the—oh, damn this. I'm not sitting around in this belly of hell waiting for the Abbot to show up. Come on, Isidore." And suddenly there's light—more light—as he flings open another door. I can see his silhouette, dark against the brightness of the cloister garth. "We'll go and wait by the southern exit," he says. "They'll be finishing Vespers soon, and that's the best place to catch them when they leave the church."

The words are barely out of his mouth before the bells start to ring. They're so loud that I can feel their vibrations through the paving stones. "There!" he says. "What did I tell you?" And he scurries across the cloister garth, which is very well designed, with a covered walkway built all around it. There are seats, and flowers, and five big book presses, off to the left. Book presses! Oh, give thanks unto the Lord, for He is good: for His mercy endureth forever.

"Here they come," says the Archdeacon, pointing at a modest little door in the southern wall of the church. A monk emerges, robed in black, his cowl pulled over his face and his hands concealed in his sleeves. Another monk follows, and another, and another. They move in single file along the eastern walkway. One of them is limping.

"They'll be going to the refectory, for a drink," the Archdeacon murmurs. His breath tickles my ear. "It's a Silent Time now, but we don't have to worry about that. We're guests." Suddenly he stiffens: he's looking at a tall, thin monk with stooped shoulders who has to duck as he passes through the door. Could that be Lord Roland? I can't see his face.

"Roland!"

The Archdeacon's voice echoes like a thunderclap. Every head turns. Every foot falters. The tall monk stops abruptly, frozen in midstep.

"Pagan . . . ?" he gasps.

So it *is* Lord Roland.

The Archdeacon is laughing. He bounds across the cobbles and flings himself at Lord Roland—actually flings himself, like a dog or a ball—and Lord Roland catches him, and hugs him, and kisses him, and they're both laughing now, laughing like fools, causing such a disturbance. What a ridiculous display. What undignified behavior. If I had a friend, I wouldn't carry on like that, no matter how long it was since I'd seen him. That sort of thing is just — it's just killing the rich and fruitful harvest of reason with the barren thorns of passion.

"Pagan! I don't believe it."

"How are you? Are you well?"

"I'm well. I'm very well."

"All the better for seeing me, eh?"

"Oh, yes."

"It's been far too long. I've been *incredibly* busy."

"Pagan . . ."

So much for Lord Roland. So much for the greatest knight in Christendom. Why, he's just an old man! A skinny old man with gray hair and sunken cheeks and lines under his eyes. Oh, why are things never, ever as good as you imagine them to be?

"Pagan!" A tiny monk hobbles over: a monk so small that he barely reaches my elbow. He has a squashed face and a stump instead of a right hand. "Pagan," he says. "It's so good to see you."

"Hello, Gaubert." (More hugging.) "Where's Durand? Durand, you old dog! Give us a smile." The Archdeacon throws his arms around a fat, balding monk with a face like a bowl of oatmeal. "How's your back? Still acting up?"

"Pagan, you look wonderful. Wonderful."

"God, Durand, your eyes must be as bad as your back. I'm a complete mess. Bones and teeth. You've no *idea* what kind of a week I've had."

Look at them all, clustering around. Why do they love him so much? He's noisy, he's conceited, he's disrespectful—and of course he doesn't even bother to introduce me. Why should he bother to introduce me? I'm nothing. No one. I barely exist.

"Father Pagan." Ah! But here's someone who doesn't look so happy. A stunted, middle-aged monk with an oversize head, a wrinkled brow, and pale, peering eyes. There's a heavy gold ring on one of his fingers.

The Abbot, perhaps?

"My lord," says the Archdeacon, bowing. So it is the Abbot. Everyone falls silent; Lord Roland steps back a pace; the Abbot frowns, and sniffs, and wipes his nose on his sleeve.

"What are you doing in here, Father Pagan?" he inquires fretfully. "You're disturbing the peace of the cloister."

"Am I?" The Archdeacon lifts an eyebrow. "Oh, well. Bear with me, my lord. You know what your

Rule says: 'Let them bear most patiently with each other's infirmities, whether of body or manner.' Chapter seventy-two, I believe."

"You should have waited in the guesthouse. I would have come to you." The Abbot flaps his hand at the other monks, in a gesture that looks like dismissal. Sure enough, they begin to move away. Even Durand. Even the dwarf.

But before Lord Roland can follow them, the Archdeacon grabs his wrist.

"I'd like Roland to stay," he says. "We have a lot to tell each other."

"I'm afraid Brother Roland was on his way to the infirmary." The Abbot sniffs again. He coughs a weak little cough. "My catarrh has to be treated. I'm going to need another poultice, Brother. Will you prepare one for me, please?"

"Wait. Just a moment." The Archdeacon lifts his hand. "I tell you what. Why don't we *all* go to the infirmary? Then you can have your poultice, and I can talk to Roland."

But the Abbot smiles a wintry smile.

"The infirmary?" he says. "Oh, no, Father. There's a sick monk in there. A feverish monk. I never set foot in the infirmary. It's not safe. My constitution isn't strong, as you know."

111

The Archdeacon folds his arms. He cocks his head. There's an unpleasant sort of glitter in his eyes.

"*Roland* hasn't come to any harm," he says in a steely voice.

"Brother Roland is as strong as an ox. Nothing affects him. That's why he's our infirmarian."

"Really? Is that so? And I thought it had something to do with his skill."

"Oh, he's skillful enough, I suppose. Although that oil you gave me, Brother—it doesn't seem to be working at all. I told you I should have been bled. If in doubt, bleed. That's my philosophy."

It's so strange, how the face can speak without words. Just as heavenly vials full of odors are the prayers of the saints, so the shifting of shadows is the language of a man's countenance. I can look at the Archdeacon's forehead, and his jaw, and the corners of his eyes, and I can see at once that he's angry—very angry. His face speaks silently, like a book. What a clever creation it is! What a miracle of craftsmanship! I will praise Thee, O Lord, for I am fearfully and wonderfully made: marvelous are Thy works, and—

Wait. Wait a moment. What's that smell?

"Isidore?"

It's the Archdeacon. His eyes are so big—his voice sounds so faint—

"Isidore? What's the matter?"

No. Oh, no.

Help me!

‡CHAPTER TEN‡

16 July 1209

I can smell something strange. What is it? Some kind of herb, filling the air like incense . . . and another smell, too. The smell of clean linen. A good, safe, peaceful smell.

Wait a moment. What am I doing lying in bed? I don't remember—I can't seem to—

Oh, God. Oh, God, it happened again. It came *again*!

"Isidore?"

That's not the Archdeacon. Who is it? Where am I? A small room, lit by two lamps resting on shelves set into the wall. Another bed, a saddlebag, a stool . . .

Lord Roland.

"Isidore?" He's sitting there with his hands in his lap. Just sitting there. "How are you feeling?" he murmurs.

How am I feeling? How am I *feeling*? I am in distress, Lord Roland; that's how I'm feeling. My bowels are troubled and my heart is turned within me.

"You chipped a tooth when you fell," he remarks in his deep, quiet voice. "You seem to have bruised your head quite badly. But by God's grace you haven't broken anything."

God's grace! That's a good one. Oh, how long wilt Thou forget me, Lord? How long wilt Thou hide Thy face from me?

"I've put you in the guesthouse," he continues. "I thought you'd sleep better here than you would in the infirmary. Brother Bernard is feverish and makes a lot of noise at night." He seems so calm. So tranquil. "Pagan will be here soon. Right now he's with the Abbot."

Oh, God. The Archdeacon. He was there, and he saw me. I've thrown away my only chance. I've ruined *everything*! O my God, I cry in the daytime, but Thou hearest not.

"Would you like something to eat, Isidore?" Lord Roland rises and comes over to the bed. "Would you like something to drink?"

Go away. Don't look at me. You don't want to look at me. Now that you've seen my devil—my accursed, ugly devil. I am a brother to dragons, and a companion to owls; my flesh is clothed with worms and clods of dust.

"What's the matter? Are you in pain?" he asks. But I can't talk, or I'll cry. And I mustn't cry, not in front of him.

Not in front of anyone.

He's hovering there, gazing down his long, straight nose (the Archdeacon was right: it *is* a long nose), his face solemn and craggy, his eyelids sagging under the weight of some everlasting fatigue. He says, "I'm glad you're with Pagan."

What?

"I'm glad that you decided to join him. He doesn't respect many people, but he respects you."

"*Me?*" It comes out as a croak. I can't believe I'm hearing this. Lord Roland nods and chases a fly from my blanket.

"Oh, yes. He's spoken about you with some admiration."

That's not true. That can't be true. You're making it up.

"He says you're like a pearl of great price. Like a treasure hid in the field. He says that you're like

116

the lost sheep found in the wilderness, and that he rejoiceth more in that one sheep than in the ninety and nine which went not astray."

He—he does?

"It's because you're so clever," Lord Roland adds, returning to his seat. He doesn't move like a monk: he moves with a kind of controlled vigor, every action neat and forceful. "Pagan is clever, too. Much cleverer than most of us. That's why he won't listen to advice. But he might listen to you, if you were to warn him against doing foolish things."

What do you mean? "What foolish things?"

"Well . . . riding around by himself, without an armed escort. It's the height of foolishness in this country." Lord Roland sighs. "There are so many brigands. So many angry heretics."

"But Father Pagan says that he can handle brigands. He says that he was trained to use a sword."

Lord Roland shakes his head, smiling slightly.

"That was a long time ago," he says. "A very long time ago."

Suddenly there's a crash from somewhere nearby. The sound of footsteps, heavy and rapid. The thud of a boot hitting our door.

It flies open; the lamps flicker; the Archdeacon is standing there, with his hands on his hips.

He marches into the room and kicks one of the stools—kicks it so hard that it bounces off the wall near my palliasse.

"By the bleeding balls of Baal!" he shouts.

Lord Roland stands up. "What's wrong?"

"Oh, nothing. Not a thing."

"Pagan—"

"You know what I need? I need a drop of fermented grape juice." The Archdeacon begins to fish around in his saddlebag; he pulls out his half-empty wineskin and almost drains it in one huge gulp. "Ah!" he gasps. "That's better." He wipes his mouth on his sleeve. "There's a remedy for every complaint, isn't there, Roland?"

"What complaint? What are you talking about?"

"I'm afraid we'll have to leave at dawn," the Archdeacon says. He's almost breathless with rage. "I've just heard from the Abbot that twelve more fortresses have surrendered to the Crusaders. Including Rochemaure and Roussillon. So perhaps it's all for the best. Can't hang around here wasting time, I suppose. Especially when your Abbot makes me want to bash my own brains out with an iron-tipped shovel."

"You're leaving? Tomorrow?" Lord Roland sounds

surprised. The Archdeacon glances at him, glances at me. . . .

And all at once it's perfectly obvious.

"It's the Abbot, isn't it?" My voice is dry and cracked, like a discarded lizard skin. Oh, why do ye persecute me? "He wants me to leave. He doesn't want me to stay here."

The Archdeacon stares; he drives his left fist into the palm of his right hand; he paces to the door and back again. At last he finds the words he's been looking for.

"The Abbot thinks you're possessed," he announces. "Well, what can you expect from such a bog-brained heap of pig's offal? That man is so stupid it's an insult. He's like something you'd scrape off the sole of your shoe. My God, I've eaten *limpets* with more sense than that moron!"

"Pagan—"

"You know something, Isidore?" The Archdeacon fixes me with a hard, intent look. "I used to wonder why you were such an angry person. But now I think I understand."

What do you mean? Angry? I'm not angry. At least—well—I suppose I can be a trifle bitter, sometimes. . . .

119

"Sweet saints preserve us! I'd be pretty angry too, if I was always getting dumped in dark corners by donkeys like that so-called Abbot. What a cess-head. What a scum-bucket—"

"Pagan, calm down."

"I just don't know how you put up with him!" The Archdeacon whirls around to face Lord Roland. "When I *think* of Abbot Anselm—when I compare him to this maggot-bag—I mean, it's a joke, isn't it? A joke!"

"Abbot Anselm is dead," Lord Roland replies in a gentle voice.

"And he must be turning in his grave, to see what old Snot-Nose has done to his precious abbey. I mean to say, no servants in the sacristy? No communicating in the latrines? And as for the money he must be spending on those relics—"

"Pagan." Lord Roland places a hand on the Archdeacon's shoulder. "You shouldn't let these things worry you."

"But it's *obscene!*"

"Please, Pagan—"

"And what I want to know is, where were *you* when he was elected?" The Archdeacon prods Lord Roland's chest with one finger. "Hmm? Why aren't *you* the Abbot? That's what I want to know."

Lord Roland smiles. "I couldn't be an abbot," he says. "It's out of the question."

"Why? You were acting Commander of the Temple, weren't you? In Jerusalem? If you ask me, you're *over*qualified."

"Pagan." Lord Roland is shaking his head. "I can't even read. How can I be an abbot when I can't read?"

That's a good point. That's a very good point. You can't be an abbot if you can't read.

The Archdeacon looks cross: he throws himself onto his bed and begins to drag off his riding boots. "Well," he growls, "I can't see, and I'm an archdeacon. All you need is a scribe to do your reading for you. Anyway, you couldn't possibly be any worse than Abbot Seguin. Do you know what he was talking about when I left? Earworms. He thinks he's got an earworm. He wants to pour some goat's urine down his ear to kill it."

Lord Roland sighs deeply. When he speaks, he sounds exhausted.

"It's a partial loss of hearing," he says. "Probably caused by a buildup of wax. I don't know who told him about these earworms. I find it hard to believe that they even exist—at least not in this part of the world."

"Well, if they're going to exist anywhere, they'll

exist inside Seguin's head," the Archdeacon observes, divesting himself of his black mantle. "There's enough empty space in there to accommodate the entire population of Byzantium, let alone a humble earworm."

"I'd better go and see what he's up to." Lord Roland runs a hand through his thinning hair. "He needs olive oil, not goat's urine. I keep telling him that, but he won't believe me."

"Don't go," the Archdeacon says. "Let him stick whatever he wants down his ear. His head is full of goat's piss, anyway—you can tell by the way it keeps coming out of his mouth. What harm can a little more do?"

"Good night, Pagan." Lord Roland gently touches the Archdeacon's head. "I'll be here tomorrow, before you leave. Good night, Isidore." He takes my hand and holds it for a while. His grip feels warm; the warmth seems to spread, creeping up my arm to my shoulder. "Sleep well," he murmurs. "If you need anything, just wake me."

And he slips out the door, padding on silent feet like a cat. What an admirable person. Quiet, but with such a strong and peaceful presence.

The room feels bigger without him: bigger and colder.

"There! What did I tell you?" The Archdeacon is carefully folding his robe. He places it in an open chest and begins to peel off his stockings. "Isn't Roland a saint? I've never met anyone as good as he is—not ever. He's one of a kind, that man."

"Father?"

"Yes?"

"Tomorrow . . ." I can't even say it. He looks up, squinting.

"What?" he says.

Oh, can't you tell? Don't you understand?

"Father, you told me . . . if I had a fit . . ." (Must I spell it out?) "Father, are you going to send me back to Merioc?"

Pause. He rolls his stockings together and sticks them under his pillow. He appears to be thinking.

"No, I'm not," he says at last. "I don't know what I'm going to do with you, Isidore, but I can't send you back to Merioc. It would be a crime." He snuggles down into bed, disappearing under the blanket. "So go to sleep, and don't worry."

Oh, thank you. Thank you, thank you! What can I say? You walk in the Lord's statutes, Father. You're like a green olive tree in the house of God.

"And you'd better be ready to go at sunrise," the Archdeacon adds in a sleepy voice. "Because mark my words, they'll be chucking us out when they empty the chamber pots. Just you wait. They won't give us time to shake the dew off the lily."

Shake the dew off the lily? What's that supposed to mean?

‡CHAPTER ELEVEN‡

17 JULY 1209

What incredible walls! They're like a great cliff, or a crown of stone encircling the top of the hill, with every tower a mighty jewel set in the diadem. Twenty-six jewels, all flying the Viscount's flag. The Narbonnese Gate is flanked by two of them, looming above us: two massive buttressed towers pierced by arrow slits, placed there to guard the open mouth of the gateway. And what a busy gateway! As a fountain casteth out her waters, so the gateway of Carcassonne casteth out people—crowds of people, clogging the thoroughfare: beggars and soldiers and people with laden mules, babies crying, hawkers yelling, someone protesting because he can't get in. He's arguing with an official-looking fellow in dark green (a toll collector, perhaps?), who takes one look at the Archdeacon and promptly waves him through.

Through the cavernous opening. Past the armed men. Beneath the jagged teeth of the portcullis.

Into the city.

"We'll go straight to the Viscount," the Archdeacon remarks. "See what he's got to say. Are you all right there, Isidore?"

"Yes, Father."

"It's just a short distance."

Praise ye the Lord! Can this be the work of man, this city? It's so big—so handsome—much bigger than Pamiers. Fine, large houses, with many windows; ditches quite empty of beggars and corpses; flapping pennants of richly dyed cloth hung out to dry above the narrow streets. Everywhere the rumble of wheelbarrows, heaped with produce. Well-dressed people laugh and shout, and hurry along with their baskets and tools, picking their way between little heaps of horse manure. A man squeezes past us carrying a live chicken, trussed and slung over his shoulder.

So many people. So much noise. And the smells! They're making me dizzy.

"We'd better get down," says the Archdeacon,

raising his voice above the howl of a nearby infant. "It'll be safer, I think." He dismounts carefully, clinging to his horse as if he's scared of being washed away by the river of people. And now it's my turn. How will I do this? There's so little space, and that woman won't move. . . . Come on, woman, you're in the way. Why don't you watch where you're going?

"That's it. That's good." The Archdeacon nods as my feet hit the ground. "Just keep close and follow me."

"Is it always so crowded?"

"On this street, yes. It's the main route from one side of Carcassonne to the other. But there are other ways."

"Where are we going?"

"To the castle. Come on."

Easy to say; not so easy to do. How difficult it is to keep out of the dung and the spittle when you're trying to avoid oncoming traffic. Dodging stray children. Falling over stray animals. Getting clouted with a bucket of water (ouch!) as somebody slips on a puddle of grease. And now my horse is nervous: it keeps tossing its head and jibbing. A horrible smell, like smoked urine. Olive pips sliding underfoot. A house with carved shutters.

127

Slow down, Father—I don't want to lose you.

"Archdeacon!" Someone is waving at us over the seething heads: someone dressed in red and blue and yellow. The Archdeacon looks around and lifts his hand.

"Master Bardelin," he replies, without much enthusiasm.

"A word in your ear, Father?"

"Tomorrow, my friend. I have business with the Viscount. This way, Isidore."

This way, Isidore. Down a side street, and we're out of the dyers' quarter. It's weavers here: I can tell by all the bits of carded wool blowing around. It smells better, too—though not *much* better. Fewer people, but a lot more garbage.

"Father Pagan." A woman beams at us from a doorstep. She bobs her head as the Archdeacon turns. "God's blessings on you, Father."

"And on you, my dear."

Giggles from somewhere behind her. The Archdeacon doesn't stop to chat: just salutes her and presses on. He seems to have a great many friends. Does *everyone* know him?

"Does everyone know you in Carcassonne?"

"Not everyone. This isn't my quarter."

"Where do you live?"

"South." He waves his hand. "Near the cathedral."

"Do you have your own house?"

"I do, yes."

"Is it nice?"

"You'll see." He smiles at me over his shoulder. "I'll take you there after we've visited the Viscount." Suddenly he sneezes, very loudly, five times in a row. "I usually don't come through here," he says, mopping his face. "All this wool . . . it bothers me."

"Pagan!"

The Archdeacon jumps like a mouse that's been trapped in a corn bin. He turns, looking back toward the cross street behind us: there's a man stepping out of the shadows, a gray-haired man, magnificently dressed. A lord, perhaps? He has gold on his sword belt; gold on his fingers; gold on the brooch that's holding his cape across his chest. Even his tunic is embroidered with gold.

He looks familiar, somehow.

"Pagan," he says in a low, lazy drawl. "What a wonderful surprise. I thought you were off wooing heretics—at least that's what your Bishop told me."

"I was."

"And now you've had enough?"

"I was summoned."

"Ah."

What a very tall man he is. Tall and heavy. And there's something about his face — his long nose — his blue eyes —

Oh, of course! Of course. He could be Lord Roland's twin. Except that Lord Roland's face is thinner, and he doesn't have a beard.

"Who's this?" Lord Roland's twin looks down his nose at me. "What happened to Julien?"

"Julien was ill," the Archdeacon replies. "I had to leave him."

"And this?"

The Archdeacon hesitates. He seems oddly subdued: I've never seen him like this before. So abrupt. So wary.

"This is Isidore," he says at last. "Isidore, make your bow to Lord Jordan Roucy de Bram. He is Roland's elder brother."

I knew it! I knew he had to be something like that. How fine he looks in those beautiful garments. How well he carries himself, for a man so full of days.

"That's an impressive head of hair you've got, Isidore," he says amiably. "Hot enough to start a fire. Where did you pick that up?"

"Isidore's parents were foreigners," the Archdeacon rejoins before I can even open my mouth. "Now if you'll excuse us, my lord, I've been summoned by the Viscount. He wants to speak with me urgently."

"Does he? How fortunate. It just so happens that I'm heading that way myself. We can walk together." Lord Jordan swings around and lets loose an ear-splitting whistle. "*Guichard! Move it!* Sniffing after skirts again, I'll warrant you. *Guichard!* He can take your horses."

Guichard saunters into the sunlight, a young man with a long neck and cheeks pitted with scars. He has lank hair and wet green eyes, and he's chewing something.

"Guichard is my squire," Lord Jordan remarks, looking down at the Archdeacon. "I don't think you've met him. He's the youngest son of Aimery-Olivier de Saissac."

"What happened to Anseric?"

"Oh, Anseric. We didn't suit." Lord Jordan smiles, displaying teeth like claws. "Guichard, you can take the Archdeacon's horses back to his place. It's right next to Saint-Nazaire—the house with the painted cross above the window. I'll meet you there later."

Guichard doesn't say anything. He simply plucks the reins from my hand and approaches the Archdeacon, who gives him a big, bright, sympathetic smile. "I know your father, Guichard," he says, whereupon Guichard removes a half-chewed lump of vegetable matter from his mouth.

"My commiserations," he replies hoarsely, and tucks the lump back into his cheek.

What a rude fellow.

"That's what I like about Guichard," Lord Jordan says, watching his squire slouch away with the horses. "We both have exactly the same feelings about his father."

"Hmm." The Archdeacon doesn't sound impressed. He turns and begins to walk up the road, muffling another sneeze against his wrist. There are shreds of white wool clinging to the skirts of his robe.

"I also like Guichard because he knows how to keep his mouth shut," Lord Jordan continues, striding along beside the Archdeacon. "Anseric was incapable of realizing that his comments were of absolutely no interest or value to anyone. It's a common fault. What's the matter, Pagan? Are you sick?"

"It's the wool."

"Ah. The wool." Lord Jordan glances around. "And what about you, Isidore? How do you like working for Pagan?"

"You leave Isidore alone!" the Archdeacon snaps. "What are you doing in Carcassonne, anyway? Why aren't you in Bram? Don't you normally ride around pestering your neighbors at this time of year?"

Lord Jordan laughs. "Oh, my son takes care of all that," he says. "My son has a natural talent for pestering our neighbors. I prefer the fleshpots of Carcassonne, myself."

"Did the Viscount summon you?"

"The Viscount never *summons* me, Pagan." Lord Jordan's voice is very calm and pleasant. "He requests the pleasure of my company, at my own convenience. I've always found him a perspicacious young man. We get along quite well."

How odd they look, from behind: the Archdeacon, so small and black, his movements as quick and sharp as a bird's; Lord Jordan, so tall and colorful in his blue cape and his crimson robe, all heavy and loose, and taking one step for every two of the Archdeacon's. He's like a peacock next to the Archdeacon's swallow.

"I hear about you everywhere, Pagan. You seem to be omnipresent."

"I get around."

"Not to Bram, though. Why don't you ever visit Bram? Anyone would think you were avoiding me."

"I saw Roland yesterday. He seems well."

"Roland? Oh, Roland. Still alive, is he?"

"Yes, he is. Why? Have you been trying to kill him?"

"My dear Pagan, what *are* you talking about?"

"Bit of a hobby of yours, isn't it? Fratricide?"

"Oh, I wouldn't say that. It would be a dull old world if we had to confine ourselves to killing our relatives. No, I prefer to describe my hobby as wholesale carnage. Much more interesting."

"Ha, ha, ha."

The road has widened, and there's a new smell in the air: the smell of freshly baked bread. Lord God of my salvation, does that smell good! And there are the ovens—over there beneath that roof, with heaps of fuel and sacks of corn, and clusters of people carrying wicker baskets.

Ahead, through thick clouds of wood smoke, you can see a fortress rising against the sky.

"Don't dawdle, Isidore." The Archdeacon has stopped: he's waiting for me, up ahead. "You'll get lost if you do."

"He's hungry," Lord Jordan observes. "He wants some bread. Don't you feed him?"

"Of course I feed him!"

"He looks half starved."

"Will you mind your own *business?*"

"What a temper he has." Lord Jordan places a hand on my shoulder. "How do you cope with it, Isidore? Is he as rude to you as he is to me?"

"Leave the poor child alone."

"You wouldn't think, would you, that he used to be a lowly squire? Someone who cleaned the shoes and shoveled the shit? He would never have *dared* talk to me like this when he was young."

Ouch! The Archdeacon grabs my arm—pulls me away—but Lord Jordan follows us, still talking.

"He hardly opened his mouth, most of the time, but of course he didn't approve of me. It was written all over him, whenever I tried to be friendly. I blame Roland, myself—we were never on good terms."

The Archdeacon quickens his pace, and I can see the castle more clearly now: a stack of towers and roofs and ramparts and huge, grayish walls, like a city within a city. How rich the Viscount must be to have built such a fortress! He must have heaped up silver as the dust, and fine gold as the mire of the streets.

"It's not a very charitable attitude, for a man of God, but I don't hold it against him," Lord Jordan is saying. "After all, he's an Arab by birth. You can't expect an Arab to be a model Christian, can you?"

"Just ignore him," the Archdeacon mutters through his teeth. "Don't pay any attention. He always does this. He's trying to make me cross."

"Why?"

The Archdeacon doesn't answer. He just marches on, fuming, toward the massive gray bulk of the Viscount's castle.

✝CHAPTER TWELVE✝

17 JULY 1209

The ceiling is lost in smoke. The walls are smoke-blackened, huge stone walls that seem to stretch on forever, disappearing into the gray haze above. The air tastes of smoke—smoke and tallow—and it's cold in here, as cold as the shadow of death, although the sun is blazing outside. People drift about like disembodied spirits, hard to see in the smoky darkness: there are men with swords, men wearing chain mail, men slumped on benches and leaning against the walls. I can hear their armor clinking. I can hear the wind whistling.

What a strange place this fortress is. What a huge, chilly, frightening place. Behold, they meet with darkness in the daytime, and grope in the noonday as in the night.

"Sounds as if your Bishop's here," Lord Jordan mutters. "I seem to recognize that squeak of his."

There's an argument going on: voices are raised down the other end of this enormous room. But it's impossible to see what's happening through all the smoke—just a faint blur of movement, and an orange flicker that could be a fire. Yes, it is a fire. An old-fashioned fire on a raised stone platform, with no hole cut in the ceiling above it. And beyond the fire a dais, covered in tables and benches and the odd carved chair. Who are all these people? Which one is the Viscount?

"Pagan!"

Oh, no. Surely *that* isn't the Viscount? He's just an old man—an old man with a few straggling gray hairs on his chin and even fewer on his head. He rises and steps forward, holding out his hand.

"Pagan," he repeats in a quavering voice.

The Archdeacon stoops to kiss his ring.

"My lord Bernard," he says.

Help! It's the Bishop! It's the Bishop of Carcassonne, and he's looking straight at me!

"This is Isidore," the Archdeacon informs him. "Isidore is my new scribe."

"What happened to —?"

"Julien was ill. I had to leave him in a village near Pamiers."

"But —"

"Don't worry, my lord. I've sorted it all out."

The Bishop's hand smells of onions. His ring is sticky. I can feel him shaking like a leaf in the wind.

"Did you bring anyone else?" he demands, looking at the Archdeacon. He keeps screwing up his eyes in sudden, nervous blinks: his scalp is covered with scaly red sores, and his cheeks droop like the wattles of a chicken. "Did you have any success with the Cathars?"

"No, my lord."

"*No?*"

"My lord, I did warn you —"

"But didn't you tell them? Didn't they understand?"

The whole room has fallen silent: everyone seems to be waiting for the Archdeacon's response. All these big, bearded men, with their swords and their scars and their golden jewelry — all of them sit and stare at the Archdeacon, who fixes his gaze on the smallest among them, a young man dressed in royal purple.

"My lord," the Archdeacon announces, "I fear that the lords of the south have so much confidence in your abilities that they disregarded my warnings. They don't believe that any army, no matter how large, will ever have the strength to get past Carcassonne. Or past you, my lord."

By the blood of the Lamb! Could *that* be the Viscount of Carcassonne and Béziers? Could that be Lord Raymond Roger Trencavel? I never realized that he was so young. His skin is smooth and unscarred, his face round and full, like a child's. When he leans forward, a lock of raven-black hair falls across his brow.

"Did you hear about the Count of Toulouse?" he says to the Archdeacon. His voice is hard and strong and abrupt. "Did you hear what they did to him?"

"My lord, I was told that he made submission—"

"They stripped him to the waist and put a cord around his neck and a candle in his hand, and they made him admit to all his faults. And then the papal legate marched him into church, beating him with a bundle of birch twigs." The Viscount narrows his long, dark eyes. "They'd have to kill me before I'd do a thing like that," he says. "Kill me and feed me to the dogs."

140

"My lord, Christ sacrificed himself to save mankind—" the Bishop bleats, but he's interrupted by a yelp of laughter from Lord Jordan.

"What a perfect analogy!" He grins. "So persuasive, too—"

"Shut up," the Archdeacon hisses, before addressing the Viscount. "My lord, you must do as you think fit. The Count has chosen to join the invaders. You, on the other hand, do *not* choose to join them. So the conditions they set may be quite different."

"They'd better be," Lord Raymond remarks, whereupon the Bishop begins to moan and fret.

"If only you'd made peace with the Count of Toulouse in January," he complains. "If only you'd abandoned your quarrels and joined him, when he asked you to, then the Pope might have backed off—"

"When I want your opinion, my lord, I'll ask for it!" the Viscount snaps. He turns to Lord Jordan. "Thanks for coming, Jordan. I need all the help I can get. Have you heard about this *other* army that's heading our way?"

Lord Jordan looks surprised. "Other army?" he says.

"The news just reached me this morning. There's

141

another band of Crusaders coming down from Agen, in the northwest. The counts of Auvergne and Turenne, Ratier de Castelnau, Bertrand de Cardaillac—"

"You mean they're coming through Quercy?" the Archdeacon interrupts, and Lord Raymond nods.

"That's right. Last I heard, they'd taken Puylaroque. God knows where they are now."

There's a glum pause. The Archdeacon mutters something under his breath. The Bishop crosses himself.

Lord Jordan smiles. "This crusade is certainly a popular outing," he observes. "Must be, to get Ratier de Castelnau off his big fat backside."

"Oh, it's popular," the Viscount says in a morose voice. "You should hear who's in Arnaud's baggage train. The Duke of Burgundy, the Count of Saint-Pol, the Count of Nevers, the Count of Auxerre—"

"I wonder if there's anyone left up north," Lord Jordan muses. "We could probably walk right in and take over. Perhaps that's what we should do. Vacate our own castles and occupy theirs."

"This is no time for jests, my lord!" the Bishop wails. "This is serious!"

"Yes, for God's sake, Jordan!" The Viscount

glares at him. "I asked you here because I need advice. *Good* advice."

"Then I advise you to opt for the birch twigs," Lord Jordan says in his slow, sardonic drawl. "A few birch twigs won't do any permanent damage. Not like a lance in the guts."

"My lord." It's the Archdeacon. His tone is compeling: it attracts every eye. "My lord, go to the Crusaders. Go to the Abbot of Citeaux, and the papal legate, and present your case. You've nothing to lose, and you may find that they'll listen."

"Yes, but what should I tell them?"

"Tell them . . ." The Archdeacon hesitates, one finger pressed to his forehead. He seems to be marshaling his thoughts. "Tell them that you're very young," he says at last. "Tell them that you were only nine years old when you succeeded your father, and that you should not be held responsible for things done during your minority. You were underage when the Bishop of Albi was imprisoned—you cannot be blamed for the burning of that unfortunate abbey, or its desecration. Tell them that you are a good Catholic—"

"Which I am!"

"Which you are, and that you have never ceased

143

to be a good Catholic, and that it was your father's choice to appoint heretics as your tutors, not your own. Assure them that it is your dearest wish to repress the Cathar forces infecting your lands, and that you had nothing to do with the brief expulsion of the Bishop of Carcassonne two years ago—"

A muffled snort from Lord Jordan. The Archdeacon fixes him with a threatening gaze and continues.

"Tell them that you have made every effort to stamp out the foul taint of heresy," he says, "but that your youth and inexperience have so far worked against you—"

"Youth and inexperience!" the Viscount protests. (He doesn't sound too pleased.) "What kind of talk is that?"

"My lord, it's an example of the technique known in rhetoric as *insinuatio*—the disparagement of ourselves or our client in order to win the good-will of the judge."

"But it's a load of garbage—"

"Of course it is." The Archdeacon inclines his head. "But as Boethius so wisely reminds us in *De topicis differentiis*, the truth or falsity of an argument makes no difference, if only it has the *appearance* of truth."

No one knows what to say to that. They all just sit there looking at each other, defeated by the Archdeacon's learning. How well educated he is. How vigorously he presents his arguments.

How I wish I could get my hands on a copy of that book he mentioned.

"Well," Lord Raymond finally remarks, "I think it would be best if *you* told them all that, Archdeacon. I don't think I could remember everything you just said."

The Archdeacon bows. "My lord, I am your most humble servant."

"And I'll come, too," the Bishop suddenly announces. He's been perched on the edge of his seat, gnawing at the skin of his right thumb. "I'm sure the legate will find my presence reassuring."

Even the Archdeacon rolls his eyes at that one. Lord Jordan grins, and the Viscount wriggles around in his chair.

"Oh, all right," he says with a noticeable lack of enthusiasm. "I suppose you'd better come, or they'll wonder what I've done to you. What about you, Jordan? Will you come?"

"With pleasure."

"Then we'll leave for Montpellier first thing tomorrow. When the gates open."

"Montpellier?" the Archdeacon exclaims in a startled voice. "Is that where they are?"

"As far as I know, that's where they are." Lord Raymond kicks moodily at a dog that's sniffing around his feet. "They're not wasting time, I can tell you."

"Then we should follow their example," the Archdeacon says. "I'll be with you tomorrow, my lord. Do we meet at the Aude Gate?"

"Yes. The Aude Gate, at sunrise."

"I'll be there."

And if he's there, I'll be there, too. O Lord, I cry unto Thee; make haste unto me; give ear unto my voice when I cry unto Thee.

For out of the north there cometh up a nation against us, which shall make our land desolate, and none shall dwell therein.

✝CHAPTER THIRTEEN✝

18 JULY 1209

There is poetry in this cavalcade—a great deal of poetry. What a vivid scene you could paint if you had Virgil's skill: if you could describe the river of gleaming horses with their flowing tails and tossing heads; the rumble of their hoofs and the glint of their gilded trappings; the standards fluttering proudly above them, some as red as the blood of grapes, others as green as the fourth foundation of the Heavenly Jerusalem. How wonderful it would be to capture those colors forever, in writing, and to resurrect the men who carry them, the knights and the squires, and the Bishop, and the Bishop's chaplain, and all those lesser folk who ride with the baggage. Some two score men, I would say—

perhaps even more—who come like the Seventh Angel of the Apocalypse, clothed with a cloud: only in this case it's a cloud of dust, thick and white, thrown up by the passage of our horses.

If I were a poet, I would compare this swift procession to a storm, and the dust to a thundercloud, and the flash of polished steel to bolts of lightning. I would compare the Viscount to Odysseus, and the Bishop to Eurystheus (the most cowardly king in all history), and the Archdeacon . . .

To whom would I compare the Archdeacon?

He's sitting there, lost in thought, and it's obvious that his limbs are working without the guidance of his brain, which is busy with matters far more crucial than the management of his reins and his stirrups. I wonder what he's thinking about. Not happy things, I'll warrant you. He's frowning, and his face seems overcast, and he's chewing at his bottom lip like a dog worrying a rat. I suppose, if I were Virgil, I would compare him to Mercury, because he's light on his feet, and to Phoebus Apollo, because he has the gift of rhetoric, and could easily argue his son back to life, just as Apollo did. But Apollo was radiant; he was as fair as the sun and as beautiful as the day. The Archdeacon looks more like Pluto, black-robed

148

and black-bearded. Except that Pluto would not have been so small. . . .

Ah, well. I'll never be a poet, in any case. You don't have to be a poet to write history. You just have to get your facts right.

"Father?"

"Hmmph?" He blinks and looks up at me. "Yes? What is it?"

"Father, will you tell me about Lord Jordan?"

"Lord Jordan?" he says, making a face. "Lord Jordan is Roland's brother. There's not much else to tell."

(Oh, yes, there is.) "But you mentioned fratricide . . ."

"Sweet saints preserve us!" He laughs and shakes his head. "You never miss a word, do you? You're as quiet as a mouse, but you soak it all up. Every single bit of it."

"Father—"

"When I first met Jordan, Isidore, his father, Lord Galhard, was still alive. So was his brother Berengar. Berengar was the eldest, then came Jordan, and then Roland. Being the eldest, Berengar was supposed to succeed Lord Galhard." There's a pause, as the Archdeacon swerves to avoid a skittish gray horse up ahead. He doesn't speak again

149

until we're safely past. "Lord Galhard died of a wasting disease, about fifteen years ago," he continues. "When he died, Berengar became Lord of Bram. But three months later Berengar also perished, in rather mysterious circumstances. Jordan maintains that it was a hunting accident. I find that hard to believe."

"Why?"

"Because Berengar was an extremely experienced hunter. It seems odd that he should have planted himself right in front of a wild boar and let it tear him to pieces. Very small pieces they were, too— or so I've heard. And no sign of his hunting sword."

"Then—"

"I'm not saying that it *was* murder. I'm just saying that it *could* have been." The Archdeacon narrows his eyes, squinting into the middle distance. "And knowing Jordan, it probably was."

God have mercy upon us. Could this really be true?

"But Father—why hasn't he been punished?"

"Oh, it's not a thing that anyone can prove," the Archdeacon replies with a careless wave of his hand. "It's just a suspicion I happen to entertain, because of certain things he's said. And certain things he's done. He's a very dangerous man, is

Jordan. Very dangerous and very clever. That's why I want you to keep away from him." Glancing at me. "Is that clear?"

"But I don't understand." This doesn't make sense. "If Lord Jordan is so bad, then why is Lord Roland so good?"

"Oh, I wouldn't say that Jordan is *all* bad. . . ." The Archdeacon's voice fades, as he becomes lost in some distant memory. But it must trouble him, because he dismisses it with a shake of his head. "As far as I can tell, Roland takes after his mother. She was a noble, pious woman, and Roland was her favorite. She had a great deal of influence over him." Another pause. "As for the other two boys, they followed in their father's footsteps."

"Lord Galhard's footsteps, you mean?"

"That's right. Lord Galhard." The Archdeacon scowls: in clear, ringing tones, he adds, "Lord Galhard was the most blackhearted butcher ever to soil the earth with his bloody crimes. May his soul be condemned, and may he spend eternity in the everlasting fires of Satan's furnace."

"Hear, hear!" Lord Jordan's voice. "I couldn't have put it better myself."

By the blood of the Lamb! Where did *he* spring from? The Archdeacon nearly falls off his horse.

He turns, and there's Lord Jordan, coming up from behind. He's riding the most magnificent black stallion, and wearing the most magnificent surcoat—red damask, lined with silk. He also wears an enormous sword and a glittering mail hauberk, and altogether looks like something unleashed by the breaking of the Seven Seals in the Book of Revelations.

Oh, but he's a glorious sight. What a glorious, glorious sight! The earth shall quake before him, and the heavens shall tremble.

"Discussing my family, Pagan?" he says in a genial sort of way. "Please do go on."

"My lord, I—I—"

"It's a fascinating subject, isn't it? Have you told Isidore about the number of wives that Berengar managed to kill off? Or about the time my father tried to cut your tongue out?" He lifts his eyes and raises his voice, addressing me over the Archdeacon's head. "My father didn't like Pagan's choice of words, so he tried to cut his tongue out. Fortunately, I was able to prevent him from doing so."

"And I'll always be grateful for that, my lord. Always," the Archdeacon mumbles, turning quite red. Whereupon Lord Jordan addresses me again.

"I suppose you've been hearing all about Roland,"

he says. "About how brave and pious and chival-rous he is, and what a good singer he is, and how his piss turns to pure gold the moment it leaves his body." A sneer lifts one side of his mouth, display-ing a full complement of small, pointed teeth. "Bor-ing, isn't it?" he says.

"My lord—!"

"Oh, I'm *so* sorry, Pagan. God forbid that I should utter the slightest criticism of Saint Roland. I'll say three Our Fathers, shall I? Or perhaps I should just nail myself to the nearest church door."

The Archdeacon looks angry now. He's sitting very straight in the saddle, and the sparks are prac-tically shooting from his eyes.

"I think that Isidore may have formed his own opinions about Roland, my lord," he says through his teeth. "I don't think your views will affect them, based as they are on ill will and prejudice."

"See what happens, Isidore? We get along quite well until we touch on the topic of Roland." Lord Jordan is riding with one hand on his hip: he looks so elegant and graceful in those beautiful clothes. On that beautiful horse. "The secret is to steer clear of Roland and talk about other people," he says. "Now this Abbot we're going to meet—the one who seems to be running everything—what's *he* like, for instance? Does anybody know him? I hear that he was down this way a couple of years ago."

"Yes, he was." The Archdeacon jumps at this opportunity to change the subject. "He came down here with the preaching mission. I met him several times."

"And what did you think?"

The Archdeacon makes a wry face. "Nothing very encouraging, my lord," he says. "Arnaud Amaury is a powerful man. He's a cousin of the Viscount of Narbonne—"

"Really? I didn't know that."

"And he was Abbot of Grandselve before he was appointed Abbot of Citeaux. Of course, Citeaux is one of the leading Cistercian monasteries, so Arnaud always has to have the last word." A sigh. "He tends to favor the fire-and-blood school of preaching."

"'And the Lord will insert burning coals into your testicles, and roll them down into the Bottomless Pit?'" Lord Jordan suggests, whereupon the Archdeacon giggles behind his hand.

"Something like that," he agrees. "'Repent, or thou shalt be smitten with the boil and the earworm.'"

154

"And what about this papal legate?" Lord Jordan raises an eyebrow. "Do we know anything about him?"

"Nothing, I'm afraid. Except that he's called Milo."

"Like the tribune who killed Clodius, and was defended by Cicero." I can't help saying it: they both look at me as if I'm a giant mushroom growing out of the saddle.

"Ye-e-es," the Archdeacon finally remarks, and turns back to Lord Jordan. "We must pray that this Milo is a reasonable man, because I tell you now that we can't expect any moderation from Arnaud Amaury. He's as vain as Venus, that fellow. Can't bear to be defeated in anything. His preaching mission was a resounding failure, so he comes back here with half the population of Europe to kick a few heads in. He's a pushy, puerile, self-centered bully."

"Well, of course he is," Lord Jordan rejoins. "He's a cleric, isn't he?"

Lord God of my salvation! What a terrible thing to say! I hope the Archdeacon doesn't let him get away with *that.*

But the Archdeacon just screws up his nose impatiently, as if he's heard it all before.

"So you're going to start insulting me again—"

"I simply want to point out that this is yet another example of what the Church so often produces. In fact I've developed a bit of a theory about it. I've been thinking that the *tonsures* might be to blame: they might be exposing the heads of young clerics to far too much sun. It's addling their brains, you see."

"Ha, ha, ha."

"But I'm serious, Pagan! If God had meant us to wear tonsures, he would have made us bald from birth—" Lord Jordan's gaze has been wandering: suddenly he stops short and bursts into a loud peal of laughter. "Oh, oh!" he cries. "By the balls of Baal, will you look at that face? Have you ever seen anything so formidable?" And he's pointing at me.

He's laughing at *me*!

How dare you! How dare you laugh! May you be delivered unto the famine and the pestilence, and may they bury you with the burial of an ass!

"Don't you approve of me, Isidore? No, don't look away. Look me straight in the eye and tell me what you think." (He's still laughing, the soulless murderer.) "Do you think I'm being too harsh on your Brothers in Christ?"

"Leave him alone, Jordan."

"Or has Pagan been telling you tales, perhaps? Warning you about my vicious propensities?"

"That's *enough*, Jordan!"

"Oh, what a pair. What a pair! If looks could kill . . ." He's grinning and gasping and wiping his eyes. "God knows you're well matched. I wish I had a couple of dogs like you. No one would ever get past them."

"Speaking of dogs—" the Archdeacon begins angrily, but Lord Jordan doesn't let him finish.

"I know, I know, I'm a dog," he says. "A real boar-baiter."

"You're a *wasp*!" the Archdeacon splutters. "A hornet! Why don't you go and bother someone else for a change?"

"Because I enjoy your company." Lord Jordan has a devil's smile: I can see that now. It's sly and wolfish and full of malice, but when he turns it on the Archdeacon, it's full of something else, as well—something akin to sympathy. "You don't know how much pleasure I get from bothering you, Pagan," he says. "It's exactly the same pleasure as I get from pulling the wings off flies."

The Archdeacon sniffs. "Well, you're not pulling the wings off *this* fly," he declares, and drums his heels on his horse's flanks. "Come on, Isidore," he adds as he surges forward. "I've got things to discuss with the Viscount. Important things. Can't loll around here all day."

Loll? *Loll?* If this is lolling, Father, I'd hate to see what you'd call a quick sprint.

Oh, Lord, how tired I am. How very, very tired. My knees ache. My backside is numb. My spine feels as if it's going to split down the middle. And we've only been riding a day!

How on earth am I going to last all the way to Montpellier?

‡CHAPTER FOURTEEN‡

20 JULY 1209

"My lords. Although I appreciate the limitations of my natural ability, I cannot deny that my experience as an orator has been considerable. And whatever benefit can be extracted from any or all of my qualifications, I feel duty bound to place it at the disposal of Lord Raymond Roger Trencavel."

A good beginning. Modest and dignified, yet with just the right touch of authority. How does he manage to sound so confident? He looks very small, standing out there in the middle of all that space: a tiny black figure on a vast expanse of red-and-yellow tiles, dwarfed by the graceful pillars holding up the chapter-house roof. And what a chapter house! How rich the cathedral of

Montpellier must be! Stained glass in the windows. Vivid paintings on the walls. Tier upon tier of stone seats, all packed with people. I've never seen anything so magnificent. So impressive.

So frightening.

"My lords," the Archdeacon continues, pointing at Lord Raymond, "I have known this young man since he was a tender child, so young and innocent that he could not tell the good from the bad. I was present when his father's death laid the burden of manhood prematurely upon him; when the child-ish playthings were struck from his hands and replaced by the sword of temporal authority. And I pitied, from the bottom of my heart, this virtuous boy, ardent in his pursuit of God's holy word, yet abandoned to the care of wicked counselors, false friends whose ways were slippery ways in the dark-ness. I mourned as I witnessed the snares they laid for him, the lies they told him. I mourned, but I blamed him not—for who can blame a child for the actions of those in whose care God has placed him?"

Lord Raymond is staring at the floor. He's all dressed up in his finest clothes, blue and gold and purple: beside him, the Bishop of Carcassonne looks rather like a reliquary, so studded with precious stones that it's a wonder he can move around. And there's Lord Jordan, resplendent in jade-green silk, as proudly impassive as a stone prophet on a church doorway. He catches my eye and winks.

"My lords," the Archdeacon declares, "it was Jesus Christ, our Lord and King, who said that a son is not guilty of the sins of his father—and if he said it, then we must agree, and anyone who condemns this doctrine must be in error. My lords, the Viscount played Jonathan to his father's Saul: for as Saul pursued David, so this man's father pursued the good Catholics of Carcassonne. And just as Jonathan said to David: 'Fear not, for the hand of Saul my father shall not find thee,' so this man, since he became a man, has made his house safe for the true children of God."

A rumble of disagreement from the Abbot of Citeaux. He's a fine, big man, somewhat heavy around the middle, but still quick and active: he has iron-gray hair and a red face, made even redder by the white Cistercian robe he wears. His hands are enormous.

"Archdeacon," he growls, "I think you have been misled. Lord Raymond's sympathy for heretics is

161

well known and widely discussed. His lands are a refuge for every kind of depraved doctrine."

"Yes, now that's very true, Archdeacon." The legate Milo is smaller and softer than the Abbot: even his voice is softer. His skin is sallow, and there are great dark circles under his eyes. "We've received many reports back in Rome," he says. "And when the preaching mission was sent to Carcassonne, two years back—"

"My lords, if you doubt me, go to his house!" The Archdeacon throws out his hands in a forceful, urgent gesture. "Search the rooms, empty the pots, uncover the beds!" he cries. "Seek out the sons of Baal—the vessels of Satan—the foul brood of the Seven-Headed Beast! You will not find them. Never, since his coming of age, has this man shared a word, a hearth, or a meal with a heretic; never was a true pilgrim, engaged in a holy voyage, ever maltreated or robbed by him, or attacked by his followers. As a man, this man has not sinned. Who amongst you would dare to accuse him and claim that, although he has not sinned, he must lose land, rent, and dues?"

The Archdeacon's voice is so strong, so compelling, that I wish I could see his face. But his movements are very expressive: every line of his

162

body seems to emphasize the message he's delivering. I wonder if those heartfelt gestures are simply part of his technique. I wonder if they're the sort of thing that Cicero would have used.

"Whether Lord Raymond is a heretic or not is of no concern to us," the Abbot announces. "What concerns us is his territory. Carcassonne is a pesthole of heretics. And Pope Lucius, may he rest in peace, declared many years ago that all receivers and defenders of heretics shall be subjected to the same punishment as heretics."

"My lord, you are unjust!" The Archdeacon's voice is like a crack of thunder. "I call upon you to prove your claims against the Viscount!"

"I'm sorry, Archdeacon, but this is not a court," Milo interrupts. (He sounds very mild and calm and reasonable.) "We don't have to prove anything here. Our Holy Father is quite satisfied that Lord Raymond is a sinner."

"And if he is a sinner—for are we not all sinners?—if he is a sinner, then surely it is our Holy Father's duty to forgive his sin?" The Archdeacon clasps his hands together: he adopts a pleading tone. "Was not the prodigal son forgiven? Did not Christ command us to forgive our brother, not seven times, but seventy times seven?"

Good point. That's a very good point. But the Abbot waves it aside.

"All priests forgive sin, in the name of God," he says. "But that doesn't prevent them from chastising a sinner. Penances must be exacted, Archdeacon."

And that's true, too. What can be said against that?

The Archdeacon takes a deep breath and plows on.

"My lords, I am a priest myself," he declares. "I too have imposed penances upon many sinners. But never, never have my penances involved war and bloodshed. Are we not the shepherds of our Lord's flock? Are we not spiritual descendants of the Apostles? And did not John of Salisbury, in his great book *Policraticus*, remind us that 'he who is greater is to diminish himself voluntarily, and is to claim for himself the duties of ministry in preference to others, *solely according to the law of peace*, dissociated from power and conflict'?"

Oh, yes. Oh, yes, that's so true. I can feel it in my heart, and I know it's right. We are men of God, not men of war. How can anyone argue against such a holy truth?

The Abbot scowls terribly and glares at the

Archdeacon from beneath his bushy gray eyebrows.

"Do you question our Holy Father?" he growls. "We follow the Pope's command, Father Pagan, in this as in all other things."

But the Archdeacon has turned toward Milo. He lowers his voice, as if he wants only Milo to hear.

"My lord," he says, "it seems to me that the Holy Father has been led astray by counselors more concerned with their own worldly advancement than with the spiritual health of Christendom. The blessed Bernard of Clairvaux, in his *De consideratione*, gave good advice to Pope Eugenius when he said: 'Tell me which seems to you the greater honor and greater power: to forgive sins or to divide estates? But there is no comparison. These base, worldly concerns have their own judges, the kings and princes of this world.'" (A deep breath; a cough; a brief, quivering silence. The Archdeacon clenches his fists and drives them into his chest by way of emphasis.) "My lord, Saint Peter himself— the Rock on which our Church was founded— thirsted for blood with fleshly desire, yet Christ bade him sheathe his sword. Should Peter's successor unsheathe it?"

165

"Archdeacon—"

"Who is more sinful than the man who casts the ministry of peace into quarrels and torment? What is the point of such great savagery? Does it lead to life? No, for its end is destruction. Does it lead to glory? No, for the glory of the men who unleash it is lost in confusion. Does it lead to this end: that they may be ennobled in flesh and blood? No, for flesh and blood will not possess the Kingdom of God!"

By the blood of the Lamb, what a great speaker he is. What a great, great orator. I never knew—I can hardly believe—he seems transformed, so much taller and nobler, so passionate and wise. Can this be his true self? Is this what's hidden beneath those crude jokes, that swaggering disrespect? Oh, if only he were always like this! If he were always like this, I would follow him as I would follow a lighted candle. I would follow him gladly, for he would lead me in the paths of righteousness.

"My lords, it was Plato who told us that Nature is the will of God," he continues. "And what does Nature teach us? It teaches us that the lion—the king of the beasts—will always show great compassion, and spare the prostrate. Is it not therefore against God's law to attack Lord Raymond, who prostrates himself before your mercy? More than that: Cicero himself reminds us that Nature holds together and supports the universe, all of whose parts are in harmony with one another. In this way are men united by Nature—but by reason of their sinfulness they quarrel, not realizing that they are of one blood and subject to the same protecting power. We are of one blood, my lords: should we slay our own brother, and spill our own blood?"

Surely this is the voice of God. Surely this is God's voice, speaking through the Archdeacon's mouth. He turns, briefly, and I can see his face: flushed, moist-eyed, the veins standing out on his temples. He raises his arms and pleads—begs— and his hands are shaking, and his cry is like the mourning of angels in heaven.

"Oh, my lords, my lords, remember the words of our Savior, Jesus Christ! 'Blessed are the merciful, for they shall obtain mercy. Blessed are the peace-makers, for they shall be called the children of God. We should not judge but love one another, because the fruit of the Holy Spirit is love, and joy, and peace, and gentleness.'" (Praise ye the Lord! Praise ye the name of the Lord!) "My brothers, I entreat you, let the peace of God rule in your souls. Raise your eyes to the light, and open your hearts to the Holy Spirit. For we shall all stand before the Judgment Seat, brothers, and when that day comes, only the righteous will eat of the tree of life. Only the righteous will enter the Heavenly Jerusalem."

Yes! Oh, yes! Oh, Father, you walk in God's statutes. You stand fast in the Lord. How could I ever have thought otherwise?

But the Abbot—the Abbot is still scowling. The Abbot is unmoved. How could he be so deaf? So blind? He turns to Lord Raymond and says, "Have you anything to add, my lord?"

The Viscount jumps to his feet. He pushes his hair out of his eyes and shakes his head. "No," he mutters. He looks and sounds like a sulky adolescent.

"What about you, my lord Bishop?" It's Milo who speaks. "Have you anything to say in the Viscount's defense?"

"Oh—ah—yes, I—if I could just—um . . ." The Bishop of Carcassonne struggles to rise, weighed down by jasper and amethysts and fold upon fold of heavy, embroidered silk. At last the Viscount has to help him, slipping a hand beneath his elbow and hauling him upright. There's a snicker from somewhere in the crowd behind me.

"My lord, I'm an old man," the Bishop whimpers. "I've done my best to guide my flock. But if I have failed, I can only throw myself on our Holy Father's mercy. I will abide by the wish of our Holy Father."

A snort from the Archdeacon. He's looking very grim. Milo nods at the Bishop, smiling in an exhausted kind of way: beside him, the Abbot gives a satisfied grunt.

"As the Holy Father's representative, I am only too happy to welcome you to his side, my lord Bishop," Milo declares. "I embrace you as I embrace any of your household who feel the same way." He turns his weary gaze on the Archdeacon, adding: "Perhaps Father Pagan, now that he has discharged his duty to the Viscount with such skill and vigor, may decide that he has an even greater duty to our Holy Mother Church? Perhaps he will take up the all-powerful and excellent arms of obedience, to fight for the Lord Christ and his representative, Pope Innocent?"

They're asking him to change sides! But he won't, will he? Surely he won't! I can't see his face, only his small, straight back, as he squares his shoulders and puts his hands on his hips.

"My lord," he says calmly, "in the words of Saint Erasmus, I would rather have my bowels ripped out of my belly and laid upon a fire."

"Are you sure of that? You're setting your face against God, you know. You're joining the forces of evil."

The Archdeacon laughs. "My lord, a certain philosopher once said to his son, 'Call him a liar who affirms that evil must be conquered with evil, for as a fire does not put out fire, so evil does not yield to evil.'" He raises his hand and points an accusing finger straight at Milo. "The Viscount came to you in peace, to make his submission, but you withheld your forgiveness. *You* are the one setting your face against God, my lord. Not I."

He turns on his heel, and it's like a signal: suddenly everyone's rising, everyone's talking, everyone's making for the door. I can hear the Viscount's yell, high above the babble, as he shakes his fist at Milo. "God curse you!" he shouts. "You'll suffer for this, you hypocrite! You bloodsucker!" What's happening? Is that all? Are we going now? So many people, squeezing past, smelling of sweat and garlic and rose oil; people treading on my heels and

170

breathing in my face and pushing me against the wall. Where's the Archdeacon? I must speak to the Archdeacon!

"Isidore." He's here at last; he takes my hand. "Come on, Isidore," he says in a hoarse and weary tone. "Let's get out of this place. It's making me ill."

And he forces a path through the crush of jabbering people.

171

‡CHAPTER FIFTEEN‡

20 JULY 1209

"Father—"

"Over here, Isidore."

"Father, wait—please. . . ." I want to tell you. I have to tell you. You're a great, great speaker: the greatest I've ever heard. You're a modern-day Cicero. "Father, what you just said—to the Abbot—"

"Was a waste of time."

"But it was *true*! All of it!"

"Well, I'm glad somebody thought so." His voice is crisp and sarcastic. "This way, Isidore; we have things to discuss."

I don't even know where we are. All these flaring torches and milling people; endless rows of carved columns; looming shadows and murky stairs. Are we in a cloister, perhaps? He drags me into a doorway, out of the noise and the bustle: I can feel the sweat on his hands.

"Listen carefully," he says, "because we haven't much time."

"Father—"

"Don't *interrupt* me, Isidore!"

But I have to tell you. You're a great man. I have to tell you that.

"The thing is, I brought you to Montpellier for a reason." He's speaking very quickly. "I would have left you in Carcassonne, only I feared the worst. Things are going to get bad there, very bad. That's why I think you should stay here with the Bishop."

What?

"He's joined the Crusaders. I thought he would. Well, you can't really blame him: he's an old man, after all—"

"But I don't want to stay with the Bishop!"

"Isidore. Listen to me." He squeezes my wrist. "You don't know what it's going to be like. Sieges are nasty things. They're no place for a boy like you. You're not strong. You'll be much better off in Montpellier, with the Bishop."

"But he's a coward!"

"Hush—"

"And anyway, he won't want me! *No one* wants me!"

"Don't be a fool." (His sternest voice.) "I'm sorry. I know he's not an ideal master, but he's the only person I know around here. And he's bound to find someone who needs you."

No. No. This can't be happening. O Lord, why casteth Thou off my soul? Why hidest Thou Thy face from me?

"Besides," the Archdeacon continues, "I'm on the wrong side of the fence now. You don't want to become an enemy of the Church, Isidore. This crusade has the Pope's approval."

"Then why aren't *you* joining it?"

A pause. I can barely see his face in the dimness: just the glitter of an eye and the gleam of his glossy hair.

"I suppose there are lots of reasons," he says at last. "Languedoc is my home. It took me in and gave me a position. All my friends are in Languedoc." Another brief silence. "Anyway," he adds, "I couldn't fight for any cause that had the Abbot of Citeaux at its head. No matter how respectable it might be."

"Well, Languedoc is my home, too, you know! And I think the Abbot *stinks*!"

174

A sudden snort. I can feel him heaving and shaking: shaking with laughter? "God, Isidore." (Gasp. Choke.) "What a find you are."

"Please. Please don't leave me. *Please.*"

"But how can I take you? You'll never make it back to Béziers. We'll be riding through the night, if we're going to get there before the Crusaders do. Riding hard, so we can warn the people to prepare." He pats my shoulder. "You'll be all right, truly. I've coped with the Bishop for ten years: he's no trouble. Just stay here, and I'll go and have a word with him. I won't be long."

No! Wait! But he vanishes—vanishes like a puff of smoke.

What am I going to do? I can't stay with that Bishop. He'll hate me! He'll hate me the way everyone hates me except . . . except . . .

The Archdeacon.

I've got to do something. I've got to think.

Everything's so confused, but there must be something—there must be someone. Someone who can help. Someone I know. Lord Roland? If Lord Roland were here, he would help me. He was *pleased* that I'd joined the Archdeacon. He said I was a pearl of great price. Oh, why isn't he here? Why isn't he here, instead of his brother?

175

Lord Jordan. Would he help? No, not him, he's a murderer. But his squire, Guichard—maybe if I rode with Guichard . . .

The crowds are thinning. They seem to be moving off toward that big door, beneath the painting of Saint Peter's martyrdom. Didn't we come through that door when we first arrived? I think we did. I think that's the way to the horses. And there's the Viscount, waving his arms, pushing people through, urgent, impatient—are they leaving for Béziers already?

I've got to move.

Hoisting up my skirts, so I can run after them. Run, Isidore, run! Under the archway, into a crowded corridor. Thrusting past the big, heavy knights; squirming between their chattering varlets. They're all talking at the tops of their voices, booming away, their angry curses bouncing off the vaulted ceiling. (Such a smell of sweat and leather!) But I can't see Guichard—I can't see Lord Jordan. Spilling into a gigantic courtyard, where the horses are already waiting, saddled up, ready to go. Tossing heads and clattering hoofs and waving torches. Where's Guichard? Where *is* he?

Ah.

There he is. Over there, near that fountain.

176

Holding two horses, gazing off into the distance, looking thoroughly bored. Whenever I see him he looks like that. Isn't he interested in *anything*?

"Guichard!"

He glances around, spots me, grimaces. But he doesn't say a word.

"Guichard, I need your help."

Grunt.

"Please, Guichard, I—I don't want to stay here. The Archdeacon wants me to stay here with his Bishop. Can I ride with you instead?"

He blinks.

"With me?" he says in a most ungracious voice.

"Please, Guichard. I don't want to stay with the Bishop. He's a coward. He's an old man. Please?"

Guichard hawks and spits. The spittle just misses my surplice.

"You'll have to ask his majesty," comes the reply. "I don't make that kind of decision."

"But—"

"Here he is now. Do you want to ask him?"

"Ask me what?"

Oh, God, it's Lord Jordan. He looks like an oak tree, in all that green: torchlight sparkles on his rings and buckles and brooches.

I have to get out of here.

"Nothing, my lord, I—it's nothing."

"He wants to ride with me."

"He *does*?" A blank, blue stare. "Haven't you got your own mount, Isidore? A very nice chestnut, isn't it?"

"Yes, my lord. I'm sorry, my lord."

"He says the Archdeacon wants him to stay here." (Oh, shut up, will you?) "He says that the Bishop's a coward."

That's it. I'm leaving. Ouch! Let go! Let go of my collar!

"Wait a moment, Isidore." Lord Jordan pulls me back. "What's all this about? What's Pagan done? He's not abandoning you, surely?"

"He—he wants me to stay with the Bishop."

"Ah." The grip relaxes. (I can breathe again.) "So that's it."

"I don't . . ." (Cough, cough.) "I don't want to stay, my lord."

"With the Bishop? I don't blame you. He always brings *me* out in boils."

"Can I ride with Guichard? Please? I—I won't be any trouble."

Guichard clicks his tongue. His master gazes down that long, aristocratic nose, which is slightly reddened by sunburn.

"If it's the Bishop's breath that's worrying you, I can always introduce you to someone else in Milo's army," he says. "The Courtenays are here—they're cousins of the Count of Toulouse. I've always found them to be reasonably chivalrous, despite their odd political alignments. If I asked, they'd probably make room for one more."

"My lord, I don't want to join the Crusaders. I don't believe in what they're doing."

"Then ask the Bishop to send you somewhere else. There's a fair number of churches in this city. Bound to be a place for someone with your skills—especially someone with a Bishop's recommendation."

No! No, that's not what I want! By the blood of the Lamb—by the blood of the blessed martyrs. "My lord, I don't *want* to stay here! I want to go back to the south!"

"Why?"

Why? Because . . . because . . .

"Why not wait until the fighting's over?" His face is completely expressionless. "It won't be pretty, I can tell you."

"My lord—my lord—"

"What?"

You don't understand! You don't know what it's

179

like! How could I ever explain—there's only one person—it's like being cast adrift, all over again, with no one to help you.

"My lord, I want to stay with the Archdeacon."

He smiles. It's a slow, subtle, indulgent smile, and it makes him look quite different.

"Well, why didn't you say so?" he murmurs. "I can understand that. Let's see, now. What can we do?" He strokes his mustache, thinking deeply. His gaze flicks from horse to horse; from my face to Guichard's, and back again.

"You'll never last as far as Béziers on your own," he says. "It'll kill you, a ride like that. You'd better double up."

"Not on *my* nag," Guichard remarks—and Lord Jordan turns on him with a look of the most profound and deadly menace.

"Did I ask for your comments, Guichard?"

"No, my lord." A mere crack of sound. "Sorry, my lord."

"I didn't *think* so." (By the blood of the Lamb! He's like a bear lying in wait. Like a lion in secret places.) "Now where was I, before I was so boorishly interrupted? Oh, yes. It would be better, Isidore, if you were to ride with me. You don't look as if you carry much weight, and Michelet, here, is as strong as a bull. My saddlebags can go with the rest of the luggage."

"But—"

"We'll put you in one of Guichard's outfits. You're about the same size. If Pagan happens to see you, just keep your head down. I'll say that you're Guichard, and that you're drunk." He turns back to Guichard. "Get out your brown tunic. And that blue cape with the hood. Take them—" He pauses, his eyes searching the courtyard. "Take them over there, behind that pillar. If Pagan comes, he won't see you in the shadows." (Flapping his hand at me.) "Go on, Isidore."

Yes. Yes, I'm going. Your wish is my command. Which pillar? This one? It's part of a portico, marching along the side of a two-story building: it's painted with weatherworn stripes of different colors, but in this light the colors are only shades of gray. I can see everything from here: I can see the Viscount and Lord Jordan, and I can see Guichard, scampering across the cobbles with a bundle wedged under his arm.

"Here!" he gasps. "Put these on!" And suddenly there are clothes everywhere, draped over my shoulders, dangling from my outstretched hands, slipping to the ground. They smell ferocious.

Guichard ducks down behind me.

"What's wrong? Why are you—?"

"He's coming!"

Help! You mean the Archdeacon? Yes, there he is! Small and dark and agitated, standing on tiptoe as he cranes his neck to scan the courtyard. He sees Lord Jordan and waves.

"Jordan!" he cries, beating a path through the crowds. Lord Jordan just stands there, stroking his stallion's fine, glossy chest: it's hard to tell what's happening, because there are so many people and the torches dance and flicker. But the Archdeacon finally emerges from a press of bodies. He grabs Lord Jordan's arm; his loud, urgent, breathless voice rises above the other voices, like a sparrow upon a housetop.

"Isidore!" he exclaims. "Have you seen Isidore?"

"Why, yes—"

"Where? Where is he?"

"I don't know." Lord Jordan's rumbling drawl is very difficult to hear from this distance. "Maybe . . ." (Mumble, mumble.) " . . . with the Bishop."

"The Bishop?"

(Mumble, mumble.) " . . . stay with the Bishop. He came to say goodbye."

"Goodbye?" The Archdeacon lets go of Lord Jordan's arm. "But he didn't say goodbye to *me*."

"I think he was angry with you."

The Archdeacon sags. His shoulders slump. His head droops. "He's always angry with me. Why is he always angry with me? I do my best."

"Ssst!" It's Guichard. He's tugging at my skirts. "Hurry up, will you? Can't you see they're going?"

Going? Who's going? You mean the Viscount? Where *is* the Viscount? By the blood of the Lamb, he's disappeared—they're all disappearing. They're moving off toward the gates, a confused jumble of mounted men, cursing and yelling and jostling for position.

I'd better get into these clothes.

"But I can't just leave him here." The Archdeacon's mournful accents. "Not without saying goodbye."

"You'll have to." Lord Jordan sounds brisk and impatient. "There isn't time to go running around looking for him."

"But—"

"Pagan. Get off your arse and *move*. Move! Or you'll never catch up!"

That's done it. He can't argue with an order like that. He turns away from Lord Jordan, and now it's my turn to move—move, move, move! Hurry, Isidore, hurry! Dragging on the tunic, buckling the belt. Guichard hovering beside me, breathing into my ear. "Give me that. And that. And that," he says, snatching up my surplice. "I'll see you in Béziers." Whereupon he slinks off into the darkness, and here I am, alone, wearing strange garments and sweating like a wineskin.

How did I ever come to this? Pinning my faith on a murderer? I must be out of my head.

The Lord is my shepherd; I shall not want. Yea, though I walk through the valley of the shadow of death, I will fear no evil: for Thou art with me; Thy rod and Thy staff they comfort me.

✝CHAPTER SIXTEEN✝

21 JULY 1209

"Isidore."

Ugh.

"Wake up, Isidore—we're here. I'm getting down."

What? Where am I? Whose back is this? Some-one's fumbling at my fingers. . . .

"Let go, Isidore! By the balls of Baal, are you dead?"

That's Lord Jordan. I know him. He's all covered in sweat and dust. Why is he moving? Why is he sliding away?

I think I'll just lie down on this saddle. . . .

"Isidore!"

Leave me alone.

"You can't stay up there, boy. Come on, make an effort."

I don't want to make an effort. I don't want to move. Let go, you're hurting me—help! Help!

"It's all right." Lord Jordan's voice, booming through his chest. "I've got you. Just hold on."

"I can't walk."

"Yes, you can. If you lean on me, you can walk."

"I want to lie down."

"You will. As soon as we get inside."

Inside? Inside what? I don't know this place. It's like the bottom of a well, all stone walls and rubbish. It's dark, too, though not as dark as—could that be—?

"Is it morning?"

"Only just."

"Are we in Béziers?"

"Yes, we are." Lord Jordan's chest is shaking now. Is he coughing? No, he's laughing.

Silently.

"Can I go to bed, then?"

"Not here, you can't. No, Isidore. *No*. Wait till we get inside."

"I don't feel well. I want to lie down."

"So do we all." He keeps nudging at me with his

hip and his foot. His arm is like a rod of iron. And what's this? I've got the wrong clothes on. These aren't my clothes.

God, I feel *terrible*.

"Isidore?"

Who said that? That's not Lord Jordan. My eyes are all gummed up: everything's so murky, and my head is throbbing.

"Isidore?"

Oh, I see. It's the Archdeacon. He's all dusty, too, all sweaty and dusty

I wish he wouldn't shout like that.

"You—you—"

"Calm down, Pagan."

"How *dare* you!"

"It wasn't my idea." Lord Jordan's voice is husky with fatigue. "It was his idea."

"Where's Guichard?"

"Guichard? Oh, he's around somewhere. Keeping well out of the way."

"You're the lowest—you miserable—"

"Pagan, the poor boy didn't want to stay with your Bishop. Is that my fault?"

"Let him go!"

"I wouldn't advise it—"

"Let him go!"

Whoops! Ouch! God, it's so good to stop moving. How cool and solid the earth feels. . . .

"See?" Lord Jordan's voice, way above my head somewhere. "I told you."

"What have you done to him?"

"Oh, grow up, Pagan—"

"He's unconscious!"

"He's *tired*. So am I. So are you." The scraping of boots on gravel. "Why don't you have a drink and lie down? It might cool you off a bit."

"I can't. The Viscount needs me." Someone's hand, tapping my face. "Isidore? Are you all right? Isidore!"

Oh, go away.

"Needs you for what?" (Lord Jordan.) "What does the Viscount need you for? Where is he, anyhow?"

"He's gone off to meet the citizens."

"To tell them to stand and fight?"

"Yes, I think so. Isidore! You're going to regret this, my lord."

"Oh, I already have. Several times." Soft laughter: something pokes me in the ribs. "This has been the worst ride of my long and varied existence. Come on, Isidore, up you get."

"No! Leave him!"

"Pagan." A quick, impatient sigh. "If I leave him, he'll be sleeping right here, on a bed of horse dung. Is that what you want?"

"I'll take care of him myself."

"And the Viscount? What about the Viscount?" (Drawling sarcastically.) "Shall I tell him that you're occupied?"

Pause. There's a fly on my lip—I can feel it there— but I don't have the strength to flap it away. I don't have the strength to move at all.

I'm going to stay here forever.

"Don't worry," Lord Jordan continues. "I'll put him to bed. He can have my blanket."

"Be careful. He's not strong."

"You're telling *me*."

A grunt. A sigh. Somebody's knees crack like nutshells. No! What are you doing?

"Let go!"

"Sorry, Isidore." It's Lord Jordan again. "You can't stay here—you'll get stepped on."

"It's all right, Isidore." (The Archdeacon.) "I'll be back soon."

"Hups-a-daisy!"

"Lord Jordan will put you to bed. Just get some sleep, and we'll discuss this later."

Discuss what? The ground is lurching again—no, it's me—no, it's my stomach. If you don't put me down, Lord Jordan, I'm going to be sick.

"I'm going to be sick."

"Jesus."

Oaagh. Yurk. Retching. Heaving, God—O God, I am poured out like water, and all my bones are out of joint. My heart is like wax; it is melted in the midst of my bowels.

"Guichard! Thank Christ. Get some water, quick!"

My strength is dried up like a potsherd, and my tongue cleaveth to my jaws, and Thou hast brought me into the dust of death, O God. . . .

"Finished now?" A damp cloth, wiping my face. "By the balls of Baal, you're a delightful traveling companion. No wonder Pagan wanted to leave you with the Bishop."

"I'm sorry, my lord."

"So am I. Come on, up you get. Not much farther. Guichard, take his other arm."

Are we inside? Yes, we are inside. There's a stone floor, and stone steps—one step, two steps, three steps, four—and a window, and more steps. . . .

Someone brushes past, going in the opposite direction.

"They're putting down straw in the chapel,"

Guichard observes. "In the chapel and the kitchen and the guardroom. I heard the steward say so."

"Then I'm sure we can find a place."

"How long will we be here, my lord?"

"At a guess, about as long as it takes the Viscount to persuade this city that it's on its own."

"You don't think he'll stay here? To fight the Crusaders?"

"I'd be astonished if he did. Carcassonne is by far the biggest prize in his possession. If Béziers falls, there's always Carcassonne. But if Carcassonne falls . . . we're finished." Lord Jordan sighs. "No—you watch. He'll tell the good people of Béziers to hold out at all costs, and then he'll be off to Carcassonne like everyone else with half a brain. Carcassonne's more secure than Béziers."

A grunt from Guichard. This is all so confusing. Where are we now? The stairs have ended, but the corridors seem to go on forever: corridors smelling of smoke and urine, full of people curled up on the floor. My throat is burning. I need a drink.

"I need a drink."

"You'll get one. Be patient. Jesus, I'm lost—"

"This way, my lord."

A long, high room with an altar at one end. Candlesticks. A font. The Four Beasts of the

Apocalypse, painted above a window in red and blue and gold.

People strewn all over the place, like bundles.

"There you go." The supports are withdrawn—my knees can't take it—suddenly I'm down again; down, down, down. Straw prickling my face, blanket across my shoulders.

Bliss. What bliss.

"Right!" (Lord Jordan's voice.) "I'm going to find myself something to eat. What did you do with the horses, Guichard?"

"I left them with that steward."

"Then I'll go and make sure he's looking after them. Meanwhile, you'd better see if you can scare up a drink for this poor little puppy."

"I'm not a puppy."

"Shut up, Isidore. And maybe some milk, or some broth. Something that's easy to swallow."

"Yes, my lord."

"I'll come and get you when it's time to leave for Carcassonne."

What's that noise? It sounds like a wood-saw. No, it's a dog. No, it's somebody snoring. How strange it is: all these people, going to bed at sunrise. Everyone else will be getting up now. They'll be getting up at Merioc—Mengarde will be stoking the fire, and Father Fulbert will be washing his face. How far away it seems. Years and years and years ago . . . Ernoul's hair . . . ringing the bell . . . vegetables left on the front steps . . .

Leering faces and pointing fingers.

"Isidore." Somebody's poking me. "Isidore."

"Go 'way."

"Do you want a drink, or don't you?"

A drink! Where? It's Guichard, and he's got a wineskin. Praise ye the Lord!

"Take it easy—you'll spill it."

Praise ye the Lord for wine that maketh glad the heart of man. Oh, my throat. Oh, that's good. Lord Jordan has disappeared; Guichard is shaking his head at me.

"God, but you're a mess. Look at what you've done to my tunic."

"Thank you. Thank you, Guichard."

"Don't thank me. I didn't bring you here." He sticks the rag back into the wineskin. "Speaking of which, you want to watch yourself, my friend. His majesty doesn't do favors for nothing, you know."

Aaah. That's better. I can go to sleep now.

"Isidore? Are you listening?" (Ouch! Don't *poke*

me like that!) "A word in your ear, chum. You want to mind Lord Jordan: he's a Ganymede. And it shows, sometimes. Especially when he's drunk."

"Hnnn . . ."

"Just don't say I didn't warn you. All right?"

Warn me. Yes. You warn me . . . tomorrow . . . get up . . . I'm here . . .

Sleeping.

‡CHAPTER SEVENTEEN‡

22 JULY 1209

Hallelujah! The walls of Carcassonne! I thought we'd never make it. I can't believe we're here. Blessed be the Lord my strength; my goodness and my fortress; my high tower and my deliverer; my shield and He in whom I trust. Lift up your hands in the sanctuary, and bless the Lord.

"Praise God."

"Praise God."

All around us, murmurs of joy and thanksgiving. Even from the Cathars. Even from the Jews. At least, I suppose that's what the Jews are saying: I don't know their language, so I can only judge from their smiles, and from the way they move their hands. It's the first time they've smiled since we left Béziers—I suppose they must be sad to leave their homes behind.

Still, they should be used to it by now. Didn't God condemn them to wander in the wilderness? They're like the harts that find no pasture. ("O ye children of Benjamin, gather yourselves to flee out of the midst of Jerusalem.") I've never seen a Jew before. They're not quite what I expected. I thought they'd be bigger, somehow: bigger and louder and more richly dressed. Somebody once told me that Jews smell bad, but these ones seem to smell just like ordinary people.

Even so, it would be easy to spot them in a crowd. I suppose that's why the Viscount brought them along: to get them out of Béziers before the Crusaders arrive. If the Crusaders are trying to kill all the heretics, then they'll probably try to kill the Jews as well. In fact they might even mistake the Jews *for* heretics.

I would have done that myself, if Lord Jordan hadn't corrected me.

"Aaagh, Jesus." He's shifting in the saddle. I can feel his bones grinding as he stretches and flexes and straightens his spine. "I'm too old for this sort of thing. I should have stayed at home, with my granddaughter."

No response from the Archdeacon. He looks very tired. I wish he'd say something—even something sarcastic. It feels so wrong to have spent half the day beside him without exchanging a single word. He must be sick. Either sick or angry.

I hope he's not angry. That would be awful. But he wasn't angry last night . . . at least, I don't think he was. I don't seem to remember much about last night, except that the Archdeacon brought me some milk and dumplings. He wouldn't have done that if he was angry, would he? Oh, if only his horse were strong enough to support us both! It's impossible to talk to him from way up here, behind Lord Jordan. Because I know he doesn't trust Lord Jordan. And I know that he must be angry—of course he must—but is he *very* angry, or just a little bit cross? I wish I could tell. I wish he would say something.

"As soon as I get back, I'm going to light a candle," Lord Jordan observes. "I'm going to light a candle to the patron saint of horses—whoever that might be."

"Saint Hippolytus."

"Thank you, Isidore. I'm going to light a candle to Saint Hippolytus, in gratitude for the strength of my beautiful Michelet." He strokes his horse's neck. "I really wondered if this would be his last ride, but he's borne it like a rock. Like a rock in a storm."

Still not a word from the Archdeacon. He's peering ahead, at the towering walls of Carcassonne, as we advance into their long, cool shadow. Jagged battlements rear up against the sunset; smoke rises from a thousand kitchen fires. A shepherd by the roadside stops and stares, dazzled by the procession of flags and swords and horses, which is loose and straggling now, strung out along the road for quite some distance. And of course I'm stuck right at the very end, because Michelet is overloaded. I can't even see the Viscount from back here: only Guichard's hunched shoulders, jolting along in front of us, and the bald-headed Jew who's riding in front of him.

Guichard. He said something to me yesterday. Something about Lord Jordan being a Ganymede. I wonder what he meant by that. Ganymede was Zeus's cup-bearer in Olympus, but I don't see what he's got to do with Lord Jordan. Unless it's a vulgarism? Perhaps *Ganymede* is another word for *drunkard*. That could be it. The way you'd say "He's an Achilles" when you want to say "He's very brave."

I'll have to refer it to the Archdeacon.

"God, but I could do with a drink," Lord Jordan

mutters. "A drink and a sleep and a good, solid meal." He yawns until his jaw cracks. "What about you, Pagan? Care to empty a cask this evening? It's been a long time since we did that."

"I'm busy," the Archdeacon replies. Praise be to God! He actually spoke! But he doesn't sound too cheerful. Lord Jordan makes an impatient noise.

"Busy?" he says. "Doing what?"

The Archdeacon turns his head. His eyes are bloodshot, his beard untrimmed. He squints at Lord Jordan as if he can't believe his ears. "Doing what has to be done," he says. "There's an army heading this way, my lord. There will be refugees soon. They'll want food and beds and clothing. All these things will have to be found."

"Is that your job?"

"Of course it is! I'm the Bishop's deputy. And the Bishop isn't with us anymore."

"Ah. Of course he isn't." Lord Jordan's voice becomes smoother and slower, the way it always does when he's amused. I can't see his face, but I'm sure he's smiling. "What a fine chance this is for you, Pagan," he says. "It hadn't occurred to me before. Will you be moving into the Bishop's palace?"

"Don't be ridiculous."

"Oh, but you should, you really should. Think of the cellars there. Think of the kitchens. Think of all your faithful friends—"

"I've got far more important things to think about!" the Archdeacon snaps. And suddenly, here's the gate—the Aude Gate—and we're surrounded by hordes of people. Where did they come from? What are they doing here? All kinds of people, men and women, pushing and shouting and snatching at our feet, tugging at our clothes, straining to catch our attention. The noise is thunderous.

"My lord! My lord, what news?"

"Are they coming?"

"God help us!"

So many voices, wading like dragons and mourning like owls. So many faces, as desolate as the waters of Nimrim. Lord Jordan kicks off a clinging hand and urges his mount forward: he's cursing to himself, under his breath.

"Friends, have courage!" It's the Archdeacon. He sounds tired and hoarse, but authoritative. "The northerners are far away. Béziers stands between them and this city. Your Viscount is a brave warrior, with many valorous subjects. Be calm and return to your homes."

A surge of noise: questions and pleas and protests. Oh, why don't they listen to him? He frowns and tries again.

"Return to your homes!" he cries. "Are you men and women, or feeble children? Arm yourselves with hope, and strength, and trust in God, for the Scriptures tell us that the just man, fearless as a lion, shall be without dread." He points suddenly, and his words cut the air like a knife. "Take that woman away!" he orders. "She'll miscarry if you keep pushing her about like that! Haven't you people any *sense*?"

Ah! That's done it. They shrink back like naughty children, scolded into silence. Are they frightened, or are they shocked? Perhaps they're comforted. It's always comforting to see that there's someone in charge—someone who can make decisions and show the way.

Besides which, the Archdeacon looks so much taller in the saddle.

"Go on!" he exclaims, flapping his hand. "Go home!" It sounds as if he's talking to a pack of dogs or a flock of chickens. Around us, the mob begins to break up. People begin to move away, and the noise subsides a little—just enough to allow one man, a stunted fellow with the sharp, ravaged face of someone who has plowed wickedness and reaped iniquity, to ask a very difficult question.

"Where's the Bishop?" he inquires. "Where is Bernard Raymond de Roquefort?"

There's a pause. Heads turn; people hesitate. But the Archdeacon doesn't flinch.

"I think we can safely assume," he rejoins, "that the Bishop is where he usually is: lying in bed with a poultice on his chest and his hands in a bowl of rosewater." As the crowd laughs, he jerks his head at Lord Jordan, who digs in his spurs, and all at once we're moving. Down the street, under the portcullis, past the first cluster of houses, and into the first side street. It smells of somebody's dinner.

"Pagan! Wait!" Lord Jordan reins in. "Are you going to Saint-Nazaire?"

"Yes."

"Well, I'm going to the castle. Which means that I'm on the wrong road." He twists around to look at me, breaking my grip on his sword belt. "Off you get, Isidore. This is as far as I'm taking you."

Oh! Does that mean—?

"Go on, boy! What do you want me to do, build you a staircase?"

"Yes, my lord—I mean, no, my lord." Help! I

202

can't reach the stirrup. He's got his foot in the stirrup. How am I supposed to get down?

"In God's name!" he snaps. He's gripping my arm, and pulling me off, and I'm sliding—ouch! Help! My arm! Let go! My feet!

I can't walk. I can't stand!

"That child is a menace. He shouldn't be allowed to travel." (Lord Jordan's voice, floating down from the heights.) "I've never met anyone with so little horsemanship—or such poor bladder control. How on earth do you put up with him?"

"Same way I put up with you." The Archdeacon dismounts clumsily, staggering as his feet touch the road. "Grit my teeth and pray to Jesus. Come on, Isidore. You can ride my horse the rest of the way."

What? Oh, no. That's *your* horse.

"It's all right, Father. I can walk."

"No, you can't."

"Yes, I can."

"Isidore, will you *get on that horse?*"

"But I can walk! Look! I'm on my feet now!"

"Don't be ridiculous. You can hardly stand."

"Well, neither can you! You're just as tired as I am!"

"Yes, but I'm an archdeacon. So shut up and do as I say."

Laughter. Who's laughing? It's Lord Jordan, doubled up in the saddle. The Archdeacon turns on him furiously.

"Go away!" he cries. "Get out of here!"

"I'm going, I'm going."

"This is all your fault! If it wasn't for you, he wouldn't be in this condition!"

"Ah. But if it wasn't for *you*, he wouldn't even have come." Lord Jordan tugs at the reins, bringing his horse's head around. "See you tomorrow, Pagan. And try to get some rest. Believe me, you need it."

Smoothly, skillfully, he turns his huge stallion in the narrow street, retracing his steps until he disappears around a corner. The Archdeacon stands there, watching him go. Oh, God, he's so angry. Look at his color. Look at the way he's breathing. In Thee, O Lord, do I put my trust.

"Father?"

He grunts, but doesn't look around.

"I'm sorry, Father." (Please don't cast me off.) "I am your humble servant. I owe you my obedience. You are my master in all things. I—I'm very sorry."

He's squinting up into my face. He's shaking his head and sighing.

"What am I going to do with you?"

"I'm sorry."

"Come here." He reaches out. What's he up to? Glory to God, is this the Kiss of Peace? No, it's just—I can't—I don't know how to do this. I don't know where to put my hands.

He pats my back, his chin on my shoulder.

"It's all right," he says, and releases me. "I'm not cross. I probably would have done the same thing myself, to get away from that Bishop. But it's the last time, Isidore. I don't want you disobeying me ever again. Am I making myself clear?"

"Yes, Father."

"Good. Now get up on that horse."

"But—"

"Isidore!"

"Yes, Father. As you wish, Father."

Thy word is a lamp unto my feet, and a light unto my path.

✝CHAPTER EIGHTEEN✝

24 JULY 1209

The most terrible noise: a screeching, rending, groaning noise, like the cry of a dying basilisk. It seems to go on and on and—*crash*! The very foundations of the cathedral shudder, as half a dozen stalls collapse onto the floor of the choir.

A great cloud of dust catches everyone by the throat.

"Good!" the Archdeacon exclaims, over a storm of coughing. "That's all for the best. Now, just take it easy, because I don't want any wood split. Use your tools, not your hands. And you can stack it over there, in that corner." He jumps down from the pulpit, pouncing on the nearest tangle of wood like a lion pouncing on a lamb. His head and shoulders are covered in sawdust. "Come on!" he cries. "Hop to it!"

Slowly, reluctantly, the canons begin to move again. They pick their way through the planks, clicking their tongues and shaking their heads, as the carpenters apply themselves with goodwill and vigor. They swing their axes; they wrench apart joinery; they reduce everything to neat lengths of board, like theologians reducing the world's manifold complexities to an orderly series of declarations.

I wonder why the Archdeacon seems to be enjoying this so much.

"Isidore!" He thrusts a fragment of carved oak at me. "Put this with the rest, will you?"

"Yes, Father."

"Burchard! Don't just stand there. Why aren't you helping?"

He's not helping, Father, because he doesn't *want* to help. I don't think he understands why the cathedral choir stalls have to be dismantled. Neither do I—not really—but then I've never faced the prospect of a siege before. You have, though: you've been in one. That's why these petty-minded canons should do as you say, instead of whining and muttering and making things difficult. What

207

good are stalls if the rest of the church has been burned to the ground? What victory can there be without suffering and sacrifice? How stupid they are, these canons. The tongue of the wise useth knowledge aright, but the mouth of fools poureth out foolishness.

"Come on, Guibert! Come on, Cornelius!" The Archdeacon waves a hand at the Chancellor and the Sub-deacon, who are whispering together at the far end of the nave. "We need all the help we can get, if we're going to have this finished before Mass begins."

"Mass!" someone protests. "How can we have Mass if we have no stalls?" The Archdeacon turns, sharply, but the speaker has fallen silent. All the canons are avoiding each other's gaze; they're looking down at their feet or up at the vaults; they're dusting off their sleeves and plucking splinters out of their knuckles.

The Archdeacon wipes his hands on his skirts.

"There were no stalls at the Holy Supper," he says, frowning. "Are you all too proud to stand, brethren? We're doing this for the good of the city. The city must be protected."

"Our prayers will protect the city much better than our stalls," somebody says, and there's a mur-

mur of agreement. O ye fools! The Archdeacon takes a deep breath and puts his hands on his hips.

"I *told* you why we need to do this!" he exclaims. "Don't you understand? The Viscount wants to build galleries along the battlements, so he can protect the base of our walls from enemy sappers. Sweet saints preserve us, haven't you people read Sallust? Haven't you read his account of the siege of Zama? I thought you were educated men!"

Sallust? The siege of Zama? Yet another book I have to read. The canons shift uncomfortably: some of them look ashamed, some annoyed, some completely blank, as if they don't know what to think. Around them, the carpenters and acolytes are cheerfully carrying off great loads of lumber, their souls as peaceful as watered gardens. Why should they be unhappy? Most of the acolytes are my age—they've no particular affection for the stalls they've had to sit in, day after day, through the summer heat and the winter cold. I think they're quite pleased to tear the things down.

"Father Pagan!"

Who's that? I know that voice. Everyone turns; everyone looks. There's a small group of men standing in the shadows of the northern aisle, all in black, all tonsured. One of them is pale and squat, with a big head and no neck. Another is hugely fat, with offal-colored eyes peering out from under a fringe of white hair. And the one beside him is—

"Roland!"

The Archdeacon's face lights up like a candle. He surges forward, arms outstretched, and meets Lord Roland at the bottom of the stairs that divide the nave from the choir.

"You've come!" he crows. "Already! Where did you spring from?"

"We only just arrived—"

"Like an angel into a lion's den. What a relief!"

How happy they look. What pleasure they take in each other's presence. *Oh, such envy comes to me / Of those whose happiness I see. . . .*

But I mustn't sing that. That's a troubadour's song.

"Anyway, you've come." The Archdeacon's voice is low and intense, vibrating through the church like a bell. "I knew you would. You were wise to come."

"If I hadn't," Lord Roland rejoins with a little smile, "you would only have dragged me here."

"It isn't safe outside the walls. Not even at Saint Martin's."

"Pagan—"

210

"You can sleep in my house. You can share my room. You can have Isidore's bed—you don't mind, do you, Isidore?"

"Pagan, please. The Abbot . . ."

Yes, Father. What about Abbot Seguin? You're being very discourteous, ignoring him like this. You're being very discourteous to everyone. The Abbot's face is like the Burden of Babylon, cruel both with wrath and fierce anger: as Lord Roland points at him, he folds his arms and says, "You advised us to come here, Father Pagan. Now where do you advise us to go?"

"My lord—you're most welcome—"

"I'm feeling poorly, after that long ride. I need a drink. A soothing drink."

"And you shall have one." The Archdeacon touches his elbow. "I have arranged a room for you in the Bishop's palace. A very comfortable room. I have also enlisted the services of Carcassonne's best doctor, on your behalf."

"And what of my monks? Where will they be housed?"

"There are guest rooms in the Bishop's palace and spare beds in the canons' dormitory. If you agree, my lord, we can divide them up like this. . . ."

The Archdeacon plunges into a detailed description of the arrangements he's made for eating, sleeping, studying, praying. He's at his most sympathetic, his most agreeable. The Abbot listens with a grumpy expression on his face.

Lord Roland turns to me and smiles. "It's good to see you, Isidore," he says.

"Thank you, my lord—I mean, thank you, Father. It's good to see you, too."

"How are you feeling?"

How am I feeling? What a strange question. I'm feeling . . .

"Anxious."

"But are you well?"

"Yes, Father. I'm well."

"You look tired."

"Oh—that's just because we've been riding so much. We rode through the night, three days ago."

"You've been busy, then."

"Yes." Glancing at the Archdeacon, who doesn't look tired at all: he's talking with his usual energy, waving his hands around, swaying back and forth, flashing his teeth, and opening his eyes very wide. His face never seems to stop moving. "I *have* been busy, because Father Pagan's been busy. The Bishop isn't here, so Father Pagan is doing all his work."

Lord Roland nods. His blank, blue gaze travels over the hovering canons, the carpenters, the sawdust, the piles of wood, the gaping hole. "So I see," he remarks.

"We're tearing down these stalls because Lord Raymond needs wood for the city's defenses."

"Ah."

"Father Pagan talks with Lord Raymond every day. They discuss defenses and food supplies and all kinds of things. Father Pagan is a very good organizer. Yesterday he spoke to the communal council, and this morning he went to visit all the custodians of the city wells. There are twenty-two wells in this city."

"Is he getting enough sleep?"

"What?"

"Is he getting enough sleep at night? He's not working too late, is he?"

Working too late? I don't know. He doesn't look as if he needs more rest. And he's always the one who wakes me up in the morning.

"Try to make sure that he doesn't work too hard," Lord Roland says in a low voice. "I know it's difficult, but he may listen to you. He doesn't like it when I tell him to rest. He thinks I'm saying that he's weak."

213

"But—"

"And try to get him to eat properly. Can you do that, Isidore?"

But he's an Archdeacon! How can I tell him to eat his dinner? How can I tell him to go to bed? This is ridiculous.

"Father, I can't—it's not my place—" (By the blood of the Lamb of God!) "If he won't listen to you, Father, he won't listen to me. I'm just his scribe; I'm not his lord. *You* are his lord, Father."

Lord Roland puts a finger to his lips. He glances at the Archdeacon and waits for a moment. But the Archdeacon hasn't heard. He's still talking to Abbot Seguin.

"Perhaps you're right." Lord Roland speaks very softly. "Perhaps he won't listen to anyone. He's a man of great confidence." Looking down his long nose. "What about you, Isidore? Will *you* be staying here much longer?"

What do you mean? Of course I'll be staying here. Who said otherwise?

Unless . . .

"He told you!" (He must have.) "He told you he was going to leave me! When we were at Saint Martin's, he must have said—"

"Shh."

"I didn't *want* to stay with the Bishop. I wanted to come back here!"

"And you did." Quietly. Gently. "Which means that he must listen to you sometimes. Perhaps you have more influence than you think."

"No, I—no, it wasn't that." (Oh, why did you have to raise the subject? This is so embarrassing.) "Your brother was the one who brought me. All the way from Montpellier."

He straightens.

"My brother?" he says, his face expressionless.

"Lord Jordan is here. In Carcassonne. He's helping the Viscount."

No response.

"I don't know where he's living. I think he might be living in the castle." Why am I saying this? "He's coming here soon with some of the Viscount's soldiers. To collect the wood. So perhaps you'll see him then."

Lord Roland stares, unblinking. He looks so much like his brother. Even the lines around his mouth are the same.

"Yes," he says at last. "Perhaps I will."

"Isidore!" It's the Archdeacon. He breaks in joyfully, grabbing my arm, grabbing Lord Roland's, drawing us close. The Abbot stands behind him, waiting. "Isidore, will you take Roland to my house? Show him where your bed is, and get Centule to make up another one. And check if there's any food around."

"Yes, Father."

"I'm just going to take the Abbot to his room. Make sure he's comfortable." A big, beaming smile. "Will you come this way, my lord? It isn't far."

He begins to usher Abbot Seguin down the steps into the nave, throwing us a wink over his shoulder. But he hasn't gone more than a few steps when one of the canons calls to him.

"Father! Wait!"

It's an angry, bewildered cry. The Archdeacon stops and swings around.

"Father, you can't just leave us. What are we supposed to be doing?"

"Doing?" He sounds astonished. "Why, keep working. I've told you what has to be done. You don't need *me* here, surely?"

Oh, but they do, Father. They need you as they need a lamp, because the wise man's eyes are in his head, but the fool walketh in darkness.

And these canons are fools. Manifestly, they are fools.

"Sweet saints preserve us!" The Archdeacon's

216

eyebrows snap together. He throws up his hands and casts about him. "Isidore, will you take—"

"Yes, Father. I will take Abbot Seguin to the Bishop's palace."

"Bless you. Bless you, Isidore. I'll be along in a moment."

And he turns back to those hopeless, helpless, incompetent canons.

‡CHAPTER NINETEEN‡

25 JULY 1209

If I had a house, with my own furniture in it, I would have a chair just like that one: a noble chair with a carved base, and a high back, and a red cushion on its seat. And I would have a little footstool, just like that one, only mine would have a cushion on top of it—a cushion embroidered with gold. And I would have a bigger bed, with hangings (red hangings), and my chest would have gold on its lid. And as for my walls, I wouldn't just have red stripes and red flowers painted on the plaster: I would have the life of Saint Augustine, showing him in the schoolroom; visiting Saint Ambrose; weeping under a fig tree. . . .

"All right." The Archdeacon raises his head from his hands. "This is what we'll say. 'Pagan, Archdeacon of Carcassonne, sends greetings and paternal love in Christ to Thibault, priest of Seyrac.'"

Whoops! Where's my quill? *Paganus, archidiaconus Carcasonis* . . .

"'Your complaint against the priest of Bram is one that I found difficult to understand. However, I have made inquiries and have discovered that your account was not as full and honest as it should have been.'"

Causam tuam contra sacerdotem Bramiensem . . . My fingers are getting stiff. How many more letters are we going to write today? The Archdeacon leans back in his chair: he puts his hands together and stares out the window, frowning, his gaze blank and preoccupied.

"'I have been informed that it is your custom to forbid burial, and due rites, until the relatives of the deceased have made satisfaction to you,'" he says at last. "'Certainly the Church is always happy to receive gifts from members of its flock when they die, just as it has always received portions from them when they are alive. But to insist on payment is forbidden, as you should know. Naturally such behavior on your part has caused anger

219

and resentment among your parishioners. It does not surprise me that the priest of Bram has taken your place in their hearts, and that they are giving to him, on their deaths, those worldly goods that you believe are your due.'"

Consuetudinem vestram licentiam sepeliendi negare . . . "Wait, Father, please! Not so fast."

"Sorry." He sighs. His chair creaks. (*Sed solutionem postulare* . . .) "Ooooh," he groans in a muffled voice. "These useless, venal, petty-minded priests. No wonder we're in such a mess here."

"Shh!"

"Sorry."

On their deaths? When they die? When they die, perhaps. *Ubi pereunt* . . .

There's a knock on the door.

"Come in!" the Archdeacon exclaims. He sounds quite pleased to be interrupted. But when the door swings open, he stiffens.

"My lord," he mutters warily.

"Hello, Pagan." Lord Jordan looks pale and tired. He's wearing a simple brown tunic and no sword belt. He closes the door softly behind him. "Hello, Isidore. Working hard, I see."

"Is there anything special you want, my lord?" the Archdeacon inquires. "Because I have a lot to

220

do just now." He sits up straight as Lord Jordan wanders over to the bed and sits on it. "I have a great deal of correspondence to get through. What do you *want*, my lord?"

"Oh, many things. Many, many things. As you probably know." Lord Jordan stretches his long legs out in front of him and crosses his ankles. His tone is careless, but there's no smile on his face, or in his eyes. "I have news," he says abruptly. "News from the Viscount. He sent me here to tell you, because—well, because he's too disturbed to tell you himself."

Oh, no. What can this be?

The Archdeacon sits forward. "What's happened?" he says.

Lord Jordan sighs. He folds his arms and stares down at the floor. All at once he looks much, much older.

"It's Béziers," he says. "Béziers has been taken. They took it three days ago, on the Feast of the Magdalene."

No. Oh, no.

"Sweet saints . . ." the Archdeacon whispers. "Already? So *fast*?"

"It was a joke. A complete joke. Some idiot shopkeepers made some kind of a reconnaissance sortie through the gate overlooking the old bridge. You know the one? They started taunting a crew of French mercenaries who were camped down by the river. They waved flags and shouted insults. They weren't expecting anything: the mercenaries were sitting around, barefoot, in their shirts and breeches. But the mercenary captain—whoever he is, he must be damned good—gave the signal to attack, and they did. With a bunch of hand weapons. They forced the shopkeepers back through their gate, and got inside the walls."

"Sweet saints preserve us."

"Once that happened, it was finished. Bernard de Servian brought his garrison up to defend the ramparts, but the gates couldn't be closed. All the noise had alerted the rest of the Crusaders, and they just waded in. Took everyone by surprise. It was over in a few hours." Lord Jordan suddenly strikes the bed with his fist. "The fools, the fools, the God-damned fools! They could have held out for weeks, but it was over in a few hours!"

Oh, Father. Oh, Father, what will we do? He's put his hand over his mouth, and he's staring—staring at Lord Jordan.

"Christ," he mumbles.

"And that's not the worst of it." Lord Jordan suddenly raises his eyes. They're pouchy and red-rimmed, and they're looking straight at me. "Perhaps," he remarks, "it would be better if Isidore left the room."

What? No! The Archdeacon's hand falls. "Left the room?" he echoes faintly. "Oh, my God . . ."

"No! Don't make me leave! Please don't make me leave!"

"It would be better," Lord Jordan says in a voice full of meaning, and the Archdeacon suddenly snaps back to life.

"Yes," he says. "Yes, of course. Off you go, Isidore."

"Father, don't send me away!" (You can't do this! You can't *do* this!) "I have to know! You have to tell me!"

"Isidore! Get out of here! *Now!*"

"They're dead, aren't they? They're all dead, every one of them!"

A shocked silence. The Archdeacon looks at Lord Jordan. Lord Jordan looks at me. His face is so still, I know that it must be true. The worst thing—the very worst thing—and it's actually come true.

"No," he says at last. "Not *every* one of them. If everyone was dead, we wouldn't know what had happened. But most of them, yes. Almost all of them." He turns back to the Archdeacon, who's shaking his head—who's clutching the arms of his chair so tightly that his knuckles have turned white.

"Oh, no, my lord. No. That's not possible." He sounds as if he's going to be sick. "I can't believe that."

"Believe it, Pagan, it's true. Thousands and thousands of people, Christians and heretics. Men, women, and children. Some of them were taking refuge in the cathedral—the Crusaders killed them there, on consecrated ground. They killed the clergy in front of their own altar."

Oh, God. Oh, God. The Archdeacon covers his face with his hands.

"Then they burned the whole place," Lord Jordan continues, remorselessly. "Looted it and burned it. Well, some of them did. I'd wager my inheritance that most of the damage was done by mercenaries. They're all scum, those mercenaries. Probably did most of the killing, too. They feed on blood."

Blood. Blood on the altar. Blood of children, screaming children—blood flowing down the steps. A sea of blood. And the third part of the sea became blood . . . and there followed hail and fire, mingled with blood. . . .

"Isidore."

They're going to kill us. They're going to kill every one of us. He that abideth in this city shall die by the sword . . . and the sword shall devour, and it shall be made satiate and drunk with our blood. . . .

"Isidore!" It's Lord Jordan; his hand is on my shoulder. "There's no need to panic," he says. "Carcassonne is not Béziers. Do you understand? What happened in Béziers was a fluke. An accident. It won't happen here, because the Viscount won't let it." (Shaking me, hard.) "You shouldn't have listened. Didn't I tell you to leave? I knew this would only frighten you."

"Saint . . . Saint Ambrose . . ."

"What?" He leans down. "What did you say?"

"Saint Ambrose told us that it is a brave man's duty not to dissemble when some danger looms, but to meet what is to c-come with careful forethought and lofty vision of mind."

He gasps and his hand tightens; I can hear him choking and snorting. Finally he says, in a slow, quivering drawl: "You're one of a kind, Isidore, I have to admit it. You're really something."

Suddenly there's a knock: *rat-tat-tat!* A sharp, angry knock. The Archdeacon uncovers his face, which looks gray and pinched; he swallows, licks his lips, wipes his forehead. "Who is it?" he croaks.

"The Chancellor."

"Come in, Guibert."

The door opens, and the Chancellor comes in. He's small and round and strutting, like a quail or a bantam, heavy with his own importance. A proud man; his spine is as stiff as a hyena's.

He glances at Lord Jordan, sniffs once, and turns away.

"Father Pagan," he says, "a very disturbing rumor has reached my ears. I've been told that you wish to demolish our refectory. Surely this cannot be true?"

The Archdeacon has to think for a moment. He blinks, and bends his mind to the question with an effort that's written clearly on his brow.

"Yes," he replies. "Yes, it is true."

"Father, I must protest. This is going too far."

"I'm sorry, but there's no alternative. Lord Raymond needs the stone for his fortifications."

"And *we* need our refectory for our meals, Father! I find it incredible that you should disregard our rights in this way. You haven't even presented your request to the cathedral chapter for consideration—

you've just gone ahead and ignored us completely! The Bishop would never have allowed this."

"The *Bishop* is in Montpellier! The *Bishop* has forfeited his authority by running away to hide, like a snake in the grass!"

"I hope you're not implying—"

"Shut up!" The Archdeacon jumps to his feet. "Just shut up! I've had it up to *here* with you people! Would you rather give up your refectory, or have your guts ripped out and trampled all over the church floor? Because that's what's happened to the canons at Béziers! That's what's happened to the Chancellor at Béziers! Is *that* what you want?"

Father Guibert takes a step backward, retreating before the blaze of the Archdeacon's fury.

"At—at Béziers?" he quavers.

"They've slaughtered all the clergy there! They've hacked them to pieces on the steps of their own altar! They've killed the entire population! And you're talking to me about your miserable *refectory*? You make me *sick*!"

"Father—please—"

"Get out of here! Go on! Go and tell those bleating fools that they can either eat off their knees or have their limbs strewn all over the cathedral! And

227

if I hear *one more complaint,* I'm going to sling you all out of this city, and let you take your chances with the northern knights! See how much *they* care about your refectory when they start slicing off your fingers!"

The Chancellor bolts. He stumbles out the door backward, and Father Pagan slams it shut behind him—slams it so hard that the floor shakes. An echoing silence, taut with emotion.

Lord Jordan releases my shoulder.

"Well," he says smoothly, "I knew I could rely on you to spread the news in a gentle, reassuring way. I mean, God forbid that anyone should panic."

The Archdeacon puts a hand to his forehead. He sags against the door. He's flushed and trembling, and gleaming with sweat.

"I'm sorry," he mutters. "I couldn't—I'm sorry. I'm sorry."

"You need some sleep," Lord Jordan observes. "Either that or a cask of wine."

"I'll call a chapter." The Archdeacon takes a deep breath. "I'll call a special chapter, and I'll announce it properly. That's what I'll do." He moves away from the door and begins to pace up and down, like a cat in a cage. "But I'll need someone else as well," he continues. "Someone with a military background, who can reassure them. Will you do it, my lord?" He stops. "Will you talk to them?"

Lord Jordan raises his eyebrows. He raises his hands. "Oh, no," he says. "Not me. Clerics in large numbers make me feel ill."

"But—"

"Leave me out of it, Pagan. I've got other things to do." He reaches out, suddenly, and pats me on the back. "Cheer up, my friend. No one's ever breached the walls of Carcassonne, and no one ever will. Believe me, you're safer here than you would be anywhere else."

He smiles wearily and heads for the door. But the Archdeacon's voice stops him as he's crossing the threshold.

"My lord! Do you know that your brother is here? In Carcassonne?"

It's a challenge, not a question. It's like a slap on the face. Lord Jordan stops; he looks back over his shoulder. There's a long pause.

"Is he?"

"He's staying right here, in this house. As my guest."

"Thanks for the warning."

"Don't you want to see him?"

"No."

"But you haven't seen him for twenty years!"

Once again, Lord Jordan smiles—a strange, complex, difficult smile. For some reason, it's more frightening than a drawn sword.

"Exactly," he says, and disappears from view.

✝CHAPTER TWENTY✝

28 JULY 1209

Behold, the Lord maketh the earth empty, and maketh it waste, and turneth it upside down, and scattereth abroad the inhabitants thereof.

"Look." The Archdeacon points. "Look, the fires are still smoking."

Desolation and destruction. Vines stripped, corn trampled, trees felled. Even the floating water mills have been demolished, cut free from their hawsers and sunk into the river. To look at it, you'd think that the invaders must have come and gone.

But they haven't, of course. All this was done by the people who tended the vines, and planted the corn, and owned the trees.

They must have wept tears of blood when they did it.

"Father, do you remember that scene in Livy? Where Verginius kills his daughter rather than let her become a slave?"

"'There is only one way, my child, to make you free,'" the Archdeacon quotes, gazing out over the battlements at the ravaged fields, the smoking bonfires. "It is a bit like that, isn't it? What a terrible waste. But it must be done. We can't let the enemy have that food or that fuel."

The enemy. When will they come? What will they do? What does an army look like, encamped around a city?

I've read so much, but I just can't imagine it.

"This really takes me back," the Archdeacon observes, stopping at an embrasure. "This takes me back to the siege of Jerusalem. I remember standing on the walls of Jerusalem with Roland, watching Saladin's army approach."

"How long did that siege last?"

"Oh, about ten days."

"And did—did you have to eat mice, then?"

"What?" He swings around to face me. "What on earth are you talking about?"

"Did you have to eat mice and weeds, and chew leather thongs?"

A pause. He's squinting in the glare; he puts his

hand up, to shade his eyes from the sun. It's so hot on this parapet.

"All right," he says at last. "What have you been reading?"

"Father—"

"I'm not stupid, Isidore. What is it, Livy? You mentioned Livy. Are you reading *The History of Rome*?"

"Book Twenty-three. The siege of Casilinum."

"Who was that? Remind me."

"It was Hannibal, Father, and—"

"Hannibal!" he exclaims, and laughs. "In God's name, Isidore, if Hannibal were heading this way, I really *would* be worried!" He reaches out and takes my hand. "Listen. You've got to stop all this reading. I'm going to have to put my foot down."

"But—"

"No wonder you've had so many fits these last few days. I realize it probably has something to do with the heat—that's why I brought you up here, because the air's always fresher on the walls—but I'm sure it's partly all that reading. You know what I've said about reading."

"Yes, but—"

"Besides, you're just scaring yourself. The siege of Casilinum! This isn't Casilinum, and Arnaud

233

Amaury isn't Hannibal, thank God. Though even if he were, I wouldn't despair for a moment. Lots of cities resisted Hannibal. Puteoli, for instance." He drops my hand and grips my arm, pulling me toward the embrasure. "Look at those barbicans. Look at those galleries. Look at the *walls*. You don't understand military engineering, so you don't know what a marvel we're standing on. I've seen a lot of cities in my life, and not one of them was as well fortified as Carcassonne. Not one of them."

"But Father, it takes more than walls to defend a city." (Livy himself said that. He said that good fighters wish to defend their walls with their arms, rather than themselves with their walls.) "It wasn't the weakness of its walls that defeated Béziers. It was the foolishness of its people."

The Archdeacon turns his head. He peers into my face, intently, silently, almost fiercely. "By God," he says at last. "By God, you're a wonder."

"But isn't it true?"

"Of course it's true! You're absolutely right. There are fools everywhere, even in Carcassonne. Fortunately, however, they're not in charge around here."

He begins to walk again, heading north; sunlight flickers on his black robe as he passes embrasure after embrasure, arrow slit after arrow slit. Apple cores and nutshells, scattered underfoot. Lots of dirty sawdust. A distinct smell of urine (someone's been pissing against the wall). The next tower is one of the old ones, small and round, with lots of red brick inserted between the gray stones. Didn't someone say that the Romans had built it? Through a postern, and into the murky guardroom beyond, which is full of wood and tools and animal skins. (Why animal skins?) An even stronger smell of sawdust here, sawdust and leather. Someone's talking in the room below, but I can't quite make out what he's saying.

Leather buckets, lined up under the window.

Bang! Bang! Bang! What's that? Is that hammering? Out into the sunshine, and here's the next wooden gallery, slung out over the huddled roofs of the Bourg. I wouldn't like to be living in the Bourg right now. It looks so vulnerable, pressed against the base of the city walls, like a child clutching its mother's skirts for protection. Not that it doesn't have its own walls—it does—but they don't seem very sturdy. And poor old Saint Vincent! Sprawled over there beside the river, no walls, no towers, no nothing. Why would anyone want to live in a suburb? You'd feel so *exposed*.

"They're doing a good job here," the Archdeacon says admiringly. He pauses to examine the nearest joist, and gives it a satisfied pat before moving on. (I wonder if that joist used to be a choir stall.) Two men in helmets stare as we pass: they're carrying a ladder between them, and they move aside to give us more room.

All these preparations. Should we be making it so obvious? In *The History of Rome*, the inhabitants of Casilinum all hid and were silent, so that when the Carthaginians arrived, they thought that the town was deserted. And when they came up to the gate to force it open, the people of Casilinum suddenly burst out and cut their enemies to pieces.

Of course, those particular Carthaginians were only an advance party. But shouldn't we be following Casilinum's example? Shouldn't we be taking the Crusaders by surprise?

"If you have to read books, Isidore, I don't want you reading Livy," the Archdeacon suddenly remarks. "I'm going to lock that book away and give you something else. Horace's *Odes*, perhaps. Something light and frothy, about the gods of Olympus. No history or politics."

Olympus. That's it. I knew I had a question to ask him.

"Father?"

"Yes?"

"What's a Ganymede?"

He stops in his tracks. His mouth falls open.

"A *what*?" he says.

"A Ganymede. What does it mean when you call someone a Ganymede?"

He's gone all red. He seems lost for words. Why doesn't he answer? Why is he looking away?

"Does it mean that you're a drunkard? Is that what it means?"

"No, I . . ." He clears his throat. "No," he says again. "No, it means something else. Um . . . let's see, now. How shall I put it?" He gazes around at the drifts of smoke; at the afternoon sky; at the roofs of Carcassonne. "Do you know Leviticus, chapter eighteen? Do you know where it says 'Thou shalt not lie with mankind as with wom-ankind: it is an abomination'?"

By the Lamb of God! It can't be—it's not possible—

"Do you know what that means, Isidore? That verse?"

A sodomite?! Lord Jordan?

"It means men fornicating with other men. Lust-ing after other men." He's staring at the ground

237

and running his fingers through his hair. "And . . . um . . . well, as you know, Zeus was so taken with Ganymede, who was a beautiful young boy, that he carried him off. The way the Romans abducted the Sabine women. And that's why certain men— especially younger, more effeminate men—are often called Ganymedes. They're also called hyenas, because hyenas change sex from year to year. And mules, of course. Mules being eunuchs."

It can't be true. Lord Jordan? But Lord Jordan is *married*. He has a wife and a son. He's a warrior. No, I must have misheard. I was so sleepy, I must have misheard. Either that or Guichard was lying.

"Isidore?" It's the Archdeacon. He's squinting at me. "Has someone called you a Ganymede?"

"No, Father."

"Has someone called *me* a Ganymede?"

"Oh, no, Father!"

"Then who's the Ganymede?"

"No one." (I can't tell him; it's too embarrassing.) "No one, Father, I just heard somebody say it. On the street. I didn't understand."

"Mmm."

He doesn't seem to believe me. I can feel the hot blood rising in my face. What an ugly, squalid subject—can't we leave it alone? I don't want to talk about this.

"What direction will they be coming from, Father? The Crusaders, I mean. Which road will they take?"

"You know, you mustn't fret about this kind of thing." He's still staring at me. "Even Ganymedes are God's creatures, and they're generally pretty harmless. I've met one or two in my time, so I know what I'm talking about. But if you're worried—if there's someone threatening you—"

"No, no!" (God, can't you leave it *alone*?) "I don't know any sodomites! I've never even met one!"

"Well, you can't be sure of that," he says with a little half smile. "Sodomites tend to look just like ordinary people."

"They do?"

"Oh, yes."

"But . . . I thought that sodomy was like a disease. I thought that it turned men into women."

"Not exactly—"

"Don't sodomites look like girls? Don't they lose their beards, and grow their hair long, and speak in high voices?"

"Not all of them, no."

"Then how can we know who they are?"

"Isidore, don't *worry* about it. They're not going to hurt you."

"But what about the Cities of the Plain? God overthrew them with fire and brimstone for harboring sodomites!"

"If we're going to be overthrown, Isidore, it's much more likely to be the Crusaders who do it. Now *calm down*. Sweet saints preserve us, I've never met such a worrier." He takes my elbow and points. "To answer your question, the Crusaders will be coming from the northwest. That direction."

"Do sodomites get married?"

"What?"

"Do sodomites get married and have children?"

"Isidore—"

"I just want to know!"

"Why?" He shakes my arm. "What is this? Mmm? Have you been reading something? You'd better tell me."

Should I? Should I tell him? If it's all a lie—if Guichard has been lying—what will I look like, passing on such tales? Lord Jordan will despise me. The Archdeacon will laugh at me. There's already a twinkle in his eye as he stands there, peering up into my face.

The bells are ringing for Nones: we'll have to go back soon.

"Father—"

"Shh!" He lifts his hand. He turns his head. Somebody's shouting: it's the watchman stationed on top of the tower. He's pointing and jabbering and waving down the wall, and the other guards spill out of their guardrooms, hoisting themselves onto the embrasures, shielding their eyes from the sun.

What is it? What's happening?

"I can't see!" The Archdeacon's shoving me from behind. "What is it, Isidore? What are they pointing at?"

"I don't know—"

"*Look*, damn you!"

I'm looking, I'm looking! Plumes of smoke from the Bourg: beyond them, flat yellow fields and green forest. Mountains in the distance. Wheeling birds.

A glint, like water. No, it can't be water—that's the river, over that way. It's a kind of flash, like sun on glass. Or like sun on—sun on—

Steel?

"It's them!" There's a soldier nearby: he's dancing up and down with excitement. "They've come, they're coming! Sound the alarm! Ring the bells! Summon Lord Raymond!"

"Father—"

"Yes. Yes, I know." The Archdeacon sounds breathless but confident. He reaches up and pats my shoulder. "It's all right, Isidore. We're going to be all right."

Deliver me from mine enemies, O my God: defend me from those who rise up against me. Deliver me from the workers of iniquity, and save me from the bloody men.

Unto Thee, O my strength, will I sing—for God is my defense, and the God of my mercy.

‡CHAPTER TWENTY-ONE‡

2 AUGUST 1209

Chaos in the bailey: men limping, men laughing, men collapsed on the ground. Wild-eyed horses tossing their heads. Faces plastered with sweat and soot. A dense cloud of smoke—thick, gray smoke—scattering ash all over the blood-soaked earth.

They must be torching Saint Vincent.

"God. God. God. God. God." A man to our right, gasping as he lies there, his quilted corselet dark with blood. Yellow face. Blue lips. Glazed eyes. Curled up like a baby, shivering in the hot sun.

O God of my praise. O God of my praise.

"What do you think?" the Archdeacon murmurs. Lord Roland falls to one knee: he feels for a pulse, and his hand comes away drenched in blood. Even as he peels back the first layer of soggy linen, the man falls silent. His eyes are open, but empty. Lord Roland shakes his head.

"It's too late," he says, and crosses himself. The Archdeacon instantly kneels beside him, tracing a cross in the air. *"Ego te absolvo in nomine Patris, et Filii, et Spiritu Sancti . . ."*

For that which befalleth the sons of men befalleth beasts: as the one dieth, so dieth the other. Have mercy on us, O Lord.

"Come, Isidore," Lord Roland says, rising. "Father Pagan will join us shortly." How can he be so calm? He rinses his blood-caked hand in the basin I've been given to carry, and dries it on the skirts of his robe—so serene, so deliberate, while around him people cough and curse and wail, and clutch their wounds and nurse their weapons and cry out for water. It's so hot out here. So terribly, terribly hot.

"Give us a drink," somebody croaks. He's tugging at Lord Roland's skirts, slumped against the wall of the bailey. "Give us a drink, will you?" He's wearing a mail hauberk, and there's something wrong with his left knee. . . .

Oh, God. The knee. I think I'm going to throw up.

"Here." Lord Roland uncorks his water bottle and places it to the man's cracked lips without spilling a drop. He holds the man's head, his hand perfectly steady.

But I mustn't look. I can't look. There are flies crawling all over that knee. White bone—something dangling—

Closing my eyes, very tight.

"We lost Saint Vincent," the wounded man mumbles. "They took Saint Vincent."

"I know," Lord Roland replies softly.

"But they paid the price. They paid the price in their own blood."

"Of course they did."

"Lord Raymond isn't to blame. He's a good fighter. He fought like a lion. But you can't defend a place without walls."

"No, you can't."

"And now we're cut off from the river—ouch!"

"Shh . . ."

Opening my eyes, cautiously: Lord Roland is flapping the flies away. He reaches into his bag and draws out a clean square of linen. He turns his head.

245

"Isidore?" he says in his deep, slow voice. "Are you all right?"

"Yes, Father."

"Are you sure?"

"Yes, Father."

"Then look at the sky and say a prayer. Say a prayer for the wounded."

A prayer for the wounded? But I don't know any, do I? The sky is angry with smoke and sparks: there's no comfort in the heavens today. My basin shudders as Lord Roland dips his linen into the water. Perhaps Psalm Twenty—perhaps that will do?

"The Lord hear thee in the day of trouble; the name of the God of Jacob defend thee. Send thee help from the sanctuary, and strengthen thee out of Zion."

"Ow! Good Christ!"

"We will set up thy banners . . . um . . . He will hear him from His holy heaven . . ."

"Save me, Jesus, save me!"

"Some trust in chariots, and some in horses, but we will remember the name of the Lord our God."

"Isidore?"

It's Lord Jordan. I'd know that voice anywhere. Look around, and there he is: huge, filthy, encased in chain mail. He's even wearing mail shoes. Mail shoes, mail leggings, mail hauberk, and a big steel helmet tucked under his arm. His surcoat is spattered with blood; his face is smeared with it.

"Where's Pagan?" he says in a hoarse voice— and suddenly stops. He's caught sight of his brother. He's staring at his brother, who's dabbing at the wounded man's knee, intent, absorbed, cleaning out the dirt and splinters.

The man groans; his teeth are clenched.

"Is that you, Jordan?" Lord Roland speaks calmly, his gaze never leaving the wound in front of him.

"Yes, it is."

"Are you hurt?"

"No, I'm not."

"Is the Viscount hurt?"

"Not as far as I can tell." Lord Jordan seems fascinated by his brother's profile. He stares and stares. "Don't you eat in that abbey? You're just a nose on a stick."

"As a matter of fact, I eat very well."

"Then you must be feeding worms, my friend. Or are you following in the old man's footsteps?"

"I'm not ill, if that's what you mean." Once again Lord Roland fishes around in his bag. He produces a small leather pouch tied with a drawstring.

When he opens it, the smell is enough to make your eyes water. He scoops out a dab of greenish paste and smears it over the bloody wound. That done, he begins to bind the wound tightly with more clean linen.

"You must go to bed," he declares as his patient groans and hisses. "Go to bed, drink plenty of water, eat as much as you can before the fever sets in. I'll visit you—where do you live?"

"Right here." (Gasping.) "In the castle. I'm part of the garrison."

"And your name is?"

"Gerard."

"I'll visit you, Gerard. I'll bring you something for the pain." Lord Roland begins to rise, but the man reaches out, grabs his robe. "Wait!" he yelps. "Who are you? You haven't told me who you are!"

"I'm Roland. Brother Roland."

"God bless you, Father. God bless you."

Lord Jordan sniffs. Even through all this noise, I can hear him. When his brother stands, they're almost nose to nose—Lord Jordan is just half a hand taller.

They study each other's expressionless faces.

"Is that blood your own?" Lord Roland finally asks.

"Is it ever?"

"You look tired."

"A brilliant diagnosis."

"Is there anyone you'd like me to help?"

"Not a soul," Lord Jordan replies as his gaze slips away from his brother, toward the approaching Archdeacon. "Ah! There you are. I was wondering where you'd gotten to. Care to join me for a sip of wine?"

But the Archdeacon doesn't seem to hear. "What happened?" he demands, fixing his red-rimmed eyes on Lord Jordan. "Is the Viscount safe?"

"Of course he is. I was looking after him myself."

"Did we lose any knights?"

"About half a score."

"*What?*"

"We weren't playing hot cockles, Pagan. It was a very hard fight."

"But you were outnumbered?"

"Dramatically."

"And now they're burning Saint Vincent?"

"It would appear so."

"Where's Guichard?"

"I'm not sure." Lord Jordan glances around at the turmoil. "Off hiding his plunder, I suspect."

"What plunder?"

"Well, you know what it's like in a house-to-house, Pagan. Always time to check under pillows. And a dead Crusader doesn't need his rings anymore."

Robbing the dead? Oh, no. How disgusting. A small hiss from Lord Roland, who obviously doesn't approve. His brother lifts an eyebrow.

"You'd prefer our *enemies* to have the spoils?" he says. "That's very generous of you."

"If our men had spent more time fighting, instead of pillaging, we might have saved Saint Vincent," Lord Roland replies. But his brother simply sneers.

"Half our men only fight because of the plunder they get from it," he says. "Grow up, Roland. You're not in a monastery now."

"What about casualties on their side?" The Archdeacon sounds impatient; he wants more news. "Anyone we know? Anyone who'll make a difference?"

"Oh, I think they'll *all* be missed, Pagan. Wasn't it Jesus who said: 'Even the very hairs of your head are all numbered?'"

"Damn it, you know what I mean! Did you kill any knights?"

"Not personally."

"Did anyone?"

"You'd better ask Guichard. He always keeps track of knights' corpses. Better pickings on a knight."

"My *lord*—"

"Pagan, I can't tell you. I saw a few go down, but I'm fairly sure that we lost more than they did."

Oh, no. O God, Thou hast cast us off, Thou hast been displeased; O turn Thyself to us again.

The Archdeacon stamps his foot and hammers his right fist into the palm of his left hand.

"Damn it!" he cries. "Damn it, if only—I can't just stand by and watch. Perhaps I could help. I've got a sword. I know how to use it. So does Roland."

Lord Jordan bursts out laughing.

"*You?*" he exclaims, and the Archdeacon scowls ferociously.

"I was a squire once. Roland was a knight. A *great* knight."

"Pagan, that was twenty years ago. A pair of old cloister cockroaches like you two . . . believe me, you'd do more harm than good."

"We're both younger than *you* are, my lord!"

251

"And with age comes experience. I'd feel a lot safer if you stayed away from sharp weapons, my child. You might hurt yourself—or others."

How insulting Lord Jordan can be, with his contemptuous smile and his patronizing drawl. The Archdeacon is red with anger. But when he opens his mouth to express himself, Lord Roland interrupts.

"God has given each of us our duties," he says. "Your duties are with the people of this diocese, Pagan. Mine are with the sick. We must exert ourselves where we are most useful. Besides," he adds, "I took an oath that I would never again wield a sword. How can I break that oath?"

He's staring at the Archdeacon, who appears to be calming down. I hope he's calming down. I don't like it when he's angry. There's a pale powdering of ash on his black hair and his black woolen shoulders. There's blood on his hands and his face, and it makes him look different, somehow—not just dirty and disheveled, but wild. Uncivilized.

Heathen.

"Father?"

He blinks, and seems to notice me for the first time.

"Why don't you wash your hands, Father?"

"My hands?" he says. Around us the bailey is filling up fast, as people pour through the gates: weary combatants, ministering monks, townsfolk desperate for news. Here and there wounded men are borne past by their friends and families, some leaning on arms and sticks, some reclining on makeshift stretchers. In the distance, toward the south, cathedral bells start to ring.

"I have water here, Father. You can wash the blood off your hands."

"Wash your hands, Pagan." It's Lord Roland speaking. "Wash your hands and attend to your duties. There's enough work here for all of us."

The Archdeacon frowns. He looks at his hands; he looks at Lord Roland; he looks at me. Finally he steps forward and dips his hands into my basin.

"Very well, then. If it will make you happy," he says.

Under a film of ash, the water turns a deeper shade of pink.

‡CHAPTER TWENTY-TWO‡

3 AUGUST 1209

How cool it is in here. Perhaps that's why so many people have come to church. Hundreds and hundreds of people, packed into the nave like piglets at a sow's teats, crushed against the walls and spilling out of doorways. I can see vast ripples of movement as they cross themselves. I can hear babies whimpering and old men spitting. I can smell garlic and bad breath and unwashed bodies.

If one more person tries to get in, I'm sure the whole building will collapse.

"*Propitius esto, exaudi nos, Domine,*" the Archdeacon intones. "*Ab omni malo . . .*"

"*Libera nos, Domine.*"

"*Ab omni peccato . . .*"

"*Libera nos, Domine.*"

All the canons sound tired and apathetic as they chant the responses. Beside me one of them sighs, shifts his feet, and grimaces. I don't think he likes having to stand throughout the entire service.

"*Ab ira tua . . .*"

"*Libera nos, Domine.*"

"*Ab insidiis diaboli . . .*"

"*Libera nos, Domine.*"

The Archdeacon looks very noble in his rich vestments. The back of his chasuble is embroidered with golden-winged cherubim, and the Four Evangelists, and Christ the Universal Creator. His alb is of the finest silk. Even his slippers are testaments to the Living God, each bearing a cross of gold on a field of blue.

He's concentrating very hard, his face solemn and devout, his voice clear and strong.

"*A peste, fame et bello . . .*"

"*Libera nos, Domine.*"

"*A morte perpetua . . .*"

"*Libera nos, Domine.*"

BOOM!

A distant noise. The floor shakes. What is it? Everyone exchanges looks; some of the canons begin to mutter.

"What was that?"

"God help us!"

"The walls!"

"Per mysterium sanctae incarnationis tuae," the Archdeacon continues firmly. He's glaring at some of the louder canons, but they ignore him; they're too busy asking questions. It's Lord Roland who chants the response, his tranquil voice rising over the squeaks and whispers.

"Libera nos, Domine," he sings, and the Archdeacon smiles at him gratefully.

"Per adventum tuum . . ."

"Libera nos, Domine."

BOOM! Another violent noise, like a clap of thunder. What is it? Is it the wall? Make haste, O God, to deliver me; make haste to help me, O Lord. A babble of voices fills the church: high, fearful voices. But the Archdeacon doesn't look scared. He looks pensive. He glances at Lord Roland, whose face is completely expressionless.

Somewhere in the crowd, a woman shrieks.

Oh, God. Oh, God, what's happening? It's like a signal—like an alarm. There's a roar of voices. Some of the canons fall to their knees. The Archdeacon scowls and moves forward: he descends the three steps from the high altar, passes through the choir, and reaches the stairs to the nave. Below him stretches a sea of milling heads.

"Silence!" he bawls. "You are in a house of God! Be silent at once!"

"She's a heretic!" somebody cries. "She shouldn't even be in here!"

"That's not true!" (A female voice.) "I'm a good Catholic!"

"We should throw her to the Crusaders! We should throw them *all* to the Crusaders! If it wasn't for them, we'd be safe!"

"Silence!" The Archdeacon stamps his foot. "Let go of that woman! Let *go* of her!"

Woman? What woman? Oh—I see. There, beside that pillar: someone's got her by the hair. She's fat and flushed and sweaty, and her veil's come off.

The Archdeacon turns. Behind him the deacons and acolytes are gathering, too scared (and too curious) to remain by the altar. Some hold candles; one is clutching a hand-bell. The Archdeacon snatches it from him and rings it as loudly as he can.

"Quiet!" he bellows. *"Be quiet!"*

People falter. The din subsides. Even the canons stop talking.

And the bell is muffled as the Archdeacon seizes its clapper.

"Brothers and sisters! What madness is this?" he exclaims. "We are allies, united against a common enemy! We shouldn't be fighting among ourselves!"

Angry muttering from somewhere to the left. A man's voice says: "Our enemies are the enemies of God. The *Cathars* are our enemies, not the Crusaders."

"Oh, really?" the Archdeacon sneers. "Perhaps the good Catholics of Béziers should have pointed that out, before they were slaughtered like dogs in their own cathedral." He lifts a hand and points. "Your enemy is outside the walls, my friends. Your enemy will make no distinction between you. To them you are all sheep to be shorn, whether or not you are fellow believers."

He takes a deep breath, and raises his voice. "My friends," he continues, "there is an old, old saying: 'Only when brothers fall out is the sword driven home.' Dissension will *always* lead to defeat. It is a sign of weakness. The mightiest of Nature's creatures, the wolves and the lions, turn their ferocity only against beasts of other kinds. My friends, would you sin against your fellow citizens?

Saint Augustine himself has told us that war between allies is a great crime. The Preacher has told us: 'Woe to him that is alone when he falleth, for he hath not another to help him up.' Be wise and stand united."

I wish I could see his face. Once again, I'm in the worst possible position: all I can see is the back of his head, and the heels of his shoes, and Christ the Universal Creator hanging from his shoulders. I wonder what he's thinking. I wonder if he's afraid. He looks very lonely, standing out there in front of that huge crowd.

But the crowd has fallen silent. The crowd has yielded, drinking down the honey of his rhetoric. What a mighty gift! When I am old, I shall say: In my youth I saw the Archdeacon of Carcassonne tame a thousand raging souls with words as sweet as the bread of angels.

"Come," he says. "Let us bow our heads in prayer. Let us pray for strength and wisdom and—"

"The Bourg has fallen!" A breathless cry, faint but clear, from outside the church. "They've taken the Bourg!"

What's that? They've taken the *Bourg*?

"They've taken the Bourg!" (Other voices, picking

259

up the refrain.) "The Bourg has fallen! The Bourg is lost!" A terrible groan, mounting toward the vaulted roof. Oh, God. Oh, God, be merciful unto us.

The Archdeacon turns his head and looks at Lord Roland: it's as if he's reassuring himself.

Lord Roland simply nods. (I wonder what that means.)

"Brothers and sisters!" the Archdeacon shouts, swinging back to face his audience. "Brothers and sisters, do not despair!"

"The Bourg is lost! The Bourg has fallen!"

"The Bourg is *nothing*! We are well rid of it!" The Archdeacon lifts his arms. "Do you think that the Viscount would have surrendered it so easily if he hadn't wanted to? The Bourg was a parasite—a flimsy pile of sticks and stones, draining us of our strength! Every soldier manning the Bourg garrison was weakening the garrison of Carcassonne! What a pointless exercise, to strengthen the garrison of an indefensible suburb at the expense of its mother city! What foolishness! What suicidal tactics! No, my friends, this is news we should be *pleased* to hear!"

Is it? Is it really? Everyone's exchanging puzzled glances: everyone except Lord Roland, who's staring at the floor. The Archdeacon presses on.

"My friends, the Bourg is only a suburb," he

declares. "It is not defended by the invincible walls of Carcassonne. Come, call to mind the great name of this city, your fathers' valor and your own. Remember that Carcassonne withstood even the mighty Charlemagne: for five long years he besieged it, and could he break it? No! Are you going to betray your courageous ancestors? Are you going to offer yourselves up to the weapons of the enemy—offer up your homes, your children, your fathers' graves? Of course not! In courage you are your enemy's equal. in necessity, which is the last and chiefest weapon, you are better than they."

That last phrase sounded familiar. That sounded like something I've heard before. The Archdeacon takes a step forward, leaning over the heads of the crowd as if in supplication.

"My friends," he cries, "would you abandon this beautiful city, which nurtured you, and protected you, and gave you everything necessary for life? Would you see her fair walls shattered, and her streets ravaged, and her wells poisoned? Because you will, if you succumb to base fear and the counsels of cowardice. To fear your opponents is to grant them the victory they seek. The Scriptures tell us: 'As for the fearful, their lot shall lie in a lake of fire and brimstone.' Fear not, my friends, and be victorious!"

A cheer from somewhere down the back. Another from a little old man near the door. "They'll not be getting *my* shop!" he howls. "I'll kill every one of them before they set foot in it!"

"And how are you going to do that?" his neighbor demands. "Fart on them?" Whereupon the whole church erupts into laughter.

"That's right!" the Archdeacon urges. "Laugh, all of you! Laugh out loud, and let the enemy hear you laughing! Laugh in their faces, and their hearts will be faint within them. For how can they hurt an opponent who laughs at their puny efforts?" He pauses, and adds: "Not to mention their puny genitals."

More laughter. The Archdeacon turns and mouths something at the Precentor, who nods and begins to sing.

"Omnes sancti et Sanctae Dei
Intercedite pro nobis. . . ."

Oh! That's clever. That's very clever. A good, rousing canticle, calling on the saints for help. Other voices begin to join in as the Archdeacon flaps his hands at us. Sing! Sing! . . .

"Sancte Michael, ora pro nobis.
Sancte Gabriel, ora pro nobis. . . ."

Now all the canons are singing, and the chorus

is like a benediction: glorious, dramatic, full of hope and courage. The Archdeacon moves back toward the high altar, passing so close that I can see the sweat trickling down his cheeks and the tremor in his limbs. Suddenly he looks exhausted, drained; he stumbles on the hem of his chasuble, and Lord Roland puts out a hand to steady him.

"*Omnes sancti angeli et archangeli, orate pro nobis. . . .*"

All the sainted angels and archangels, pray for us.

✜ CHAPTER TWENTY-THREE ✜

8 AUGUST 1209

God, I'm hot. I'm so *hot*. How can a person sleep when it's this hot? How can Father Pagan sleep? Snoring away, over there by the door. Doesn't he mind the heat? Doesn't he notice the mosquitoes? These mosquitoes are driving me mad. And the tansy leaves aren't working, either. They might work for Lord Roland, but not for me. I suppose my skin is too tempting—too thin and white.

Oh, I can't stand this. I can't stand the heat and the flies and the smells—the smells! Everything seems to smell of corruption, of sewage and corpses and unwashed bodies. And where are all these mosquitoes coming from? That's what I can't understand. The wells are almost empty, they say, so where are the mosquitoes breeding? In the river?

That's the bell for the Prime service. Sunrise already, and I've hardly slept a wink. I'm like Job, full of tossings to and fro until the dawning of the day. I should have gone with Lord Roland when he got up for Nocturnes. At least I would have been doing something useful, instead of lying around in a pool of sweat. And the church is probably cooler than this room is, although . . . ugh, it's all too early. Much, much too early. I wonder how the monks endure it, getting up in the middle of the night. I know *I* wouldn't last long if I had to keep those hours. Thank heavens I'm an acolyte. I wouldn't be a novice for anything.

BOO-OO-OOM!

Sweet Jesus.

"Wha—?" The Archdeacon's voice. He sits straight up in bed. "What's happened? Isidore?"

"Oh, Father—oh, Father—"

"What is it?"

"I don't know!" God preserve us. "A huge noise . . ."

"Christ." He scrambles to his feet and gropes around for his drawers in the dimness. "I hope it's not Castellar."

265

Castellar! The very last suburb! They've tried so hard to take Castellar: first the scaling ladders three days ago, then the siege engines yesterday. What else can they possibly do?

"It could be a mine," the Archdeacon mutters. "Jordan said there were sappers at the Castellar wall yesterday, under a wheeled hut. We burned the hut with blazing arrows, but we may have been too late. They may have had time to mine the wall."

Mine the wall? Is that the same as *undermining* the wall? I remember reading about undermining in Livy: I remember reading that the Romans dug a tunnel under the walls of Ambracia. "You mean they've dug themselves a path into Castellar? You mean they're coming in under the walls?"

"Oh, no." He's pulling on his boots. "They don't dig a tunnel to get in. They dig it so that there's nothing supporting the wall *over* the tunnel but planks of wood. Then they burn the wood—"

"And the wall collapses!"

"Exactly." His head emerges from the collar of his robe; he smoothes his tousled hair. "I hope Jordan's all right. He joined the Castellar garrison yesterday. I hope he doesn't do anything stupid."

"Wait! Father! Wait for me!"

He stops at the door. "You're not coming," he says.

"But you can't leave me here!"

"Isidore—"

"If you don't take me, I'll go by myself!"

He stamps his foot. "By the beard of Beelzebub!" he exclaims. "Why are you doing this? Anyone would think I wasn't coming back!"

"My boots—I have to put on my boots—"

"Well, hurry up, then. I can't wait around all day."

There! Done it. He grunts as I stand, and throws open the door: the kitchen fire is just a pile of glowing ashes; cockroaches flee in every direction.

"Father!" It's Centule, standing there as naked as Adam before the Fall. He's clutching one of his precious cheeses. "What's happening, Father?"

"I don't know. Go back to bed."

"Are they coming?"

"Of course not!"

"How can you tell?"

The Archdeacon turns to face his whimpering servant. "Because I'm not a fool!" he snaps. "Now go back to bed—or at least put some clothes on. Come on, Isidore."

Out of the kitchen, into the square. Pounding

footsteps. Raised voices. The dark mass of the cathedral, with people spilling from its southern entrance. Most of them seem to be monks: they stare and cluster and point at the nearest fortification, the tower of Saint-Nazaire, a great, four-sided tower simply crawling with people.

"Roland!" The Archdeacon raises a hand. "Roland! Over here!"

Lord Roland looks around and sees us. He strides across the square with the long, firm strides of a military man. He's frowning a little.

"What is it?" the Archdeacon demands. "Is it Castellar?"

"Apparently."

"Have they made a breach?"

"I don't know."

"We have to get up there." The Archdeacon lifts his gaze to the tower of Saint-Nazaire, to the gesticulating men strung out along the walls on either side of it. "We have to see what's going on."

"I doubt we'll be given access."

"Where's the Viscount? Have you seen the Viscount? Damn it, I have to get up there!"

He shoots across the filthy cobbles, weaving his way between makeshift huts erected by the refugees. In one of them a baby is crying: its mother

268

is trying to offer comfort in a high, hysterical voice. Panic-stricken people are rushing around, bundling up their valuables and heading for the church. They brush past a naked child—a toddler—who stands wailing in a puddle of her own urine.

Lord Roland stops. He reaches down and picks the child up, settling her onto his hip with the ease of a wet nurse. "Where's your mama?" he says. "Where's your papa?" But the child can't talk.

"Roland!" It's the Archdeacon: he's over by the tower, waving his hands. "What are you doing?" he yells. "Come on!"

"Is this your baby?" Lord Roland inquires, stooping to look into one of the shelters. A garbled response, and he moves on to the next one. "Is this your baby?"

"Maa!" The child begins to wriggle; an old woman emerges with her arms outstretched. Surely *she* can't be the mother? Lord Roland murmurs something and surrenders the child. He smiles at me as he straightens. "I'm told that you're an orphan, Isidore."

"Yes."

"You have my sympathies. I only wish that I could have restored you to your mother as easily as I just restored that child to hers. Every day, at sunrise and sunset, I thank God in his mercy that I knew my mother for sixteen years. Sixteen years of my life. It is the greatest gift that can ever be bestowed." He looks across to the tower of Saint-Nazaire, but the Archdeacon is already on his way back. (Don't tell me they wouldn't let him through!) "Hmm," Lord Roland remarks in a quiet voice. "I thought so."

"What are you doing? Why didn't you come?" The Archdeacon is breathless from running. "We're not allowed up there. We have to go to the Aude Gate."

"The Aude Gate?"

"That's where the garrison will be coming in. The Castellar garrison. They're retreating right now."

"Jordan—"

"Yes, that's right. Including Jordan. Come on, hurry!"

Hurry, hurry! Everyone's hurrying. Armed men, pouring past from every direction: men with swords, men with crossbows, men with shields and maces and spears. Where are they going? Up to the wall? People everywhere—half-dressed people hanging out of windows, frightened people shouting questions. The crowds get thicker and thicker.

"Father, what's happened?" An elderly man grabs the Archdeacon's sleeve. "Are they coming?"

"Go back to bed, Master Aimery."

"They're not coming?"

"Not as far as I know." The Archdeacon pushes on, burrowing through the closely packed bodies, using his feet and elbows to clear a path. Behind me, Lord Roland mutters apologies to the Archdeacon's victims: angry men with crushed toes and bruised ribs. A high voice rings across the milling heads. "Clear a way! Clear a way!" Suddenly there's space, and air, and bloody specters stumbling out of the shadows.

Panting, staring, trembling men. Some supporting others. Some dazed, stupefied, their drawn swords still clutched in their hands.

The remnants of the Castellar garrison.

Have mercy upon us, O Lord; have mercy upon us. Give us help from trouble, for vain is the help of man.

"Jordan!"

No, it can't be. That staggering figure—staggering like a newborn calf—his arm wrapped in something . . . a cloak? Red with blood, heavy with blood, leaning against a wall—

"Jordan!" The Archdeacon reaches him first. "Is it your arm? Show me!"

Lord Jordan opens his eyes, looks down, and smiles. Even his teeth are red.

"Pagan . . ." he croaks.

"What happened? Is it bad? Show me, for God's sake!"

"I've lost a couple of fingers," Lord Jordan remarks. "But the other fellow lost more. Lost his head."

Lost his *head*?

"Quick! Roland! We'll take him back to my place—"

"I took his head off with an axe. He looked pretty surprised, I can tell you." A horrible laugh. "I would have brought the head back with me, if I'd had two hands. Cured it like bacon. Sold it to a leech."

"My lord? Just put your arm around Roland." The Archdeacon is panting under Lord Jordan's weight. "I can't hold you up alone, my lord— you're too heavy."

"They killed Guichard." Lord Jordan blurts it out. "They sliced him open like a pig."

Oh, my God.

"Tripping over his own guts. He didn't even

notice at first. Too busy trying to get out with his plunder." Lord Jordan's bloody grin is like the gates of hell. "Just looked down. 'What's this?' he said. I couldn't even—I was trying—" Suddenly he begins to sob. Tearing sobs. Standing there with his mouth open and the tears running down his cheeks.

No. Oh, no.

"Jordan." (Lord Roland's soft voice.) "Come with me. Lean on me. Come along."

" . . . looked up . . . couldn't help . . ."

"I'll give you something to ease the pain."

"No. Not you." Lord Jordan turns his head. "Pagan."

"I'll be coming, too, my lord. Don't fret—I'm right here. Isidore? Look at me. It's all right. Are you listening? It's *all right.*"

This is terrible. I can't stand this.

"You've got to be strong. You've got to be *strong,* Isidore."

Oh, Father.

"Now I want you to run home and tell Centule that we're coming. Tell him to make up another bed, in my room. Tell him to put my pillow on it, the feather pillow, and to heat up some water. Can you do that for me?"

"Yes, Father."

273

"Are you all right now?"

"Yes, Father."

"Good boy. Off you go. And *be careful.*"

Yes, Father. Oh, yes, Father. I will run the way of thy commandments.

Whatsoever thy soul desireth, I will even do it for thee.

‡CHAPTER TWENTY-FOUR‡

10 AUGUST 1209

What's happening? Is it time to get up? But it's as black as sackcloth outside. And that smell . . . surely that's not wood smoke? It doesn't smell like a kitchen fire to *me*.

Footsteps, hurrying past the window. A distant shout. More footsteps.

"Father?"

"He's not here." Lord Jordan's voice, from out of the gloom. "They've both gone."

"Gone?" What do you mean? There's a lamp by his pillow: I can see his face in the flickering light. I can see big drops of sweat sliding down his forehead. "Gone where?"

"Gone to see the show." He licks his dry lips. "I didn't feel up to it myself."

"What show? What's happened?"

"Don't ask me. I'm an invalid."

"But—but—" (He didn't wake me up! He just *left* me here!) "Why didn't he wake me? Why didn't he tell me?"

"Perhaps he thought you needed your rest."

"But he woke Lord Roland!"

"Well, of course he did."

"But—"

"Isidore, let me tell you something." A hoarse, feverish croak. "My damned brother will always come first with Pagan. Always, always, always. And there's nothing you can do about it." He rolls his head around, flapping a feeble hand across his face. "Hell and damnation!" he snaps. "Curse these mosquitoes. Why don't they go and bother someone else for a change? As if I haven't lost enough blood already!"

What do you mean, there's nothing I can do about it? Why should I want to do anything about it? Of course Lord Roland comes first: that's his rightful place. He's a great man, and he's Father Pagan's own lord. I don't understand what you mean.

Unless . . .

Oh, no.

You're not *jealous?*

"I feel as if I'm lying in a swamp," Lord Jordan complains. "Maybe I'll move to Roland's bed and wait for this one to dry out." A snort of laughter. "If they're so worried about the water supply around here, they should come and wring out my palliasse. There must be enough sweat in this thing to fill all the wells in the city."

"My lord?"

"What?"

"You . . ." (Come on, Isidore, out with it.) "You really like Father Pagan, don't you?"

He turns his head. He squints at me.

"Don't *you?*" he says.

"Yes, but . . ."

Pause.

"But what?"

Gulp. It's that voice—the voice he used on Guichard. What am I doing? I must be out of my mind. He's going to blow upon me the fire of his wrath, and I shall be melted in the midst thereof!

"N-nothing."

"Been listening to gossip, Isidore? Been sniffing around in dirty corners?"

"No—"

"I thought better of you, my friend. I thought you were above such things."

"I am! I mean—I didn't—I know it's not true. I know you'd never—never—"

"Never what?"

Oh, God. How can I say it? "Never defile yourself with the concupiscence of Onan."

He bursts out laughing. "Do *what*?" he chokes. "Christ, but you've got a way with words, Isidore, I'll say that for you."

Wait. What's that? A cheer. A roar. Something's happened. Something's happened, and I can't even see! I can't see a thing from this window because the church is in the way!

"Isidore! *Isidore!* Come back here!"

"My lord, I can't just sit around waiting! What if there's a breach?"

"What if there is? Do you think you'll be able to help, with no clothes on?"

Oh.

"In God's name, get dressed." He pushes himself up, using his good arm, and swings his feet to the floor. "I'll come with you."

"No!" (You can't!) "You're still sick!"

"If I let you go alone, Isidore, Pagan will skin me

alive," he says, smiling crookedly. "And if I stay here any longer, there won't be anything left of me *to* skin. The mosquitoes will have finished me off."

"My lord—"

"Besides, I need you to protect me." (This time it's more of a sneer than a smile.) "Now that I can't protect myself."

The lamp. We should take the lamp. Where's my surplice? Ah, there it is. Poof! It smells so awful—I wish there were enough water to wash it in. Lord Jordan groans, and mutters something under his breath.

"Help me with these boots, Isidore."

Boots? Oh, yes. You need two hands for boots. His legs are thin and pale and hairy, and covered in ancient . . . *teeth* marks?

"What—what happened to your—?"

"Dogs. Just dogs. Hurry up, will you?"

Dogs? It looks as if they've been savaged by a pack of wolves. He staggers when he tries to stand, staggers and blinks and gropes for the wall. "Get out of my way," he says.

"But—"

"If I need your help, I'll ask for it. Now get out of my way."

Very well, then, I *won't* lend you an arm. He

279

wobbles to the door and drags it open: the logs on the kitchen fire are still burning, but Centule is nowhere to be seen.

"Servant gone," he gasps. "Wonder why?" His knees seem to give a little every time he puts his foot down. The front door is standing slightly ajar; beyond it, shadowy figures scamper about, squeaking like rats. Smoke everywhere. Torches in the distance. "Stay close," he says, and nudges my shoulder.

I don't like this. I don't like this at all. Show us Thy mercy, O Lord, and grant us Thy salvation.

"Bertrand!" (Lord Jordan, raising his good hand.) "Bertrand? Over here!"

Bertrand? Who's Bertrand? A man with a torch stops in his tracks. His hair is so white that it seems to glow in the dimness; his face is black with soot. "My lord?" he says, grinning. "You're on your feet, then!"

"What's happened?"

"We did it, my lord! We burned the bastards out!"

"You what?"

"The Viscount, my lord! By God, there's a man. Led the whole thing himself."

"Led *what* himself?"

"The raid, my lord! Those fools withdrew for the night. Can you believe it?"

"From Castellar?"

"Yes! Left a holding garrison! Lord Raymond takes one look: 'They're not getting Castellar,' he says. Sneaks out the Aude Gate—catches the garrison by surprise—wipes out every one of them. Burns the whole suburb! Not a stick left!"

"But he got back safely?"

"Oh, yes, my lord. No trouble." Suddenly the man whoops; he's caught sight of a friend. "Isoard!" he cries. "What a fight, eh? What a fight!" They start to punch each other, laughing merrily. "That'll teach them! That'll teach them to mess with *us*!"

How very strange.

"Well, I'll be damned," Lord Jordan remarks. He sounds surprised. "Who would have thought?"

"Thought what, my lord? I don't understand. Is it a victory?"

"No-o-o. No, I wouldn't call it a victory." He's peering across the moonlit square, toward the southern ramparts. "But it's not a bad move."

"Have we retaken Castellar?"

"No, Isidore. We've simply made sure that there's nothing left to take."

Oh.

"Let's see if we can find the Viscount." He stumbles forward, hissing as another joyful, sooty soldier brushes past him, jarring his injured hand. "Watch it, you fool!" He's heading westward, away from Castellar.

I suppose Lord Raymond must have returned via the Aude Gate.

"Are you there, Isidore? Don't lose me."

"No, my lord." Lose you? How can I lose you? You're as slow as a snail. Step by step, from ever-lasting to everlasting. This trip is like the name of the Lord God Almighty—it shall be continued as long as the sun.

Or shall it? All of a sudden he stops and inclines his head. "Wait a moment," he says. "Listen to that. I recognize that voice."

So do I. That's the Archdeacon's voice. High and angry, somewhere off to the right. Down that street over there, with the smithy on the corner.

Torch light glinting on helmets and chain mail and rows and rows of fierce, gnashing teeth.

"What's going on?"

"I don't know." Lord Jordan puts out a hand, steadying himself on the smithy wall. "Isn't that the well of Saint-Nazaire? Looks like another rationing fight."

"Over water, you mean?"

"Naturally."

"But where's Father Pagan?"

"I've no idea." Lord Jordan studies the turbulent crowd of heavily armed soldiers. "If you ask me, that lot are just back from Castellar. Probably think they deserve an extra ration for their trouble."

"Look! Look, there he is!"

I can see him over the steel-capped heads· he must have climbed up onto something. The well, perhaps? Somebody waves a torch in his face and he flinches, beating it back with his arm. There's a scuffle going on, but I can't make out what's happening. Shouts and thumps and surging bodies. The clink of chain mail.

"We've got to help him!"

"How?"

"Can't you—can't you just—" Oh, no. Of course he can't. His sword arm is still in a sling. He looks down his nose at me and lifts his lip in an utterly mirthless smile.

"What do you want me to do?" he says. "Bite off their kneecaps?"

Twee-ee-ee-eet!

By the blood of the Lamb! Who did that? Was that the Archdeacon? I didn't know he could whistle like that!

Everyone is shocked into silence.

"All right!" he yells. "Have you finished now? Have you thoroughly impressed each other, poncing about, flexing your muscles? Because *I'm* not impressed, I can tell you! And neither are those ladies there!"

He points up at a first-floor window, where a couple of women are hanging over the windowsill, watching. One of them quickly ducks back inside.

"Who else needs to prove he's a man? Hmm? Who else is feeling small because he didn't kill anyone in Castellar?"

An angry rumble of voices. Someone shakes a threatening fist. "Say that again! Just say that again!"

"Why? Didn't you understand me the first time?"

"You dare to insult—you cowardly priest—I ought to punch your head in—"

"Oh really? And what's that going to prove? That you can wipe the floor with a midget in long skirts?" The Archdeacon pauses as a ripple of laughter passes through the crowd. "If you want to impress the rest of us, my friends, you'll do it by showing how strong you are. Only strong men can do without water. Extra water is for children and invalids, not for valiant men at arms."

Murmurs of agreement. But not everyone is convinced.

"That's all very well for you to say!" (A high, harsh, nasal whimper.) "*You* haven't been lighting fires! *You* haven't been running and fighting!"

"Is that you, Renaud Galimard?" Suddenly Lord Jordan speaks. He's drawling through his nose, but somehow he manages to make himself heard. "I'm surprised to hear that *you've* been running and fighting," he says. "I don't think I've seen you do that since you chased that whore of yours down the Street of the Saints."

This time it's a great yelp of laughter, drowning Renaud's protests. The Archdeacon peers in our direction, dazzled by the light of the torches, which dip and sway as the crowd turns to stare at us.

"I'm looking for the Viscount," Lord Jordan continues. "Can anyone tell me where he is?"

Utter confusion. Scores of voices, all talking at once. Some of the men peel off from the crowd, hurrying over to speak to Lord Jordan. ("I'll take you, my lord." "It was a romp, my lord." "My lord, you should have seen us!") He stoops quickly and puts his mouth to my ear.

"Tell Pagan I'm meeting the Viscount," he mutters. "Tell him he can save his sermon for Christmas."

"But—"

"Sorry, Isidore. I'm not hanging around here to be scolded."

What? Wait! Where are you going? A shove from behind—men pouring past—and all at once I'm facing the Archdeacon.

"You *wretched* boy!"

"Father—"

"What do you think you're doing? What does Jordan think he's—my lord! *My lord!*"

"He's gone to see the Viscount, Father."

"But he should be in bed! *You* should be in bed! What are you doing, dragging him around like this? Can't you see he's a sick man? As for you—in God's name, Isidore, this is no place for you! Can't I leave you alone for *one single moment?*"

By the blood of the Lamb of God. "You didn't tell me I had to stay in bed."

"That's because you were asleep!"

"Then you should have woken me up! I didn't

know what was happening! I didn't know where you were!"

"Isidore, if I've told you once, I've told you a thousand times—"

"You should have woken me! You *should* have! There could have been a breach! You could have been killed! How would you like to sit in a dark room waiting and waiting, with people screaming outside and no one there to tell you what was going on?"

"Shh. Calm down."

"Then don't shout at me! It's not my fault! I get scared, don't you understand? I get *scared*!"

"I'm sorry. I didn't think. Just calm down." He's holding my arms—squeezing my arms. "I'm here now; you're perfectly safe; there's no need to get upset. All right?"

"Just don't leave me! You're always leaving me!"

"Well, I won't do it again, I promise."

"That's what everyone . . . I mean . . ." Oh, it's no use. How can you possibly understand? They always go away, all of them. Only the books stay. Only the books are always there, and they're always the same.

"Isidore? Listen to me." He speaks slowly and clearly, squinting over the flame of my lamp. "I'm

287

not going to abandon you, Isidore. I'll never do that. So you don't have to worry about where I am, because I'll always come back for you. All right? That's a promise."

Promises, promises. How many promises have been made to me? A promise is like a broken tooth. A promise is like a foot out of joint. Unreliable.

"Now, I have to go and find the custodian of this well, because it's not being guarded properly." He glances at the men still clustered around it, little groups of men who seem to be exchanging war stories. Lord Roland is standing among them: he nods as he catches the Archdeacon's eye. "So can you go home, Isidore, and wait for me? Because I won't be long."

"Yes, Father."

"And if you don't want to sleep, you can get a book out of my book chest. You know where the keys are."

"Yes, Father."

"No military histories, mind. Something nice and uplifting. *The Letters of Saint Jerome*, perhaps. Only be careful with that book, because it doesn't belong to me."

"Father?"

"What?"

"Father, don't be angry with Lord Jordan. It was my fault that he got out of bed. He wouldn't have done it if I hadn't."

The Archdeacon blinks. An enormous grin spreads across his face, from ear to ear; his teeth gleam in the lamplight.

"Do you think Lord Jordan's *scared* of me?" he says.

"I—I don't know—"

"God, Isidore. What a find you are." Slapping my shoulder. "Don't worry. I promise that if anyone's going to give Jordan a kick up the backside, it certainly won't be me."

And he walks away, laughing.

✝CHAPTER TWENTY-FIVE✝

11 AUGUST 1209

"I saw them myself," Centule insists, wiping the sweat from his nose. "A whole family, lined up there on the street: mother, father, and six children. All dead—pop, pop, pop. Just like that." He begins to knead the dough again. "I said to my friend Amiel, 'It's the fever,' I said. 'You watch. I know the fever when I see it.'"

Oh, Lord. "Maybe they ate something. Something poisoned."

"Maybe. Maybe. But I've got a hunch." He sprinkles more flour onto his dough. "I can always smell the fever. I can smell it in the air."

Can you? All I can smell is excrement. This whole city stinks of latrines. "Where did they bury them?"

"Bury them! No room to bury them. They'll probably throw them over the wall."

"But they can't do that!"

"Well, maybe not. Maybe not." He's sweating into the bread dough: his hands are big and cracked and dirty. No wonder there are always black spots in our bread (not to mention wiry brown hairs and bits of grayish fingernail). But I suppose we should be glad that we're eating bread at all. So many people in this town are going hungry.

"I've heard tell," Centule continues, in mournful tones, "of sieges where the people in the city ended up eating their own dead."

"Oh, *Centule*."

"That's what I've heard."

"Well, I don't believe it!"

"Some things *are* hard to believe."

Suddenly there's a knock at the door: a knock and a rattle, as the person outside tries to open it. But Centule has put the bar up, for some reason (to stop people from stealing his bread dough?), and it's impossible to get in.

"Come on!" Lord Jordan's voice. "What are you playing at? Is anybody home?"

Whoops! Mustn't keep Lord Jordan waiting.

"One moment, my lord." This bar's so heavy . . . there. That's done it. He looks pale and tense, and pushes past as if I didn't exist.

Wait!

"My lord!"

He pauses, halfway to the bedroom.

"Please don't disturb him, my lord—"

"He's in there?"

"Yes, but—wait! He's asleep!"

"At this hour?"

"He sleeps when he can."

"Then he can sleep later. I've got some news."

News? What news? It's dark in the bedroom, because the shutters are closed, but there's enough light to make out the Archdeacon's huddled shape. He's still fully dressed, boots and all; he must have come in here, thrown himself on the bed, and gone straight to sleep.

Why didn't he call me? I would have pulled his boots off for him.

"Pagan!"

"Nngrr . . ."

"Wake up!" Lord Jordan pokes him in the ribs. "It's the King! Do you hear me? The King has come!"

The *King*? What king?

"Wha . . . ?" The Archdeacon rolls over, bleary-eyed. Grimacing. "Jordan?"

"Get up, for God's sake! It's King Pedro! He's arrived!"

King Pedro? You mean—King Pedro of Aragon?

The Archdeacon sits up, rubbing his hand over his face. "King Pedro?" he says.

"They spotted his colors from the wall. There must be at least a hundred knights with him. He's in the Crusaders' camp right now, but he's bound to head this way soon—if they'll let him."

"They'll have to." The Archdeacon is blinking, and smoothing down his ruffled hair. "They can't afford a fight with the King of Aragon." (So it *is* the King of Aragon!) "Does Lord Raymond know?"

"He thinks they might want to treaty. He's calling for you."

"In the castle?"

"Hurry up!"

King Pedro of Aragon. A real live king, and he's coming here. Oh, if only I could see him!

"Father . . ."

"What?" He's dragging a comb through his hair, as Lord Jordan hovers impatiently on the threshold. "It's all right, Isidore, you don't have to come."

"Oh, but can't I just—? I won't get in the way."

"You mean you *want* to come?"

"I've never seen a king before."

"Well . . ." He glances at Lord Jordan. "Oh, all right. Who knows? There may be letters to dictate."

"Shall I bring your satchel, then?"

"Yes, yes, just get a move on."

I'm moving, I'm moving! Where's his satchel? Under the bed. Lord Jordan has already vanished: he must have grown sick of waiting. The Archdeacon has to hoist up his skirts and run—out the door, through the kitchen, into the square.

Hold on, Father, wait for me!

"Father—Father—"

"What?" (He's panting.) "What is it?"

"Why has the King of Aragon come here?"

"Because Lord Raymond is his vassal."

"Is he going to help Lord Raymond? Is that why he's come?"

"I expect so."

"Perhaps he'll tell the Crusaders to go away!"

A shout of laughter from Lord Jordan, who's

striding along up ahead. "With one hundred knights behind him? It'll take more than that, boy."

"Still, it's a good sign." The Archdeacon quickens his pace. "It shows that he's worried."

"The King? Of course he's worried! Wouldn't you be worried, having a French army stomping around on your doorstep?" Lord Jordan looks around, sneering, as the Archdeacon struggles to keep up. "Pedro's not worried about us, my friend. He's worried about Aragon."

"Oh, surely not. Milo wouldn't take his army across the Pyrenees."

"*He* wouldn't, no. But what about Arnaud Amaury? That bastard's crazy enough to do anything."

The Archdeacon falls silent. Around us the air is thick and humid; people lounge in gutters and doorways, sluggish, sweaty, scratching their mosquito bites and moaning about the heat. Even the children just sit and stare as the flies crawl over their runny noses.

I feel as if everyone's looking at me.

"Didn't you say you'd met him?" Lord Jordan remarks, glancing at the Archdeacon. Around us, the castle barbican is clogged with people, all the way up to the moat. Many of them took ill—they lie dull-eyed, clutching their pitiful possessions, not making a sound when Lord Jordan kicks their feet aside. "King Pedro, I mean."

"I've seen him. I haven't met him," the Archdeacon rejoins. "He called on the Viscount once. I saw him ride through town."

"I met his sister when I was in Toulouse."

"Oh, yes. A great lady."

"They say the Count leads her a hell of a dance."

The Count? Oh, of course. The King of Aragon's sister is married to the Count of Toulouse. I forgot about that. What's going on over there, by the gate tower?

"Something tells me the King has arrived," Lord Jordan observes, and begins to run. His footsteps make a hollow noise as he crosses the wooden bridge. The guards don't even bother to challenge him.

"Curse it!" The Archdeacon grabs my arm. Pounding after Lord Jordan, over the bridge, through the gate, into the great courtyard. There are horses in the courtyard—four horses, with gilt on their saddles and stirrups, and fine cloth draped over them like cloaks. Several men are clustered around them.

"Well?" Lord Jordan stops abruptly. He's breathing very hard. "Can you see him?"

"No, I—no, I don't think so." The Archdeacon squints across the wide expanse of gravel. (How can it look so white, when so much blood has been spilled here?) "No, King Pedro has hair the color of chestnuts."

"Then he must be inside. Come on."

Past the horses. Up the stairs. Plunging into the chilly dimness of the great hall. This would be a perfect room, in summer, if it weren't so smoky. Though the fire does seem to be out, for a change.

"Which one?" Lord Jordan murmurs, and the Archdeacon strains to pick out familiar features through the gloom. I can see Lord Raymond, standing on the dais, wearing a jeweled sword belt. And there's the Lord of Pennautier, and the Lord of Vintron, and—yes! That must be him. That *must* be him. It's hard to see the color of his hair in this light, but only a king would wear such a magnificent surcoat.

"That's him." The Archdeacon points. "The slight one, next to the knight in red."

You mean *him*? But his clothes are so plain! Suddenly the Viscount catches sight of Lord Jordan:

he jerks his head, and the King stops talking and turns to look at us. He's of medium height, with a long, bony face, a broken nose, and greenish eyes that droop at the corners. They make him look weary and sad.

"Um . . . this is Lord Jordan Roucy de Bram," the Viscount declares as Lord Jordan drops to one knee. "And this is our Archdeacon, Father Pagan. He's provided me with much loyal and able support."

The Archdeacon bows very low. I suppose I'd better bow, too. Or should I? Perhaps I'd better just pretend I'm not here.

"What do *you* think of the situation, Lord Jordan?" The King's voice is quite deep for a man with such a narrow chest. "Do you see any reason to hope?"

Lord Jordan raises his eyebrows.

"My liege, there is always room for hope," he says at last, cautiously. But the King frowns.

"Not in this case. This is pointless. I don't need to be told how bad things are in Carcassonne—I can see it for myself. You're choking to death in here. People are dying. They're dying of hunger and thirst."

A long pause. The Viscount is staring at the

floor: he looks so young, so very young, to have such a terrible weight on his shoulders. The King studies him for a moment before reaching out to squeeze his arm.

"You have your father's courage," he says quietly. "I remember my own father telling me that when your father came to him, thirty years ago, and offered his allegiance, my father was happier than he'd ever been in his life. He said to me: 'That young man has caused me more trouble than all the other lords of Languedoc put together.' He was a great warrior, your father."

The Viscount nods, and blinks, and swallows. He looks as if he's going to cry.

"But your father was also a man of political wisdom," the King continues. "He knew that fighting wasn't always the answer—that sometimes it was better to lose a little than to lose all. That's why I would urge you to parley with the Crusaders. They are in a position of strength, and it would shatter my heart if your father's inheritance, which he nourished and guarded so fiercely, were to be divided like a dead hart between these dogs of France."

The Viscount clears his throat. "Yes," he says, "but they're not—how can we—?" He glances at the Archdeacon, who instantly comes to his rescue.

"My liege, these dogs, as you call them, are like dogs indeed. Mad dogs. They appear to have abandoned all reason, all mercy, all human motives. Surely you've heard what they did to Béziers?"

The King grunts. "Repulsive," he agrees, but in somber, unfriendly tones. His cool gaze rests on the Archdeacon for the space of five heartbeats: the Archdeacon straightens, and flushes, and sticks out his chin. Finally the King turns back to Lord Raymond. "What happened at Béziers was a warning," he says. "They were trying to frighten you. Consider what happened between there and Carcassonne: many towns surrendered without fighting, and the Crusaders were lenient. Forget Béziers. Parley now, while you are still in a position of advantage. While your people are still strong enough to resist." He releases the Viscount's arm and taps his own breastbone. "*I* will parley for you," he offers. "I will plead on your behalf, for I love you like a son, my lord—I love you just as my father loved your father. I would do anything to keep you here, in your father's house."

"And keep the King of France off his doorstep," the Archdeacon mutters, in a voice so low that I can barely hear it. The Viscount doesn't hear it. He looks up and says: "Lord, you may do as you please with this town and all within it, for we are your men, as we were for the King your father." He sounds very despondent.

The King smiles and embraces him.

"Your honor is my honor," he declares. "I shall go at once, and return before sunset. By sunset this city will be free of its stinking shackles." He motions to his attendant knights, who immediately head for the door. "Gird yourself with hope," he adds, "and pray to God in His mercy. Tell Father Pagan to pray for deliverance." Another cold, measuring glance at the Archdeacon. "Prayer is the best contribution he can make to our cause."

By the blood of the Lamb, what a slap in the face! The Archdeacon turns red, but says nothing: everyone watches in complete silence as the King departs. As soon as he's out the door, Lord Jordan grins and says: "I don't think King Pedro approves of you, Pagan. Perhaps he thinks that priests have no place in secular affairs." A muffled snicker. "Perhaps that explains why he's developed such a peculiar dislike of Milo's mob. Clerics in corselets. Most unattractive."

"In God's name, Jordan!" The Viscount's voice is

harsh. Stricken. Filled with the most profound despair and anger. "Must you joke about *everything*? Can't you see how serious this is? This could be the *end of Carcassonne!*"

Let Thy mercy, O Lord, be upon us.

‡CHAPTER TWENTY-SIX‡

11 AUGUST 1209

How can I rest? How can I *possibly* rest? Oh, this is stupid; I can't even read, let alone rest. My eyes just slide off the page. And the bell—that's the end of Vespers! I can't believe it's been so long. How long does it take to parley? Is it a good sign or a bad sign when it takes so long?

Perhaps I should tidy up a bit. Perhaps I should straighten the Archdeacon's bedclothes. Yes, that's what I'll do—I'll make myself useful. Push his riding boots under the bed. Smooth out his blanket. Shake out his pillow.

Wait. What's that? The front door . . . is that him?

"Hello, Centule." A muffled voice. Lord Roland's voice. "Is supper ready?"

Centule begins to speak. Don't you dare! Don't you dare tell him! They both jump when I burst into the kitchen. "Father! You'll never guess!"

"Why, Isidore—"

"It's the King, Father! The King of Aragon!"

"Calm down." (He looks so thin and tired.) "Where's Pagan?"

"He's with the Viscount. They're waiting in the castle, for the King to return. The King has gone to parley with the Crusaders!"

"King Pedro?"

"Yes! He came here, and he told Lord Raymond to parley, and Lord Raymond said he would, because we're all the King's men, and the King said he loved him like a son—"

"Wait a moment. How do you know all this?"

"Because I was there, Father! I saw everything! Only then Father Pagan sent me away." (Damn him.) "He said I was looking sick, and I should go home and rest, but how can I rest? How can I possibly rest?"

Lord Roland grunts. He stares at me with those wide, blue, expressionless eyes, and puts a hand on my shoulder. "If Pagan wants you to rest, Isidore, then you should rest," he says.

"But—"

"Come along." (Steering me into the bedroom.) "We can talk just as well if you're lying down."

"But I can't!"

"Why not? Are you like an elephant, with no joints at the knees? Will you never be able to rise again?"

"Yes, but—"

"In you get."

"But you don't understand! I'm too—I can't—if I lie down, I can't breathe."

"What?" He frowns again, and probes my wrist. "Isidore, what's the matter? You must calm yourself, or you'll have an attack."

"How can I be calm? I'm worried! Aren't *you* worried?"

"I'll give you some valerian."

"Father, why do you think it's taking so long? Why haven't we heard anything?"

"Here." He takes a clean rag from his medical pouch, and dips it into the water bucket. "Put this on your forehead. You're a terrible color."

"But what do you think the terms will be? Will they make us pay a ransom?" Ah! That rag feels nice and cool. "What about the people who don't have any money?" (People like me, for instance.) "What about the heretics?"

"Shh." His hand is on my tonsure; it's heavy and warm. "Don't say anything. Just breathe. In and out, very slowly."

"But—"

"*Isidore.*"

Gulp. Is that him? He sounds so different—so cold and ominous. He sounds like his brother.

"Just breathe," he says. "In. Out. In. Out . . ."

A noise. The door. It's Father Pagan.

He slouches into the room, dragging his feet, his dark face even darker than usual. "Isidore," he says dully. "What's wrong? Have you had a fit?"

"Father. Did they—"

"He's all right," Lord Roland interrupts. "He's just a little nervous."

By the blood of the Lamb! Look at the way he's moving! Look at the way he casts himself onto his bed! "Father, what happened? Is the King back? What did he say?"

"He said goodbye." The Archdeacon doesn't move: he just lies there, staring at the ceiling. "Goodbye and good luck."

"But—"

"Didn't I say it was hopeless? Didn't I say they were mad dogs?"

"What were the terms?" Lord Roland speaks clearly and quietly. "Unconditional surrender?"

"Almost. They said the Viscount could leave, with eleven of his men. The rest of us would have to take what comes."

Oh, God.

"Even the King saw it was hopeless." The Archdeacon utters a sour little laugh. "When they told him the terms, he said, 'That will happen when an ass flies in the sky,' and turned on his heel. I would have farted in their faces."

A long, long pause. I don't believe it. This can't be true.

"Then we fight on?" Lord Roland says at last.

"On and on and on." The Archdeacon rolls over and buries his face in his blanket. "Jesus, Roland, I'm so tired. I'm so *tired.*"

"Then you should sleep more. We should all sleep more."

"My head hurts."

"I'll give you something."

This is crazy. They're both so calm. Don't they understand? We're going to be *killed!* We're going to stay in here until we're half dead of thirst, and then the Crusaders will come and—and—

"Isidore?" Lord Roland. "It's all right, Isidore."

All right? *All right?*

"You mustn't worry." He leans down, his hand still on my head. "We won't let anything happen to you."

"No, you won't! Because you'll both be dead and buried!"

"Oh, don't be a fool, Isidore." The Archdeacon sounds cross. He sits up and rubs his face. "Come over here." (Patting the bed beside him.) "I'm going to explain something."

You mean you're going to lie about something. I've got eyes, Father Pagan. I've got ears. I know what's going on.

"Listen." He puts an arm around my shoulders. It feels frail and insubstantial—not like Lord Roland's hand. His fingers are very small and brown and thin. "You're obviously letting that imagination of yours run away with you," he says. "And you're doing that because you've had no experience of war. Now I'm going to tell you what I believe is going to happen, and I'm not trying to make you feel better; I'm telling you this because it's really what I think. And I know what I'm talking about because I've had a lot of experience. All right?"

There's a scar on his face. I've never noticed it

308

before. It's not big and jagged, like the one on his forehead; it's small and neat, and it's sitting back near his left ear.

"Isidore! I'm talking to you!"

"Yes, Father."

"Are you listening?"

"Yes, Father."

"All right." He takes a deep breath. "Now, what you saw today was not the end of the world. It was simply a bluff. Think of what happens when you go to the market: when the man selling shoes offers you a price, do you pay him that price? Of course not! And he doesn't expect you to pay it, either. At least, he's hoping you might, but he's quite happy to come down. Well, it's the same with a parley. These terms are simply the first set of terms, to test us out. They want to see if we'd be mad enough to accept them."

Is that true? Is that really true? It *sounds* like the truth, but then Father Pagan makes everything sound like the truth. What was it he said to the Viscount? "The truth or falsity of an argument makes no difference, if only it has the appearance of truth." Father Pagan is trained to persuade.

"If that's so, Father—"

"It *is* so."

"Then why has the King left? Why hasn't he stayed to negotiate the next set of terms?"

His eyes are screwed up into such a squint that I can't see into them. I can't tell from his expression whether he's lying or not. But his smile is real: it flashes through his beard like the sun emerging from behind a cloud.

"Don't you believe me, Isidore?"

"I don't know."

"Perhaps you'd believe what I'm telling you if you read it in a book."

"Don't laugh at me!"

"I'm not laughing." His teeth disappear back into his beard, but the smile remains in his voice. "The fact is, no king is going to sit around in this stinking place for the next three weeks. Not if he doesn't have to. I certainly wouldn't if I were the King of Aragon."

"Then you think he's going to come back?"

"Who knows? He might. But kings are notoriously busy people."

I suppose so. I suppose that's true.

"Isidore." The Archdeacon still sounds amused. "Don't you think, if we were in mortal danger, that I'd be a bit frightened myself? Hmm? Don't you think I'd be running around in a panic?"

"No."

"No?" He seems genuinely surprised. "Why not?"

"Because you're brave. You're always brave. You're the bravest man I've ever known." (Wait. That's not right.) "Except for Lord Jordan. He's brave, too. (Not that it means much, for someone like me to say it.) "Of course, I haven't met many people."

A crack of laughter, right in my ear. "God, Isidore, what a find you are." He squeezes me with his arm, as if I were a friend. As if I were Lord Roland. "You're the one who's brave," he says. "You're the one who chose to come. You could have stayed in Montpellier." Another sympathetic laugh. "Perhaps you *would* have stayed, if you'd known what it was going to be like."

"Perhaps." I don't know. I don't think so. Even now I don't think so. "But what would I have done, if I'd stayed?"

"Read books?"

Read books? How could I have read books? My eyes would have been turned to Carcassonne, from morning till night. "Maybe there wouldn't have been any books. Maybe things would have been worse there. 'For who knoweth what is good for man in this life, all the days of his vain life which he spendeth as a shadow?'"

"Fair enough." The Archdeacon slaps me on the back and rises. "I can tell you one thing that's good for man, though, and that's his supper. I'm starving. Are you starving?" He laughs again, through his nose. "Or perhaps that's an unfortunate choice of words, in the circumstances."

You see? He's so *brave.*

Who else would laugh in the face of famine?

‡ CHAPTER TWENTY-SEVEN ‡

19 AUGUST 1209

Look at that cockroach scurrying across the floor. It seems so full of energy. Do cockroaches drink, or do they just eat? But there's not much left to eat, either. I wouldn't have expected to see cockroaches thriving in a town where the people are hoarding every crumb.

It's not fair. Why can't I rush about like that cockroach?

"Isidore." Lord Roland is standing on the threshold. "Are you awake?"

"Yes."

"How do you feel?"

Grunt. How do you think I feel? My own clothes abhor me.

"Are you feeling any better?"

"No."

He crosses the room on noiseless feet and opens the shutters. "Let me look at you," he says. "Can you sit up?"

I suppose so. If you insist. The cockroach has disappeared, and so has everyone else. Where are they all?

"Where's Father Pagan?"

"He's at the castle."

"Where's Lord Jordan?"

"He's at the castle, too."

"Why? Has something happened?"

"I'm not sure." Lord Roland presses his hand to my forehead. "You're still very hot."

Of course I'm hot! Everyone's hot! "I think I can get up now."

"Do you?"

"I think I'll go to the castle."

But he shakes his head. "Pagan told me to take you for a walk along the battlements," he says quietly.

Pardon?

"He thinks you need some fresh air." A sigh. "I have to agree with him. The air in this city is very unhealthy. It's full of poisonous vapors."

"But what's happening at the castle?"

"Nothing that need worry you."

"But—"

"Isidore." He's feeling for my pulse. "If it was bad news, do you think Pagan would let us go up on the battlements?"

That's true. He wouldn't. "Then it's good news!"

"Perhaps."

"Then tell me! *Please* tell me!"

"Not if you're going to get excited."

"I'm not. I won't. It will calm me down "

"Oh, will it?"

"Yes, it will. Because otherwise I'll just keep wondering and wondering."

He smiles. "Sometimes you sound so much like Pagan," he says. "If I tell you, will you promise to come up to the battlements?"

"Yes, of course."

"Let's go, then."

What? But—

"I'll tell you when we get up there."

Oh, very clever. Highly amusing. He hands me my boots and heads for the door. Wait! Don't rush! I don't have the strength to rush.

These boots smell like rotten fish.

"Wait! Hold on—"

"I'm waiting."

There. Done. He's holding open the door. "You can lean on me, if you want," he says.

"It's all right."

"Where's Centule?"

"I don't know." The kitchen's deserted. "Fetching water?"

"As long as he's locked all the food up. . . ."

It's sunny outside. It's always sunny outside. If only it would rain! There's a baby crying somewhere—crying and crying and crying—and somebody's sharpening a knife on a whetstone. Smoke rises from the refugees' shanties huddled in the shadow of the city wall. A dead body has been left on the road, wrapped in a blanket; I can smell it from here.

"We'll go via the tower of Saint-Nazaire," Lord Roland remarks. "The guards there know me now."

"Father?"

"Yes?"

"Do I really sound like Father Pagan?"

"Sometimes." His eyes are screwed up against the afternoon glare. "You sound like him when he was your age."

"What was he like when he was my age?"

"Oh . . ." A pause. "Not much different from the

316

way he is now. A little quieter, perhaps. Less confident." He smiles, as if at some distant memory. "Cheekier."

"Do you think he's a great man?"

"A great man?" Lord Roland seems to ponder as he strides along with his hands in his sleeves and his gaze on the battlements. "Yes," he says at last. "Yes, I do." He looks down his long nose at me. "Do you?"

"Oh, yes." How can I explain? Of course he's not a devout person. He's not a saint or anything, he's just . . . "He's the most learned man I've ever met, but it's not just books. It's life, as well." (He has such depth of knowledge.) "I wouldn't say he was a model priest, though. I wouldn't say that."

"No." Lord Roland smiles again. "No, I don't think anyone could say that."

And here's the tower. Its entrance is a little hole punched high in the wall, reached by a ladder and guarded by a man whose face is like the seven plagues of Egypt. "Can you manage that ladder?" Lord Roland inquires.

"I think so."

"Wait here." He begins to climb, rather stiffly, and the man at the top of the ladder watches without a change of expression. They begin to talk

317

before Lord Roland has even reached him, but it's hard to hear what they're saying. At last Lord Roland turns and beckons.

"Come on!" he says.

And up we go: one step, two steps, three steps. The rungs are worn smooth, polished by the passing of so many feet. They're slippery and dangerous. Take it slowly, Isidore. (My knees are beginning to tremble.) The soldier spits, and it sails past my left ear.

"Stop that!" Lord Roland's stern voice. He leans down, extending a hand. "Grab hold of me," he says. "That's right. There."

Done it. Hooray! This room is so dark that I can barely see him: he takes my elbow and guides me toward the stairs, circular stairs leading up to the parapet. Their treads are slippery, too—greasy with lamp oil. "Be careful," he mutters. "Watch your step." Why don't they clean up around here? The light's growing stronger and . . . yes! At long last.

What a wonderful breeze. So fresh and pure.

"Breathe it in," Lord Roland instructs. "It will clear your head." He sets off along the parapet, heading east: soldiers on guard duty stare at us both, some grinning, some scowling, some blank-faced like cows. They look small and mean and dirty against the soaring, glowing background of spreading fields and blazing skies.

And there are the Crusaders. So many of them! A great ring of tents and fires, horses, mules, carts, flags, garbage. Just like a town with no houses. All the vineyards are gone, pulled up for fuel. Every blade of grass has been trodden into the dirt.

"Father?"

"What?"

"Aren't you going to tell me what's happening? At the castle?"

"Oh." He stops, and looks around. "Of course. Forgive me. It was a message from the Count of Nevers."

"Who?"

"One of the crusading lords. He wants to speak to the Viscount."

"Why?"

"To discuss terms, I presume."

"To parley?"

"Yes."

"To parley! That's good news, isn't it?"

"Perhaps."

He's engulfed by the shadow of another tower, and passes straight through it to the next stretch of parapet. More sun, more soldiers. He's taller than most of them, and broader in the shoulders: he keeps glancing at the Crusaders' camp, as if it's troubling him.

"Father?"

"Mmm?"

"Is that what's happening now? Is the Viscount parleying with the Count of Nevers?"

"No." He shades his eyes with his hand as he peers out over the battlements. "The Count wants Lord Raymond to go to *him.* Lord Raymond doesn't know if that's wise. I believe he's seeking advice from his counselors."

"Father Pagan, you mean?"

"He's one of them."

"And your brother?"

A grunt. I shouldn't have said that: he doesn't like talking about Lord Jordan. He's swallowed up by another tower—disappearing into the darkness—and there's an angry exclamation. What? What's happening? I can't see. . . .

"Are you trying to break our necks?" he barks as someone scrambles around on the floor. Who is it? Did Lord Roland fall over him? A hand on my arm, and suddenly we're in the light again: the light and the breeze. Lord Roland is muttering to himself.

"Asleep on duty . . . bad sign . . . foolishness . . ." But all at once he falls silent. He slows. He stares.

"What is it, Father?"

No reply. It's those Crusaders; they're still bothering him, for some reason. His face is set like a rock. Glancing along the wall, he releases my arm. "Stay here," he says. Up near the next tower there's a big man with a sword: when Lord Roland approaches him and speaks to him, he frowns and shrugs and begins to argue. Lots of pointing and waving. What on earth is going on?

"There!" Someone yells from behind me—a bare-chested man whose subsequent words are lost on the wind. Flurries of movement, up and down the walls. Lord Roland is running.

What . . . ?

"Run!" he cries. "Run, Isidore, run!"

Run? Where? Why? What are you—

Wh-oo-oo-oom-CRASH!

"Down! Get down!" His weight—falling—help! Flat on my belly, and he's on my back. He's shielding my head with his arms.

Wh-oo-oo-oom-CRASH! The foundations shudder.

"What is it? What *is* it?"

"Mangonels."

"What?"

"Siege machines! Keep your head down!"

Oh, God. Oh, God, have mercy upon us. "But you said they wanted to parley!"

"It's insane—"

"Oh, God. Oh, God."

People running past. People shouting. Lord Roland's breath on my tonsure. "We've got to move," he gasps. "They're clearing a space for the ladders."

"O-God-Thou-art-my-God-early-will-I-seek-Thee—"

Wh-oo-oo-oom-CRASH! Something patters down like hail. Clouds of dust—I can't breathe—a chorus of shouts from somewhere in the distance. Somewhere . . . below?

"Crawl! *Crawl!*" Lord Roland, pushing me from behind. I can't! I can't crawl! Leave me alone! *Ouch!*

"Don't hit me!"

"Then move! Crawl! They're coming!"

"Oh, my God. Oh, my God."

"To the tower! We've got to get to the tower!"

The tower. It's just ahead. We've got to get to the tower. My heart: my heart's so loud I thought it was drums.

Wh-oo-oo-oom . . . (He pushes my head down.) . . .
CRASH!

Screaming. Someone screaming. Christ on high.

"Don't stop!" Lord Roland, shouting in my ear. "Keep moving!"

But the man's there. He's right there, lying with his arms spread, and his head all . . . still pumping . . . sprays of . . .

I'm going to be sick.

"Don't look!" Lord Roland's voice. What's he doing? He reaches out and grabs the sword—the discarded sword. It's spattered with blood. Chunks of rock everywhere, splintered rock, and a hole in the defenses where they've knocked down a merlon. How are we going to get past that? Something whizzing overhead, clinking on rock . . .

An arrow.

"Where are the crossbowmen?" Lord Roland hisses. "Where is everyone? You! Sergeant! Cover that gap! This is insane. They must be insane." He grabs my collar with his free hand. "Quick! *Quick!*"

Rubble underfoot. What's that noise? Someone rearing over the battlements, blade flashing, hair flying, mouth open, screeching like a pig. A cross on his chest. No. It can't be.

No.

Lord Roland surges forward, his sword raised. *Chunk!* Down it comes. The man falls to his knees, still screeching. *Chunk!* He's dying. Lord Roland is killing him. This can't be true.

"Yaagh!"

Another. Another and another, swarming through the gap, and Lord Roland turns, and meets them, and wields his sword. *Chunk! Clang!* What's happening? I can't see—that shield's in the way. But it falls; it hits the ground with a thud. Someone staggers, bent double, groaning. Someone in blue.

"Isidore! The tower, quick, run!"

Run. Run! Bodies pushing past—men with crossbows. Our men. A tide of them, pouring out of the tower. The tower! I'm almost there! Get out of my way—let me through! O God be not far from me. A bit farther . . . a bit farther . . . done it!

"Who's that?" A shout from the dimness. "Hold fast!"

"Don't . . . oh, d-don't, please . . . "

"What the hell—?"

"I want to go home! Let me go home!"

"It's a priest."

"It's a boy."

"Let him through! Let him pass!"

Crowds on the stairway. Armor scraping on stone. My foot slips, but someone catches me. "Watch it, son." I've got to get out. I can't breathe. Where's Lord Roland?

"Don't stop." His hoarse voice, behind and above me. "Keep going."

He's there! He's safe! Bless the Lord O my soul. O Lord my God, Thou art very great: Thou art clothed with honor and majesty.

"Father—"

"Don't stop."

I'm not stopping. I can't stop. These stairs aren't wide enough to stop on. Hallelujah! At last! The light and the space—the street—the air. Frightened people milling about. What's wrong with Lord Roland?

"Father?"

He's bowed and staggering. His face is white. His hand is pressed to his stomach.

Blood. There's blood. His black robe is gleaming with it.

"You're—you're not hurt?"

"I am hurt."

"Oh, God . . . "

He reaches out. "Help me. Help me back home."

He's so heavy. He can hardly walk. He's breathing

in short little gasps, and the blood patters down onto the dust as he passes.

"Is it bad?"

"Shh."

"I'm sorry. I'm sorry, Father."

"It's all right."

Faces everywhere. What are they staring at? Which way is it to the cathedral? Shouts from the walls, but I can't look back. There's blood on my surplice.

"Wait." He stops. He sounds surprised, but not worried.

He seems to sag at the knees.

"Father?"

Something's wrong. He stares at me with wide, blue, startled eyes. "This isn't going to work," he says, and pitches forward onto his face.

"Father!" Oh, God! "Father! *Father!*" This is a nightmare. This can't be true. "Wake up! Father!" He can't be. No, it's not possible. God—you can't do this. Not to him. His eyes are open, but—

"*No! NO!*"

Please don't die. Oh, please, don't do this—you can't—you can't leave us. You mustn't. You *can't.*

"Father . . . Jesus God . . ."

There's blood running out of his mouth.

‡ CHAPTER TWENTY-EIGHT ‡

19 AUGUST 1209

"Yep, he's dead all right." The man nudges Lord Roland's limp foot with his toe. He's a dyer, a sturdy, balding man with dye on his hands and inflamed mosquito bites all over his face. "Was it one of those rocks?"

"It was—we were up there."

"On the wall?" He looks around. "What were you doing up there?"

"I don't know." Woe is me. Why died I not from the womb? Dust and ashes—I am dust and ashes. "We were walking. Just walking along . . ."

"Bad luck." He's still peering up at the battlements. "Seems to have settled down, though. No more rocks, and no more noise."

"What happened?" Another man, quite young, with a thick mop of dark brown hair and a pale, unhealthy complexion. "Did they kill a monk?"

"Yep. He's dead."

"That's a shame."

"I tell you, Gaucher, they'd kill their own mothers without blinking an eye."

"Please — please —" What am I going to do? I have to think. Oh, God, I can't believe this.

"Do you want some help?" the older man inquires. "We can take him somewhere, if you want."

Yes, we have to take him somewhere. But where? Back home? Back to his bed, and wait for the Archdeacon? Sit by the bed and wait and . . .

No. I have to tell him.

"To the castle." For I will declare mine iniquity; I will be sorry for my sin. "Can you take him to the castle?"

"The castle?" Both men exchange glances. "Is that where he lived?"

"He — his friend is there. His brother is there. His brother is the Lord of Bram."

A reverent kind of noise from the man called Gaucher. His companion looks down at Lord Roland with dawning respect.

"Right," he says. "Then we'd better take him to

his brother. You take the head, Gauch, and I'll take the feet."

God have mercy. Save me from the scourge of all sorrows. Save me from a shattered and bleeding soul. Let this cup pass from me, O Lord. I can't bear it, the way his head lolls, the way his hand falls, it's too pitiful, it's too terrible, how could you do this? How could you *do* this?

"Oof!" The young man staggers a little. "He's a big fellow, isn't he?"

"I'll go first."

"It's a shame, you know. God will punish them for this."

"Right. Lead on, Father."

Father? I'm not a Father. I'm nothing. I'm dung upon the face of the earth. I have destroyed a man beloved of God, and Father Pagan's going to kill me. He's going to hate me and he's going to kill me. God! I didn't even say the words of absolution. He died like a dog, with his sins on his soul. Why was I even born? I can't do anything right. . . .

"Father?" It's the older man: he sounds uneasy. "Don't cry, Father. He's a monk. He'll be in heaven now. He'll be with God."

"Isn't this where we turn?" Gaucher says. "Don't we turn left here?"

"Yes, we do. This way, Father."

People staring. People crossing themselves. "What happened?" somebody shouts.

"Killed on the wall," the dyer rejoins. "Killed by the Crusaders."

"Did they get through?"

"No, no."

"There were rocks! I heard rocks!"

"It's finished. We pushed 'em back. Let us pass."

He died saving me. He died like a hero. I'd be dead if it wasn't for him. I'd be dead with my throat cut, and they'd have thrown me off the wall, and the crows would have . . . would have . . .

"Odo!" Gaucher's voice. "Hold on, wait. He's sick."

"Poor little man. I'm not surprised."

My breath is corrupt; my days are extinct; the graves are ready for me.

"You just let it out, son. No point trying to keep it down."

My life is spent with grief. My life is spent with grief.

"There's nothing worse," Gaucher remarks thoughtfully, "than throwing up on an empty stomach."

I am feeble and sore broken, and my life is spent with grief.

"Finished?" Odo says. "That's the way. Better wipe your mouth, because we're almost there. Can you get past the sentinels?"

The sentinels? I don't know. Surely they'd recognize Lord Roland? Surely they've seen me enough these past few weeks? The barbican opens out in front of us, a sea of shacks and dung heaps, with goats and children fossicking for scraps. One of the children sees the blood—the limp body—the bouncing head—and begins to cry.

"What happened to him, Master?" A little boy with black curls and a sharp, inquisitive face. "Did the crossers get him?"

"Out of the way."

"Was it the crossers? Did he get hit by a stone?"

"*You'll* get hit by a stone, son, if you don't behave yourself."

A swarm of children, trailing after us like flies. Why are they doing this? Aren't they frightened? Only when we reach the castle gate do they falter, repelled by the massive stony walls and the flinty eyes of the sentinels.

"What's this?" The tallest guard has a broken

nose, and teeth as white as the Seven Angels. "What happened to *him?*"

"He was killed. On the wall."

"Did those bastards do this?"

"Please. Please let me through. I have to tell his brother."

"By my faith." The guard shakes his head in anger and disgust. "They say they're Crusaders, and they kill a man of God. I hope they sweat in hell for it." He crosses himself and waves us through. "My sympathies to Lord Jordan," he says.

Lord Jordan? Will Lord Jordan mind? I doubt it. But Father Pagan—God. I don't know if I can do this.

"Where are we going?" Odo pants, as we emerge from the shadow of the gatehouse.

"There."

"The great hall?"

"Yes."

"Good," says Gaucher. "My arms are getting tired."

"No offense meant," Odo adds. "But he's pretty heavy."

Heavy. How can a man be so heavy, when he's so thin? Is the weight in his bones? A couple of stable hands stare at us across the courtyard, but there's no one on the stairs. I suppose the rest of them are in the great hall: they generally are. Perhaps I'd better not . . .

"Can you just wait here, please?" (I don't know how to address them. Are they servants? Men of property?) "I'll be back very soon."

"Can we put him down?"

"Oh, yes. Thank you."

Sixteen stairs. Sixteen stairs up to the door of the great hall. I feel as if I'm going to faint. My throat is burning. What will he do to me? Will he send me away? The smell of smoke, the coolness, the dimness. I can't see a thing. Is he in here?

"Isidore?"

That's Lord Jordan's voice. Where is he? Is that him? A shadow, advancing over the rushes. A glint of gold; a gleam of leather. Suddenly his face appears and his gaze drops to my knees. "What happened?" he says. His tone is hard and urgent. "Are you wounded?"

Wounded? Oh. The blood.

"N-no . . ."

"Where's Pagan?"

"What?"

"He went to find you when we heard the bombardment. He went to see if you were still at his house, or if you'd left for the wall. I would have gone myself, if it wasn't for this. . . . " He fingers his bandaged hand. "What's wrong?" he asks softly. "Were you caught?"

"Forgive me. Forgive me."

"What is it?"

"Come—look—"

Out into the sunshine. You can see he's dead, even from this distance. It's the way he's lying, all twisted and bent. It's his open mouth and his half-open eyes.

Lord Jordan freezes. He swallows.

"I'm sorry. I'm so sorry. It was all my fault."

More tears; I can't see where I'm going. Fumbling my way down the stairs, following Lord Jordan, who's found the use of his limbs again. He reaches the bottom and stops: Odo and Gaucher bow nervously.

"My lord."

"My lord."

He doesn't seem to hear them. He's staring down at his brother, his face completely blank.

"My lord, we were stuck on the battlements. We were trying to get to a tower, but there were men coming over the wall. He killed at least one—I don't know what happened—"

"Were they driven off?"

"P-pardon?"

"The Crusaders! Were they beaten back?"

"Yes, my lord, I think so."

"Hmm." He's frowning. "It doesn't make sense. Why attack, when you're trying to arrange a parley? Unless . . . well, it could have been a warning. Either that, or somebody's bungled. Somebody didn't tell the right hand what the left hand was doing. Wouldn't be the first time."

"My lord—"

"Listen to me." He presses my shoulder. "We can't let Pagan see this. If he sees this, he's finished. And we can't afford to lose him now because the Viscount needs him. The Viscount wants to parley, and they've told him he can bring nine men along. He wants Pagan to be one of them."

"You mean—"

"Most of the wells are dry. We've *got* to parley. But if Pagan sees this . . . " (A jerk of the head.) "He'll be no good to anyone."

"But how can we hide—?" This is crazy. "Father Pagan would never leave, not without knowing what's happened to his lord. Father Roland was his lord!"

"We'll say he's looking after the wounded. We'll

tell a lie. The Viscount will be leaving soon—Pagan won't have time to check." He looks down at me, frowning. "You'll have to change your clothes before he sees you. Change your clothes and wash your face."

"My lord—"

"But where shall we hide Roland? That's the question. Can't take him back to Pagan's place." He ponders, stroking his mustache. "Not the chapel: there might be prayers before we go. Not the cellars—too many rats."

By the blood of the Lamb of God! "My lord—"

"In fact, we'd better stay out of the main building altogether. Stables? Too risky. Barracks? Too crowded. Ah!" He narrows his eyes. "That's it. The gatehouse. Nice and private. You!" he barks, gesturing at Odo. "Both of you! Pick him up and follow me."

The two men scramble to do his bidding. I can't believe this. This isn't right. As Lord Roland is lifted, his arms flop loose, trailing on the ground; Lord Jordan bends over and takes both the bloody hands in his. He places them on his brother's chest, one on top of the other, and stands there for a moment, studying the lifeless face that looks so much like his own.

"Poor old Piglet," he says softly, before closing his brother's eyes. There's a brief, solemn pause. Odo and Gaucher look embarrassed; Lord Jordan turns on his heel. "Come!" he snaps, and heads for the gatehouse.

"My lord." Wait. Wait for me. "My lord, if you do this, Father Pagan will hate you. He'll never forgive you, never."

"So what's new?"

"But it's *wrong*, my lord! To lie to him about something like this."

"We're going to need him, Isidore. We're going to need all the help we can get." Suddenly he stops. He catches his breath and winces. "Oh, Jesus," he chokes.

Someone's coming through the gateway: someone small and wiry and dressed in black. As he steps into the sunlight, his gaze alights on Lord Roland.

"Pagan." Lord Jordan moves forward, his arms outstretched. "Pagan, listen to me—"

But Father Pagan doesn't listen.

He just falls.

"*Father!*" (Oh, God, no!) "The Archdeacon! He's dead!"

"Don't be a fool." Lord Jordan reaches him first. Turns him over. "He's fainted. Damn! His head."

There's blood on his brow, where it hit the gravel. He looks so small. Oh, Father—oh, Father—

"Well, that's the end of that," Lord Jordan remarks in a toneless voice. But his hand trembles as he lifts the thick black hair away from the wound. As he strokes the bearded cheek, so gently, so fondly, so—so—

By the blood of the Lamb of God. It's true. It must be true. Look at his face! Guichard was right. He was *right*!

"Come on." Lord Jordan gathers up the small, inert figure and rises to his feet. "We'll forget about the gatehouse. We'll take them home."

Home. Yes. We'll take them both home.

‡CHAPTER TWENTY-NINE‡

19 AUGUST 1209

How long has it been? How many tears can one person shed? That patch of sunlight has moved all the way from the bed to the chair, and he still hasn't stopped. First the whispering, then the yelling, then the pounding—pounding on the bloody chest: *"How could you do this to me?"*—and now the groans and the tears, on and on and on, his face buried in Lord Roland's neck, his voice muffled, his whole body racked with violent convulsions. Bare, bloody patches on his scalp, where he actually tore out his hair: it's floating about on the floor now, like feathers. I've never seen anyone do that before. I've never seen anyone throw back his head and howl at the ceiling.

I've never seen such pain.

Search me, O God, and know my heart: try me, and know my thoughts. I didn't realize . . . How could I fathom such depths? He must have loved him as his mother and father. He must have loved him as his own soul. How could I know that? How could you do this? Look at what you've done—look at how you've hurt him. That's Father Pagan, lying there. That's what you've reduced him to, that damp huddle, that broken, noisy, demented—that *creature*. Look at him! You've got to bring him back. You can't let him stay like this.

"Father?"

He doesn't hear me. He's deaf and blind, as deaf and blind as his dearest friend. He only has ears for one voice—eyes for one face—and he keeps pleading and pleading: "Talk to me. Say something." But Lord Roland will never say anything, ever again.

I wish Lord Jordan would come. Haven't they finished their parley? Lord Jordan's voice might do it. His face might do it. His face is so similar, his eyes are identical. . . . Why doesn't he come? He said he would. He said he'd come as soon as he got back. Surely he must be back by now?

A fly buzzes through the window. It's so hot. We'll have to bury him soon, or—or—But how are we going to do that? Father Pagan will want a proper funeral. It's too difficult. I can't think.

Someone's shouting in the distance, but the words all run together. Another voice joins in. Could that be a sign? Has the Viscount returned? I could go and see what's happening, but I don't like to leave him in case—in case—I don't know what he might do. He might hurt himself. The way he was staggering about earlier, banging his head on the wall . . . he seems to have lost all sense of where he is.

More shouts. A shutter slams. I can hear Centule's plaintive cry: "What's happening?" When I open the door to the kitchen, he's already disappeared.

Must have gone to ask for news.

I'll wait till he returns. I'll get Father Pagan some water. There's still some left at the bottom of the jug, but is there enough to wash Lord Roland? Probably not. Just enough to clean his blood off the Archdeacon's hands, and his face, and his tonsure. It's smeared all over him.

"Father?"

No reply. He's sobbing into Lord Roland's ear: "What am I going to do? What am I going to do?" I can't bear it. If only I could—this is worse than— but what can I say? What can I possibly *say*?

Gird thee with sackcloth and wallow thyself in ashes; make thee mourning as for an only son, most bitter lamentation. For Lord Roland Roucy de Bram is dead.

"The children! Get the children!" Wailing from outside. People run past the window; a woman weeps piteously, moaning and beating her breast. Somehow the sound of it reaches Father Pagan, and he begins to howl again, howling until he runs out of air, until he can't force anything through his open mouth except a tiny hiss. His face is red and contorted.

"Father, please—" You've got to control yourself. Something's wrong out there, I can feel it. Something bad has happened. I'll have to ask—I'll ask that man there.

"Wait! Stop!"

He wheels around and stares up at the window.

"What is it?" (My voice sounds so squeaky.) "What's all the noise?"

"Get out!"

"What?"

"Get out! They're coming!"

"What do you mean? Who—?"

But he's gone. He's run away. "What's *happened*? What is it?" What do you mean, get out? There

342

must be some mistake. Where's Lord Jordan? A soldier is coming across the square—a garrison soldier. There's a cluster of people around him: one, a woman, is on her knees. She's clinging to the skirts of his tunic, and he's shouting and waving his arms. Finally someone pulls her off; someone else reels away from the soldier, holding his head, shaking his head, in pain or sorrow or disbelief.

I've got to find out. I've got to ask.

"Sergeant? *Sergeant!*"

He hears me. He turns. And he must recognize the house, because he comes straight over.

"Is the Archdeacon there?" he pants.

"Yes, but—"

"Tell him the siege is ended. Tell him to leave. Leave, but take no property. If we leave our property, they won't kill us."

"Did the Viscount—?"

"The Viscount is taken prisoner."

"*What?*"

There are tears in his eyes. "They lured him in and took him prisoner. Him and the nine knights who went with him. Ah, Christ, those faithless . . . may they rot in hell."

No. Not Lord Jordan.

"If you leave now, they'll let you through. Don't

try to take any property. *No property.* And don't stay, or—well, you know what happened at Béziers."

He moves away, and the people follow him, weeping, questioning, protesting. I can't—oh, no. No.

It can't be true. Not Lord Jordan. How can I leave, when—but I've got to leave. I've got to think. Don't panic. Be calm. Concentrate. Just concentrate.

"Father?"

He doesn't look up. He doesn't hear me. Oh, Jesus—

"Father!" (Listen, damn you!) "Father, we've got to go! The Crusaders are coming! If we stay, they'll kill us!"

Still nothing. He's lying there, tracing a line down Lord Roland's nose with the tip of his finger. Totally absorbed in the lifeless profile.

"FATHER!"

As loudly as I can, and he doesn't even twitch. What can I do? Should I pull his hair? Slap his face? Or—

Wait. I know.

He gasps as the water hits him—gasps and blinks and sits up.

"Father, listen—"

"Go away."

"The Crusaders are coming. The Viscount is captured. We can't stay, or they'll kill us."

"Leave me alone."

"You're not listening! Didn't you hear what I said? The *Crusaders* are coming!"

"Let them come."

What?

I can hardly recognize his swollen face, it's so plastered with blood and sweat and tears. I can hardly see his eyes or hear his voice.

"Father, what are you saying?" (It's me, Isidore! Don't do this to me!) "We've got to go!"

"*Go?*" A savage look. "Do you think I'd *leave* him?"

"But—"

"If *you* want to go, then go! Get out!"

"But he's dead, can't you see? He's dead, Father."

A terrible silence. The Archdeacon covers his mouth. He closes his eyes, and his chest heaves. At last, however, he manages to control himself. "Roland may be dead," he declares hoarsely, "but he's still here. I'm not leaving him. *I'm not leaving him.* He's my lord. He's my father and my mother—

they won't have him—they'll never—I can't—
no . . . " And he begins to cry again, like a child,
rocking back and forth with his hands hanging
loose and his head thrown back, and it's breaking
my heart. It's breaking my heart.

"Please, Father, please, you've got to come.
Please." What can I say? "If you don't come, they'll
kill you, Father."

"Oh, God." He's moaning. "Oh, God, oh, God,
do you think I care?"

"Father—"

"Go away. Just go away, run away, I don't care, I
don't care anymore."

"But—"

"Go!" he screams. *"Get out!"*

Go. I've got to go. If I don't go, they'll kill me.
Where shall I go? Through the kitchen, into the
square. Everyone's heading toward the Aude Gate:
women dragging their children, monks tripping
over the hems of their robes, one man carrying his
aged mother or grandmother on his back. No
property, no bundles, no goats or carts or horses.
Just loaves and bottles and cabbages tucked under
their arms.

I know that monk. That's Brother Gervaise. I

346

could join him and follow him to the nearest monastery. That's what I'll do. That's . . . at least . . .

No. I can't do that. I can't leave my Father, how can I? How can I go away and never know—never see—it's impossible. What kind of a life would I have without him?

"Father!" There must be some way. "Father, I know what we'll do. We'll take him with us. Do you hear me?"

Back into the bedroom. He's lying beside Lord Roland, his face on Lord Roland's chest. He doesn't move or speak. If it weren't for his breathing, you'd think that he was dead, too.

"Father, we'll make a hammock. We'll get two sticks and tie a blanket between them. We'll carry him like that."

No response.

"Father, please, we've got to hurry, we've got to go *now*!"

Nothing.

"Father!" Look at me, damn you! Listen to me! I'm Isidore, I'm here, I'm not dead, I'm alive! I'm alive, and I need you! "Answer me! *Answer me!*" Pounding on his back, but he doesn't make a sound, nothing, not a single word—

347

Wait. What's that? A scream. Someone's screaming, screaming in terror. They've come, I know
they have, they've come and I can hear—I can
smell—they're lighting fires. No, wait, that's
not—that's—

Help!

‡CHAPTER THIRTY‡

19 AUGUST 1209

"Isidore?"

Go away.

"Isidore?" Someone's tapping my cheek. "Isidore, wake up. You have to wake up."

Wake up? Is it morning? No, it's not morning; there's something wrong. Where am I?

"Isidore, wake up. We're leaving. Come on."

It's his face, hanging there, all wet and dirty. But if that's his face, and that's his chest, then my head must be on his lap.

Yes. And the rest of me is on the floor.

"You've had a fit," he murmurs. "It's all right. You've just had a fit."

"What—?"

"Can you get up? You can't sleep now, we've got to go."

Go. Yes.

Yes! God! "The Crusaders!"

"They're not here."

"Quick—quick—!"

"It's all right. Calm down. They're not here yet; we still have time." He puts a hand under my elbow and wipes my mouth with his sleeve. "Take it slowly. Don't hurt yourself."

The Crusaders. We've got to go. My knees are trembling. Lord Roland . . .

He's been covered up. There's a blanket over his face.

"You—you—" You're standing. You're talking. "Aren't we going to take him with us?"

Father Pagan shakes his head. His eyes are still red and swollen, but they're seeing things again. "We're on our own now," he says.

"I'm sorry. I'm sorry, Father."

"No. *I'm* sorry. You've nothing to be sorry for."

"It was for me! He was trying to save me—"

"That's because you're worth saving." Suddenly he closes his eyes, and grabs my hand, and presses it to his cheek. For a moment it seems as if he's going to cry again.

But he doesn't.

"Can you walk?" he asks.

"Oh, yes. I'm not dizzy. I've got a headache, but I'm not dizzy."

"Then we'll go." Dropping my hand, he puts his arm around my shoulders. "Come on. I'll help you. Lean on me, and you'll be fine."

It seems to take forever to cross the room. When we finally reach the threshold, he turns back, looking at the shrouded body—that long, gray shape on the bed—with a look that lays bare his very soul.

And he closes the door behind us.

‡EPILOGUE‡

After occupying Carcassonne, the Crusaders slowly moved through the rest of Languedoc. Some towns were conquered; some surrendered. Everywhere the local lords were deprived of their rights and lands, which were bestowed on knights from the north. Many Cathars were burned at the stake. The bloodshed lasted for years, surviving the death of Pope Innocent in 1216, and in 1226 King Louis VIII of France himself came south, triggering a fresh wave of violence. In 1244 the last Cathar stronghold was taken, and in 1249, when the last Count of Toulouse died (leaving no male heir), the lands traditionally held by him, and by the Viscount of Carcassonne and Béziers, became permanent possessions of the kings of France.

Lord Raymond Roger Trencavel died of dysentery soon after being taken prisoner. Lord Jordan Roucy de Bram also died a captive, and his son was killed defending Bram against the Crusaders. Bram held out for three days, and when it surrendered, one hundred prisoners had their eyes gouged out and their noses, lips, and ears cut off. They were then allowed to leave under the guidance of a man who had been blinded in only one eye: he led them to the fortress of Cabaret, which defied the Crusaders until 1211.

Dominic Guzman remained at Prouille. Three times he refused bishoprics, preferring to devote himself to the foundation of the Order of Friars Preachers (or Dominicans). He died in 1221, and was made a saint in 1234.

Isidore Orbus escaped from Carcassonne and followed Pagan Kidrouk to Prouille, and thence to Montpellier, where Pagan spent many years lecturing at the university. Isidore studied under him at Montpellier, and then moved on to the University of Bologna, where he became a professor of canon law. During this time, the frequency of his epileptic fits diminished greatly. At the age of thirty-nine he was appointed papal chamberlain. He wrote several books, including *A History of Noble Men, Concerning the Theological Virtues* and a study of papal law.

Pagan Kidrouk remained at Montpellier until 1223. That year he went on a pilgrimage to St. James of Compostela, and upon returning, retired to a monastery near Marseille. Here he devoted himself to writing a book on the life of Lord Roland Roucy de Bram, emphasizing the Christian lessons that could be learned from it. He died in 1227, at the age of fifty-six, leaving the book incomplete.

Isidore was with him when he died.

GLOSSARY

acolyte One of the minor orders of the church (below that of deacon or priest), entrusted with duties around the altar

alb A full length garment worn by a priest during the celebration of Mass

archdeacon A bishop's deputy, superintending the diocese and presiding over the lowest ecclesiastical court

bailey A courtyard enclosed within the outer protective walls of a castle

barbican The outer defense of a city or castle

basilisk A mythological beast

canon A cleric living in a community of clerics who serve in a cathedral and follow certain rules of behavior

canticle A hymn used in church services

Cathar A member of a sect holding beliefs fundamentally opposed to the doctrine of the established church

chancellor One of the four chief dignitaries in a medieval cathedral, in charge of correspondence, legal documents, and such.

chapter A general assembly of monks or canons

chasuble A sleeveless mantle worn by a priest over the alb during Mass

cloister A covered walk or arcade within a monastery or other building

cloister garth The open space or courtyard enclosed by monastic buildings; a covered walk or arcade

corselet A piece of defensive armor covering the body

deacon One of the major orders of the church (below that of priest)

embrasure The opening in a crenelated battlement, through which arrows can be fired

emerods Hemorrhoids

gallery A long, narrow passage or platform

garrison A body of soldiers stationed in a city or fortress for its defense

hauberk A long military tunic, usually of chain mail

hellebore A medicinal plant, once used for treating mental disease

Infidel Someone of the Muslim faith

keep The innermost and strongest structure or central tower of a castle, serving as a last defense

legate A representative of the Pope

mangonel A military engine for casting large stones

manticore A mythological beast

merlon The solid portion on either side of an embrasure

Nocturnes Early morning service (about 3 A.M.)

Nones The church service held on the ninth hour of the monastic day (about 3 P.M.)

novice Someone received into a religious house on probation, before taking the vows

palliasse A straw-filled mattress

parapet A low wall or barrier at the edge of a platform, balcony, or roof

portcullis A strong frame or grating, suspended by

chains and made to slide up and down in vertical grooves in the gateway of a fortress or fortified town

postern A doorway or opening distinct from the main entrance

precentor One of the positions in a monastery or cathedral; the precentor is responsible for singing and services within the church

Prime The daybreak service in a monastery

refectory In a religious house, the hall or room where eating takes place

reliquary A container, often jeweled and ornate, for holding religious relics

sapper A soldier whose duty concerns the building or destroying of fortifications

scribe A secretary; one who writes at another's dictation

secondary A cathedral dignitary of second or minor rank

See The office or position held by a bishop or the Pope

seigneurial rights The entitlements of a lord

squire A young man, usually of good birth, attending a knight

sub-deacon One of the orders of the church, below that of deacon or priest

surcoat An outer garment often worn by armed men over their armor

surplice A loose vestment of white linen, often full length, with wide sleeves

syllogism A three-part argument used in the classical art of rhetoric

tithe The tenth part of an annual produce of agriculture, usually paid to the church

troubadour A poet and musician of southern France

varlet An attendant or servant

vellum A fine parchment prepared from calfskin

vernacular The native language of a country or district

Vespers The second-to-last service of the monastic day

villein A peasant